Book

Giant Wars Series
Loving His Fire
Grounded By Love
Melted By Love
Wicked Flames of Desire

Galactic Courtship Series
Xacier's Prize
Claiming His Champion
Captivating the Doctor
Escaping the Hunt
Abducting the Ambassador
Wicked Prisoner
Seducing the Enemy
Cuff Me Now
Challenging the Arena
Dark Desires in Space
His Fallen Star
His Human Temptation
Racing Toward Desire
Zro'eq's Fallen Star
His Human Doctor

Ice Age Alphas
The Sabertooth's Promise
The Sabertooth's Mate

The Sabertooth's Mate

Lily S. Thomas

Cover created by SelfPubBookCovers.com/ KimDingwall

www.lilythomasromance.com

ISBN: 9781088811313
ISBN: (ebook)) B07VWTZ3GN

Dedication

To all my lovely readers, thank you so much for your continued support and lovely reviews! I hope to share many more amazing journeys with you!

Chapter 1

"Are you alright?" Aiyre bent over at the waist and placed a comforting hand on Ezi's shoulder.

Ezi glanced up and sent her friend and clanmate a broad smile. "Yes." When she saw the lines of worry stay firmly planted on Aiyre's face, she explained a bit more. "The baby is just kicking. It is nothing to be concerned about."

Aiyre stood there, her face mere inches from Ezi as she searched her face for the truth. Ezi squirmed under the intense gaze of her friend.

"I'm fine!" Ezi forced a chuckle as she rubbed a hand over her rounded stomach. In these final stages of pregnancy, she hadn't been able to shift into her pronghorn form, and she could feel her other half itching to escape her human form.

This child was a treasure… or so she kept telling herself, but the closer she drew to the birth, the more she fretted about raising the child on her own.

It would never know its father, but she would be sure to tell it about Drakk. That man had been the kindest she'd known, and although they'd only had one night together before the sabertooth attack, she would forever treasure that memory in her mind. It had been a brief, awkward joining in a cave in front of all the gods.

Ezi sighed as she watched the flames of their village bonfire dancing with flickering glee. A glee she was envious of because it'd been many moons since she'd enjoyed a pleasant humor. She'd found a seat on a log right next to it, and despite the unseasonably warm spring, she found the warmth welcome. It wrapped its comfortable arms around her and eased the tension out of her body.

Kicking out a leg, Ezi eyed the blue beads on her leather moccasin and did her best to relax, but that last kick from the baby had been painful. She rubbed her stomach through her tanned leather shirt. This child was eager to escape, but she hadn't felt a single cramp yet, and the healer had been certain she'd feel something soon.

Aiyre plopped down beside her. "Are you sure everything is good? Your face keeps scrunching up like you might be in pain, and I've noticed you rubbing your stomach a lot."

"I'm fine," Ezi repeated. It was nice of Aiyre to be so concerned about her, but the hovering was beginning to irritate her. It'd been non-stop in the last few days. It wasn't like she didn't enjoy her friend's company, but it was hard to see Aiyre so happy living among the same clan of sabertooths that'd killed their clan… killed Drakk and her family.

At that exact moment, one of the sabertooths in the clan walked past, and Ezi warily eyed the man. He could pass for human or even any other shifter, but lurking under his skin was a predator unmatched. And it scared her that she would never know when it would rear its ugly head and rip off her hand.

"There's a line that forms between your eyebrows every time your baby kicks." Aiyre raised her finger to Ezi's forehead and traced a fingertip down between her eyes, distracting her from her racing fears.

Reaching up, Ezi smacked her friend's hand away from her face as her irritation got the best of her.

"The baby is eager to leave and see the village, and I can't say I blame it." Ezi frowned. "It feels like years have passed since I knew I was with child. I'm just as eager to give birth. My ankles hurt when I walk." The extra weight she'd gained hadn't been easy on her body.

Aiyre studied Ezi's stomach. Her eyes were filled to the brim with longing. "I must admit I'm envious of your good fortune. Daerk and I still haven't produced anything," Aiyre rubbed her own stomach, a distant look entering her eyes, "and there hasn't been a lack of trying." She laughed, and Ezi cracked a smile.

"The gods will deliver it to you when it is time." Ezi had to believe that because Aiyre would make a great mother, and although Daerk was a sabertooth shifter she had no doubt he would be a doting father. The man had been good to them.

"Eron has been helping us by asking the gods to bless us." Aiyre nodded her head, her brunette braid bobbing with the movement. "I can't count the number of rabbits he's sacrificed for us."

Ezi patted her friend's thigh, "It will come. After everything we've gone through the gods owe us good fortune."

"Sometimes," Aiyre looked over at her before glancing back at the bonfire, "I wonder if the gods will ever do enough to make up for the destruction of our clan. How can they?"

Ezi was in full agreement. The father of her child, Drakk, hadn't deserved to die. None of their pronghorn clan had deserved to die, and now they were living here with the same sabertooths who'd destroyed their clan in a single horrible night.

Glancing around, she watched the clan around her. The people here were good at heart, and they'd proved it over and over again. Ever since Brog, the leader, had been kicked out, Ezi and Aiyre had been accepted into the clan fully. Without their evil leader here to taint them, they'd come to realize the error of their ways… but it was too late.

An entire clan had nearly been wiped out.

Although she'd been reassured over and over again that no one would harm a single hair on her head, Ezi sometimes flinched when one of the sabertooth shifters shifted into their animal form. Violent nightmares still plagued her every time she closed her eyelids. She was born a prey shifter, while this clan was full of natural predators, and it unnerved her. At any moment, one of them could decide to rip out her throat, and there'd be nothing she could do about it.

She closed her eyes and sucked in a calming breath. There was no need for her to panic. The gods may not be able to atone for that night, but they had been blessing this clan with new life and filling their meat tent once more. The winter had been scarce, and Brog had been convinced killing her clan would give them a better chance at survival, but he was gone now.

"And Brog?" Ezi opened her eyes and glanced over at Aiyre who was using a bone needle to finish sewing a pair of pants back up for Daerk who'd ripped them while out hunting. Aiyre wasn't just good at being a hunter, but she was even skilled with her hands. Ezi would be lying if she said there wasn't a little jealousy inside her. She wasn't a hunter, and her other skills were limited.

Aiyre heaved a sigh as she continued with her task. "Nothing yet." She drove the bone needle through the tanned leather with a light pop.

"I worry about him coming back to retake the clan from Daerk." It was one of the nightmares that plagued her at night. That man loved blood, and there was no doubt in her mind he would be back.

"We all do, even the sabertooth shifters." Aiyre glanced up her brown eyes scanning over Ezi. "But don't worry about him for now." Aiyre sent her a smile that was meant to comfort. "He's gone, and he won't be welcomed back."

"Ooo!" Ezi pushed a hand against her stomach as another pain seared through her abdomen.

"Are you okay?" Aiyre dropped the garment she was sewing, rushed to Ezi's side, and dropped to a knee. Placing a hand on Ezi's leg, she asked again, "Are you okay?"

"Yes, I think s–," Ezi groaned as another pain rolled through her.

"You aren't fine." Aiyre darted to her feet, glancing around frantically as she searched for someone to help her.

"I'm fine!" Ezi didn't want anyone worrying about her. "Aiyre… ooo!" Another pain screamed through her. Gritting her teeth, she squeezed her eyes shut.

"Daerk! Daerk!" Aiyre hollered at the top of her lungs as she spun around in a tight circle.

Ezi's eyes popped open at Aiyre's hollering. Everyone near them stopped and turned. If

Ezi hadn't been so focused in on her protruding stomach, she might have felt a bit of embarrassment crawl over her face, but at the moment she was too distracted to care.

"What is it?" Daerk ran out from behind a hut and rushed over, his hands taking a hold of Aiyre's shoulders as he searched her face.

Ezi would have laughed at the overprotective nature of these sabertooth mates if another pain wasn't rolling through her and curling her toes in her moccasins.

"It's Ezi!" Aiyre pointed over to her.

"What's wrong?" Daerk's panicked golden eyes skimmed over Ezi. He'd been just as watchful as Aiyre these past few moons. The two of them were worse than a pair of birds looking after a nest of eggs.

"I'm fine." She had no idea how many times she would have to repeat that until someone finally believed her.

"It's the baby. I think it's coming. We need Eron… and your mother." Aiyre smacked Daerk's shoulder when he just continued to stare at Ezi in horror. "Go and get them! Now!"

The moment he fled the area in a scramble of panicked steps, Ezi shook her head. "Men."

Aiyre nodded her head as she bent down beside Ezi. "The moment a child is being born, they lose their ability to think. Perhaps it's a good thing I'm not with child yet. I don't think I could deal with him being a fretful mess."

"I'd do anything to have Drakk being a fretful mess over me." Ezi sent Aiyre a wobbly smile as she longed to feel Drakk's embrace once more. Now that the baby was coming, she worried she wouldn't be able to do this without Drakk by her side.

"I know." Sadness gripped Aiyre's voice. "Now, wrap an arm over my shoulder so I can help you over to the birthing hut. It will be more comfortable for you and give you a place to relax without prying eyes."

"Yes, thank you." Ezi grimaced again as another sharp pain shot through her. She didn't need to be attracting attention from the sabertooth shifters. She'd done her best to disappear into the shadows of the village since arriving here. She could barely name half the village.

"Help us." Aiyre waved over another clan mate. A sabertooth clan mate.

The woman rushed over and took Ezi's other side as they guided her through the village huts. Smoke trickled up and out of most all of the tents, and as they passed by Tor's tent, Ezi couldn't help the flashback.

Tor had been one of the sabertooths to save Aiyre and herself, after their clan was attacked and killed by the former leader of this sabertooth clan. He'd declared her as his mate, but it had been too soon after Drakk's death, and she'd rejected him, harshly. Tor had been gone for nearly nine moons after learning she was already with child and still in love with Drakk… too in love to even give him a chance. She knew some in the clan blamed her for his disappearance, but they didn't understand what she'd gone through, what she was still going through.

Another pain seared through her, and she gasped for air as her legs buckled a bit and brought her back to reality.

"We're almost there." Aiyre encouraged as they continued to guide her past huts.

She understood the sabertooth shifters had mates, but she was a pronghorn shifter, a mateless species. She'd been unable to accept Tor after Drakk's death… it'd been too soon… not that she thought any amount of time would change her mind. How could she mate with someone from this clan? What would Drakk think of her if she chose to mate with a sabertooth?

Another pain had her doubling over at the waist as her mouth opened on a silent cry.

"A few more steps." Aiyre continued to encourage her forward.

Ezi pushed past the pain. Nothing was more painful than the emotional pain she'd endured the night Drakk had been murdered. Nothing. She gritted her teeth and continued to move her feet.

The three of them pushed past the birthing hut's fur flaps, and she sighed when she saw the bed of furs waiting for her inside. Soon she'd be relaxing on those furs while Eron, the healer, and Tira, Daerk's mother, took care of her and guided her through this process.

A rush of hot liquid seared past her thighs, and Ezi paused.

"What is it?"

"My waters," Ezi said dumbly as her head dropped, and she spotted the dampness of her leather pants.

"We'll change your pants once you are laying down and comfortable." Aiyre pulled her along with the help of the other woman.

When they reached the bed of furs, they slowly let her down until she was lying comfortably on her back against the thick pad of furs.

"Relax." Aiyre smiled down at her.

"I'm not sure the baby will let me. It seems eager to join this world." Ezi shook her head sadly.

"What is it?" Aiyre asked as she undid the leather strings of Ezi's pants and whipped the garment off of her.

"This baby has no idea how sad and cruel this world can be." Despair rose inside her chest. If Drakk was here, she might feel more optimistic, but right now all she felt was panic.

Aiyre shook her head, her brunette braid swinging behind her back. "I know the pain this child will bring back," Ezi opened her mouth, but Aiyre was quick to raise a hand and toss her a stern glance, "but this child will also bring you copious amounts of joy. Joy you can't imagine right now, but it will."

"I'm here!" Tira rushed into the tent with several leather bags thrown over her shoulder. "Let's get her into a dress. It will make the birth easier."

Aiyre rushed to the other side of the birthing hut, and Ezi relaxed, knowing the women around her would see her through this. It was her first birth, and although she'd been around other pregnant women, she'd never seen the process. She'd be lying if she said she wasn't a bit scared. Many women lost their lives during the birthing process, and she still wasn't sure if the gods were done casting ill upon her head.

"Breath," Tira instructed her. She raised her hand and then lowered it as she demonstrated breathing. "The pain will only get worse from here, but you need to remember to breath. We don't need our new mother fainting because she was panicking."

Ezi tossed her a tentative smile. She wasn't exactly happy to hear that things were going to get worse before they got better, because it already seemed pretty terrible to her.

"Now let's raise these legs." Tira smacked her calves lightly until Ezi raised her knees into the air.

Aiyre rushed over a dress clasped in one of her hands.

"Lean up," Tira instructed Ezi, and she did as she was bid.

Aiyre gripped the hem of her shirt and stripped it off her before slipping the dress over her head in a matter of seconds.

"Now lay back down." Tira smiled at her, and despite the golden eyes of the sabertooth shifter staring at her, she calmed a bit. This was Daerk's mother after all, and she'd helped Aiyre and Ezi merge into the clan seamlessly.

"What else can I do?" Aiyre looked more worried than Ezi felt.

Right now, there was more for her to focus on, like giving birth to a new life.

"Boil some water. We will need to brew all sorts of teas for her, and I should have everything else we need." Tira pulled one of the leather bags towards her before digging through the supplies. "The goddess of fertility will look after you." She placed a statue of a large-breasted woman with a plump figure near Ezi.

"What's wrong?"

Ezi barely heard Aiyre's panicked voice over her scream of pain. Something was wrong. Something was terribly wrong. Sweat poured off her brow, and when the pain stopped, she laid her head back down. She needed to rest, but every time she thought it was over a searing pain like someone was spearing her through the middle would course through her.

She cracked open her eyes and saw Eron stride in through the entrance of the hut. He should be in the caves, asking the gods for a safe birth.

"This is no place for a man!" Tira barked as she darted to her feet, looking ready to shift into her sabertooth form and drag Eron out with her teeth if he dared to refuse.

He held up his hands as his wide wise eyes took in the angry woman before him. "I need to be here, Tira. This birth needs the gods in the birthing hut."

Tira looked divided as her golden eyes flickered from Ezi over to Eron.

"No one else in the clan can call upon the gods and their generosity." Eron's sky blue eyes dared Tira to disagree with him. "They can be cruel if we don't honor them properly."

Ezi could care less who was in the birthing hut with her. Another pain ripped through her abdomen, and she screamed as her eyes slid shut and more sweat poured down her spine and forehead.

She was going to die.

Aiyre had been wrong. Clearly, the gods owed them nothing, because she wasn't going to survive this. The pain was unbearable, and no matter what tea Tira brewed, nothing worked, and the baby refused to come out.

"Fine. You may stay inside the hut, but stay on the other side." Tira rushed back to her side as her vision blurred with black dots.

"Save my child." Ezi panted out. She couldn't live knowing she'd lost Drakk and the baby he had left for her.

Tira leaned in until her face was close to Ezi's face. "I am going to save both of you."

Chapter 2

Tor panted as he plodded through the forest. His fur coat brushed up against low hanging branches. His sabertooth's head turned in every direction as he sniffed and processed all the scents floating through the air. It'd been too many moons to count since he had shifted out of his sabertooth form. He wasn't even sure he could change back into his human form.

A growl rumbled out of his chest as his sabertooth instinct remembered the hurt Ezi had delivered to them both.

She'd rejected him. Rejected him because of his sabertooth side. He'd never resented his other half until she'd wandered into his life. Never before had he wished that he was something other than a sabertooth, then, maybe then, his mate would accept him.

A growl ripped up his throat, rumbling low in his chest. She hated him for what he was, even though he'd never done anything to warrant her hatred. He only wished she'd give him a fair chance at winning her heart. All he wanted was to wrap his arms around her and protect her from the cruel land they called home.

But not only had her rejection stung, but he'd seen the depth of her hurt, and every instinct inside him had screamed at him that she wouldn't ever accept him. What his clan had done to hers had created a rift that he wasn't sure he could fix. It wasn't like patching the tear in a piece of clothing.

Tears in the heart were a lot harder to repair.

It would take time and patience, something he wasn't sure he could give her, so he'd left the village. Only distance would keep him from ruining things between them even more.

He glanced up at the sunlight streaming through the shifting tree branches above him. By now, Ezi should've had her child. A child another man had put inside her. It'd been before him, but still, he couldn't help the jealousy that reared its ugly head, but there was also some eagerness. He hoped the child would bring her copious amounts of joy. After everything she'd lost, he hoped this would give her something back. Give her a spark in her eyes.

The father of Ezi's unborn child had been able to win her over, and yet Tor feared the gods wouldn't be so kind to him. The gods were waving his mate in front of his face but had given her to him damaged. If it was a test, then he wasn't entirely sure he would pass it.

Eron, the healer of their village, always said the gods wouldn't give them more than they could handle, but Tor had a hard time believing that wise old man. Tor couldn't handle being around Ezi. The mistrust in her eyes had cut him to the bone.

His sabertooth growled in displeasure at the direction his thoughts were headed. It didn't want to relive the rejection, but what else could he focus on out here? Thoughts of Ezi plagued him like a bad hunting season.

A light breeze picked up, rustling the leaves overhead and wafting a scent straight past his sabertooth nose.

A wholly rhinoceros.

He would recognize that scent anywhere. There was a muskiness to them that no other animal possessed, and it was hard to describe but distinctive. It filled the air and crinkled his nose in disgust. Those hairy beasts weren't known for their cleanliness. Tor swore there were more creatures living in their thick fur than he would ever see in his entire life.

Despite their stench, they did make a great challenge for a skilled hunter. The rhinoceros were known for their foul temperaments and willingness to fight back.

The opportunity to distract himself from thoughts of Ezi had arrived.

A smile curved the lips of his cat head as he plodded his way through the forest. His large paws crushed fallen leaves, but the pads of his paws deafened the sound as he moved across the forest floor. As the stench of the wholly rhinoceros grew stronger, he crouched low to the ground. His lightly colored belly skimmed over the fallen leaves and grass as he made no sound.

If he wanted to take out one of these rhinoceroses by himself, then he needed to catch it by surprise, and even then, it would be quite the fight. But it would take his mind off Ezi and relieve some of his boredom.

Creeping forward, one slow paw at a time, Tor weaved his way through the tall green grass. It waved around him as he crawled through it, but wholly rhinoceroses weren't known for their eyesight. What he had to worry about was their sense of hearing or smell.

When his paw began to press down on a brittle piece of wood, and he heard the creak of wood, he pulled it back and chose to take a different path through the tall grass. One wrong sound and the rhinoceros would either bolt or charge the sound, and he didn't want to be on the wrong end of one of their horns.

A light wind brushed over the fur on his back, tickling his skin.

He froze.

But the wind was on his side. It was blowing his scent in the opposite direction of the wholly rhinoceros, and a smile played across his cat lips. The gods were on his side. As he broke through the tall grass, he finally caught sight of his prey.

The wholly rhinoceros was larger than he'd remembered them being, but he was determined to take it down. He'd never hunted such a large creature by himself, but he had faith in his sabertooth form. If his sabertooth thought they could do it, then he would believe it.

The grayish-black fur on the animal waved in the light wind as it shuffled a foot in the dirt, searching for the spring shoots that were popping out of the ground. Something that'd be easy to digest after such a slim winter they'd all lived through.

Testing the scent on the wind, Tor found the rhinoceros by itself.

His heart thundered under his ribcage with the task ahead of him.

Now all he needed was the rhinoceros to shift its lumbering body so that he could get a good angle for the attack. Although he best keep in mind that though this animal might look like a lumbering beast, he'd seen one of them trample a man in the blink of an eye before. They were much faster than anyone could ever imagine just looking at their short legs and ginormous bodies.

As if reading his mind, the wholly rhinoceros turned away from him and began lumbering off in search of some more young plant shoots to munch on.

If he was going to take on this beast, then this was his chance.

Tor's muscles bunched up in his hind legs as he launched himself, dirt flying wildly behind him as he tore off. His claws dug into the ground as he used them to gain some grip and speed.

Then as he neared the rhinoceros's rear end, his hind legs bunched once more, launching his large cat frame into the air. His front paws reached out wide as he zeroed in on the target below him.

As he landed on top of the massive animal, he dug his claws and the long canines in his mouth into the rhinoceros's back, trying to sever the spine or hit the jugular, but the animal startled the moment his claws landed on its skin.

Holding on for his life as the animal tore into a high-speed bolt, Tor growled in frustration as the long hair on the rhinoceros's neck tickled the back of his throat as he attempted to get a better hold of the massive animal under him.

This animal was refusing to go down easily.

But that was fine with him. He was up for a bit of a challenge. All thoughts of Ezi had fled from his mind, and his only goal now was to stay alive and bring down this brute of a beast.

It began to zig-zag, tossing his body around until he was braced on its side. As he looked around without releasing his grip on the beast's neck, he saw, too late, what the wholly rhinoceros was up to with its zig-zagging ways.

It slammed its side into a thick tree trunk, and a loud snap reached his ears at the same time that pain rammed through his entire body. His grip on the beast weakened, and he slipped down the side of the rhinoceros until he was laying on the ground in a heap.

His long pink tongue rolled out of his mouth as he panted in pain. Glancing up, he saw the beast had turned itself around and was now bearing down on him. Its large bottom horn aimed straight for him.

Frantically, Tor got his feet back under him and bolted right before the rhinoceros barreled past him, ramming the horn on its nose into the thick tree trunk. Wood chips flew through the air, and a shiver spread down his spine as he realized how close to death he'd been.

The rhinoceros wasn't done with him though.

Turning, it barreled down on him again. The large beast was in a blind rage, and its sole focus was Tor.

Tor leaped to the side, but this time he wasn't quick enough when one of his paws slipped on a patch of mud. The wholly rhinoceros filled his vision, and he feared it would be the last thing he would ever see.

Chapter 3

Ezi's vision blinked back to see Tira bending over her, stroking a hand over her sweating face. Even through all the pain, she could feel that her hair was stuck to her scalp from the amount of sweat pouring off her. If childbirth didn't kill her, lack of water might.

"We are almost done," Tira promised sweetly as she wiped another hand across Ezi's brow.

"Am… I dying?" She managed through the pain that was radiating up from her abdomen.

"We won't let you." Tira smiled down at her. "I will save both the child and yourself. The gods will have to look elsewhere if they are seeking a soul to join them in the Eternal Hunting Grounds."

Ezi's head lolled to the side, and then she spotted Eron, the sabertooth clan shaman, burning incense and chanting to a small stone statue in front of him. The statue was that of a pregnant woman, her thick legs spread wide and her immense bosom welcoming all the children of the land. Eron bobbed up and down as he worshipped the statue with his hands outstretched in a pleading manner.

She had to be dying.

Eron, a man, wouldn't be allowed in the tent unless the situation required extra guidance from the gods, which meant things weren't going as they should.

A lone tear carved a path from the corner of one of her eyes, down over her cheek before plopping onto the thick furred blankets under her. She felt mixed about the possibility of passing. She'd been raised to believe the Eternal Hunting Grounds would be a land full of food, warmth, and loved ones, like Drakk, but she wasn't sure she wanted to be rejoined with Drakk so soon.

The unknown scared her. Terrified her. Her heart thundered inside her chest.

"Ezi?"

Shifting her head to the other side, Ezi's eyes landed on Aiyre. Her friend's brunette eyebrows were drawn down over her eyes in worry.

"Take care of my child." Ezi pleaded with her friend. She needed to hear the words from Aiyre's mouth. She couldn't join the gods when she didn't have the promise. If she did end up seeing Drakk again, she wanted to be able to say truthfully that she'd left their child in good hands.

Aiyre shook her head, a brunette braid rolling over one shoulder. "You will take care of your child, Ezi."

"I'm dying." She croaked, her dry throat hating her for even trying to speak.

"You won't die." Aiyre shook her head, refusing to believe what was right in front of her face.

"Please." Ezi pushed the darkness that was calling her name away. She couldn't leave this world for the Eternal Hunting Grounds, not when she didn't have a promise. She needed someone here to promise to take care of her child. "Please."

Aiyre reached out of her line of sight and took hold of one of Ezi's hands and squeezed it. "You will live."

Despair slowly choked her. Aiyre wasn't

going to let her fade away. It was like her lifelong friend, and clanmate knew she wouldn't die until she got the promise out of someone.

"Place this in her mouth." Tira handed a wooden bowl of green mash of herbs to Aiyre.

Aiyre sniffed it before her nose crinkled in disgust. "What will it do?"

"It will relieve some of her pain." Tira glanced down at Ezi, and she could see the pity in the other woman's eyes. "We aren't done yet, but we are getting close."

Close.

Ezi clung to that word. Soon this would all be over. Her life was in the gods' hands, and maybe in Eron's hands as well. Her head lolled to the side again, and she watched Eron, letting him distract her from what was happening around her.

He was bowed over the statue of the pregnant woman with a stick of dried herbs burning, filling the tent with its comforting floral scent.

Fingers pressed something against her lips, and she opened her mouth only to choke on the taste of whatever was being pushed into her mouth. Quickly, she swallowed before the paste overpowered her taste buds. If Tira said it would take some of her pain away, then she would choke it down while smiling.

"Push." Tira encouraged her. "Push. Your baby wishes to enter our world."

Ezi heaved every time Tira told her to give a push. Sweat continued to pour off her. It ran down her back in streams as her body quivered with her tiredness. She had no idea how long she'd been in labor.

In what seemed like several lifetimes of panting and pushing, the crying of a baby reached her ears, and a smile spread across her face as everything went dark.

All Tor felt was the front horn of the rhinoceros tearing through the flesh on his leg. The pain seared up his spine, and his teeth ground down as a growl of agony tore through his throat. Then the wholly rhinoceros tossed its head back, flinging him through the air by his leg, and he felt his flesh tear with the force.

A roar of pain and shock left his sabertooth mouth as he flew through the air, his paws stretched wide as they tried to find a grip in the air. Birds scattered in the trees above at the horrific sound below them.

Then he landed. Hard. Pain rocked through him, and lights danced across his vision. Instinct kicked in. He had to save his life by getting away from the wholly rhinoceros. He'd picked a fight he was incapable of winning, and now he needed to get out of the area or die. And he had no intention of dying.

Heaving himself to his paws, he pushed through the pain in one of his back legs, trailing blood as he searched for a safe place to assess his wound.

The ground below him trembled. Dumbly, he turned his cat eyes to the ground and watched a couple of stones bounce wildly near his front paws. When Tor glanced up his cat eyes widened as he saw the rhinoceros charging back at him. Its horns were once more lowered, and he knew it was coming back for the kill. Pushing through the pain that tried to knock him off his paws, he shoved himself to the side, this time before the rhinoceros could trample him.

The beast rumbled past going too fast to slow down and change course.

Without waiting to see what it would do, Tor shot off, each step radiating pain up to the base of his skull. If he didn't push past the pain, the rhinoceros would most definitely come after him.

The ground under him rumbled again. Little rocks on the ground beside him jumped into the air as if trembling in fear of what was bearing down on them.

A growl ripped out of Tor's throat as he whipped around and found the rhinoceros bearing down on him once more. He knew he'd started this fight, but he needed it to be over before he died due to his stupidity for thinking this would be an easy or fair match.

As the rhinoceros aimed its horn at him, Tor tensed his muscles waiting for the right moment. At the very last second, he threw himself to the side, pain ripping up his leg with the movement, but this time instead of fleeing he readied a clawed paw and swiped at the beast's face as it galloped past.

His claw connected, hooking on the flesh of the rhinoceros's face.

It let out a bellow of pain before turning tail and fleeing the area.

Tor sighed in relief as he slumped over on the ground. He couldn't deal with the pain anymore, so he receded into the back of his mind and let his sabertooth instinct come to the front. It would take care of him. It always took care of him.

Tor didn't come back to the front of his mind until his sabertooth had found them a safe place to stay the night. It wasn't much. It was only a tree, but there was something familiar about it like he knew it from somewhere, but he was unable to place it in his current state of mind.

Slumping onto the ground, he licked the wound on his leg. Tor knew he was going to pass out again, but he wanted, needed, to get his wound cleaned. Slowly, his vision blacked out, and before he lost consciousness, he thought to himself, *I'm going to die, and my mate won't even know or mourn the loss.*

Chapter 4

Blinking, Ezi glanced around the hut and caught sight of Aiyre standing off to one side. She swore that woman was always around. The woman lurked around like a mother bear, always watching and waiting for the cry of her cub. She wished Aiyre would realize that she was a grown woman who knew out to take care of herself.

"You… are still… here?" Ezi asked, her throat a bit hoarse and painful. After delivering her child successfully, she'd passed out for a couple of days. Tira and Aiyre hadn't slept a wink in that time as they'd taken care of her and her newborn child, and Ezi wasn't sure how she would repay them.

"Only until you are ready for your child." Aiyre moved closer.

Ezi frowned as her eyes slid down to the bundle of furs Aiyre had grasped in her arms. "No."

Aiyre's lips turned down in a frown as she slowly walked across the hut. "Please. Just hold her once, Ezi. I think you will fall in love the moment you see her small nose and big eyes."

"No." Ezi placed her hands behind her, stiffly pushed herself into a sitting position, and glanced away from them. It should have been Aiyre who'd become the mother, not her. "You were meant to be a mother more than I."

"But she is yours, and she is beautiful." Aiyre cooed down at the baby in her arms as she wiggled a finger at the child.

"She will only remind me of what I've lost." Ever since waking up from her fever-induced sleep a couple of days ago, she hadn't wanted to hold her child. Before the birth, she may have been excited to meet her child, but now that the baby was here, she feared the memories it would bring back. The hurt it would bring back. There was no father for her to celebrate with over the successful if scary, birth.

"Ah."

Ezi glanced back over at Aiyre, who was gently jiggling the baby in her arms. "What?"

"You are afraid she will look like Drakk." Aiyre stared down at the face in her arms, while wiggling a finger in the giggling baby's face. "I suppose there is a hint of him in there, but she might also help you to overcome his death. She's a part of both of you."

Ezi just wasn't sure she was ready.

"How are we today?" Tira popped her head inside the hut before striding in with a small leather pack slung over one of her shoulders.

Ezi smiled, thankful for the interruption. Out of the corner of her eye, she watched Aiyre move away from her, the baby still clutched in her arms, and a pang of jealousy crept into her heart. She wanted to love that child as much as Aiyre did. She really did.

"I'm feeling much better, and I'm hoping to get out of here." She waved a hand at the hut that surrounded her. She'd spent so much time in here recovering that she now knew exactly how many stitches there were in the fur-lined sides of the hut and how many bones held up the structure.

"Good." Tira beamed down at her. "I'm hoping to get you out of this hut for some fresh air."

Tira bent down next to her. "Has Aiyre let you hold your baby yet, or is she being greedy?"

Aiyre frowned at Tira for her teasing. "I've tried to give her the child, but she refuses to take it from me." Aiyre's lips fell down in a flat line.

"Some mothers need a little time, especially after such a difficult birth." Tira eased the tension in floating through the air. "Thankfully, Eron's prays to the goddess of fertility and women worked." Tira sent Ezi a relived smile. "The birth could have ended in two deaths. I've seen it end in deaths before. Is there a name for the child yet?"

Ezi shook her head. She had tried her best not to even think about the child. Before the birth, she'd somewhat been looking forward to the child, but now that it was here it scared her. All the emotions it brought back were so hard to handle. How could she be expected to give it a proper name when she wanted nothing to do with it?

"We must name the child, and we must introduce her to the gods." Tira gave her a stern look, "You must introduce her to the gods."

Ezi shook her head again.

"You would risk angering the gods and endangering the child's life? How can they help to protect her when they don't even know her?" Tira's head shot back in surprise. "They helped me and Eron save the both of you. You owe them the respect of naming and introducing her to the gods."

Ezi didn't even know how to answer that. It was true. The gods needed to give the child their blessing so she could hopefully live a long and fruitful life, but that would mean Ezi would have to hold the child, look at the child.

"They will be patient with you to a point," Tira relented, "but they will expect you to show them the newest member of this tribe."

"We should let her rest." Aiyre placed the baby in a nearby fur-lined reed basket before walking over to them. "Ake will be in soon to feed her if you still don't feel like it."

Ezi shook her head. She couldn't even feed her own child. Her breasts felt heavy and uncomfortable with all the milk still inside, but the discomfort wasn't intolerable. Not yet.

Aiyre nodded her head as she ushered a reluctant Tira out of the hut.

"Make sure to eat some of the food I brought and eat some of the herbs," Tira called out over her shoulder as they both left the hut.

Once they were gone from sight, Ezi sighed in relief and relaxed back on her bed of furs. Her eyes sunk closed as she laid there, but the silence and peace didn't last long.

Soon she could hear shuffling and mewing noises from the bundle of furs nearby. Then the child let out weak little cries. It pulled at her heart because she knew the child was hungry, and she was more than capable of feeding the child.

Her breasts were near bursting with the milk in them.

And there was only one way for her to release the pressure.

Rolling over, Ezi gave her back to the child that laid not far away. She couldn't look at that child's face. At Drakk's face. The child would do nothing but remind her of what she couldn't have, and for the first time, she resented Drakk. He'd left her here in this world with a baby that would only remind her of him.

It had been cruel of him.

As she shut her eyes once more, she did her best to ignore the little sounds coming from behind her. But the baby wasn't having it. Its cries grew louder, and an instinct she couldn't ignore reared its head inside her.

Rising from her bed, Ezi stood on shaky feet. She'd been close to death only a few days ago, but the gods and Tira had been able to bring her back from the brink. Every time she though the gods had given up on her, they'd brought her back from the brink, and she believed it to be a bad joke.

From where she stood in the hut, she couldn't see the child among the fur-lined basket, but as she crept closer with tentative steps, she finally caught sight of the chubby-faced child.

The baby glanced over, and a gurgling smile beamed up at her from the basket.

Ezi's steps faltered as she stared down at the child. She could see Drakk's eyes staring right back at her. Her heart shattered inside her chest. The child raised its hands, almost seeming to recognize who she was to it.

"I can't promise to be perfect." Ezi bent down next to the fur basket and slowly pulled the child out, cradling her head. "You remind me so much of your father, and I only wish he was here now to see you."

Pulling aside a part of her animal skin shirt she wore, she bared a breast, and without any encouragement, the child latched on the moment Ezi pressed the child's lips to her nipple. She sucked hungrily, and relief washed through Ezi. Her breasts felt like they would burst at any moment like an overfull animal intestine water sack, and she was thankful for the relief.

Walking back over to her bed of furs, she took a seat while the child suckled at her teat.

"I want to love you." Ezi longed for nothing more.

Running a hand over the sun-streaked patch of hair on the child's head, she wondered if it would darken like hers and Drakk's. Little brown eyes looked up at her, trusting, dependent.

It pulled at Ezi's heart, but she distanced herself from the feelings. If she wasn't careful, she would end up reliving her loss of Drakk over and over again. If she was going to love this child, then she needed to learn how to separate her feelings, so there'd finally be room in her heart and mind to accept the child.

"I'm here to feed the child." Ake's head popped inside the hut.

"I'm already feeding her. You may leave." Ezi was quick to respond as she glanced up.

She watched as Ake's eyes widened, and then a slow smile spread across her lips as her eyes landed on the child in Ezi's arms.

"You may leave." Ezi was getting tired of being watched by everyone in this clan. Didn't they have anything else to do with their lives? She could think of plenty of activities that needed to be done around the village.

Ducking her head, Ake left without another word, and the hut flap waved behind her.

Ezi didn't need anyone drawing conclusions about her feeding the child in her arms. Her breasts were full and heavy with milk, and this feeding was nothing but a way to relieve the throbbing pain. Her teats had begun to leak milk just a day ago.

Pulling the child's head away from her first breast, she switched the baby to the other breast before the baby filled its stomach. The child latched onto the second breasts just as eagerly as it had to the first.

Ezi allowed herself to relax against one of the mammoth bones that supported the hut. Her eyes closed in pleasure as relief swam through her.

Then a couple of images of Tor flashed through her mind.

No one had seen Tor in many moons. He'd disappeared right after she'd rejected him, and there were many in the clan that wondered if he was even alive. Even Ezi wondered. She wasn't sure how long someone could stay away from their clan. If he was alive, then his ability to live on his own was impressive. There was no way Ezi could leave her clan for such an extended period.

She felt nothing towards his loss in the village. If anything, she was thankful his intense eyes were long gone, but it was strange that he hadn't come back. A clan was the safest place to be in this world of dangerous animals and unknowns.

One moment he'd been here professing his desire to be her mate, and then he'd disappeared.

But despite all the time that'd passed, she could still recall what he looked like clearly. His piercing sky blue eyes would be hard to forget, especially when they'd always been so centered on her. And his head of full black hair with a bushy beard covering the bottom half of his face. It was like he was standing right in front of her. She remembered him so clearly. If she reached out, she was sure she'd be able to feel the prickle of the hair on his face.

Ezi's eyes shot open as she growled in frustration. Drakk's memory was quickly fading, to the point where she doubted she even remembered his face correctly, yet she could clearly see Tor. And it annoyed her. Tor was nothing more than a sabertooth shifter, and a part of the clan that had ruined the life she'd known and loved.

"Ezi?"

Glancing over to the entrance of the birthing hut, Ezi's eyes landed on Aiyre.

A smile spread over her face, and Ezi frowned at her.

Clearly, Ake had decided to spread the news about her feeding the baby. "My breasts were hurting, and this provides them with relief." She said a little defensively.

The smile dropped off Aiyre's face for a second, but then a smaller one replaced it. Making her way into the hut, Aiyre plopped down beside her and gazed longingly at the baby in Ezi's arms.

"Would you like to hold her?"

Aiyre shook her head. "I held her enough while you recovered. It is time for the both of you to bond." Her clan mate hugged her with one arm around her shoulders, "We do need to do an introduction ceremony for the gods though. She will need them in her life to help guide her and look after her."

"I have to be there for it. No one can take my place?"

Aiyre shrugged a shoulder. "You don't have to be there. I figured you would like to be there though, and it might bring this little one some comfort when Eron spreads ash paste across her body."

Ezi glanced down at the baby as it pulled away from her breast, having suckled its fill. Placing her shirt back into place, Ezi propped the baby up against her shoulder as she lightly jiggled it. She had no idea what she was doing, but she figured she'd let her instincts take over when it came to handling the child.

"Can I tell Eron we will do the ceremony?" Aiyre pressed.

After a couple of seconds, Ezi breathed, "Yes."

Aiyre smiled in relief. "Good. If you can meet us at the caves, I can fetch Eron from his hut."

"Now?" Ezi was surprised it would be so soon. She hadn't expected them to be ready, but then again, what had she expected from Eron? When it came to the gods that shaman was always ready to communicate with them.

"You know Eron. He is always prepared for anything." Aiyre rose from her seat. "Will you meet us there?"

"Yes," Ezi said because she knew no one was about to let her stay inside the birthing hut in peace and quiet. She also knew she would be kicked out of the birthing hut and forced to go live in the communal women's hut.

Without another word, Aiyre rose and left the hut.

With a sigh, she glanced down at the child's head. Shifting the baby back into her arms, she stared down at the smiling baby face. It was so cute and chubby, and there was a rosy tint to its cheeks.

She wanted nothing more than to be close to her child, but despite her wishes, she was still unable to feel close to the baby. She'd much rather have Drakk beside her than this child. She didn't blame the child for Drakk's death, because she fully realized it was the sabertooth shifters that killed him, but she was still left longing for his tender caresses.

The baby swatted at a leather strap on her shirt that dangled down with a couple of deer bone beads on the end. The chubby hands hit the beads, sending the string flying through the air in back and forth movements.

A smile spread across her face as she watched the joy that filled the baby's eyes.

"I know you're having fun, but we must introduce you to the gods and let them name you," Ezi told the baby even though she knew the baby wouldn't understand a single word she was saying. "Or Eron will be cross with us."

Rising from her position, she bundled the child up in her arms and left the hut. The bright sunlight seared her eyes, and her eyelids slammed shut as she paused right outside the hut. It'd been days since she last left the hut, and her eyes had trouble handling the sudden sunlight.

Slowly, Ezi cracked her eyes until she could handle the bright light of the outdoors. She glanced around the village, getting her bearings. It felt like an eternity since she'd last been outside, but nothing around the village had changed reassuring her that it'd only been a few days.

"Are you ready?" Tira came up beside her, her voice soft and motherly.

"Yes. You were right about the child needing to meet the gods." This was her way to try and get closer to her child. Maybe if she pleased the gods, they would lessen the hurt of Drakk's death and open her heart to love the child in her arms.

"Eron will be waiting for you in the caves. As you know, it will be just you, Eron, the child, and the gods."

She nodded her head. The ceremony of the sabertooths wasn't that different from her pronghorn clan. Although, if her mother had still been alive, she too would have been welcomed into the ceremony.

More despair came up to choke her. It hadn't only been Drakk she'd lost, but her entire family. None of them had made it out of the sabertooth attack alive. Her mother, father, and her brother had been lost. Their deaths also weighed heavily on her, and she questioned why the gods had allowed her to live while taking so many.

Quickly, she glanced over at Tira's eyes. Brown eyes with golden flecks in them, eyes that hid a predator.

Unnerved by where her thoughts were once again leading, she left Tira behind. Ezi weaved her way through the village of huts. And as she walked through the village, people would stop and stare, trying to get a glance at the newest addition to the clan.

A woman strode up to her. "May I see?"

Ezi loosened her grip on the baby so that the woman would be able to see the child more clearly.

"Beautiful." The woman cooed, her head descending close to the baby.

Suddenly flashes of sabertooth teeth from the night of the attack flew through her mind, and she yanked the child back, away from the woman.

A startled gasp escaped the woman before she leaned away.

Ezi rushed away with quick steps, not wanting to explain the sudden change in her mood. She might not like the memories the baby dredged up, but it didn't mean she trusted any sabertooth shifter around her child.

The child cried out a few times at all the jostling as Ezi's hurried steps carried them away.

Rushing through the huts, she didn't slow down until she left the village behind and made her way towards the cave system nearby.

The baby calmed down the closer they neared the cave system, seeming to sense they were about to commune with the gods.

"I wonder what they will name you." Only the gods knew, but she still wondered about it. She could name the child, but she wasn't sure she should be trusted with such a decision. A name had importance. It could shape the entire child's future.

As she walked the well-traveled path leading from the sabertooth village to the caves, she found the silence peaceful. Some of the stress left her shoulders. Until the sabertooth attack, she'd always been relaxed and comfortable about the world she lived in, but now she found herself always afraid. She felt like a skittish rabbit, and she wasn't fond of the feeling.

Soon a cliffside rose up in front of her as some of the trees disappeared. The mouth of the cave gaped wide in front of her, threatening to eat her whole. But it was another place that she didn't fear. This was where people like her could communicate with the gods. It was a safe place.

Ezi broke into the caves, the dark dampness encompassing her with a welcoming embrace. She'd seen the inside of this tunnel before, several times in fact, and she knew there was nothing on the cave floor to trip her. It'd been rubbed smooth by the many generations of sabertooth shifters who'd used this cave for all their ceremonies.

Then a small orange flickering light further down the cave tunnel called to her.

"Almost there." She said to the baby.

In just a few moments, Ezi broke out into a main chamber where she found several small fires around the inside of the cave. Eron was standing in the middle of the cavern, smiling at her. Firelight flickered off the older shaman, giving him a godly appearance, especially with his large shadow standing on the cave wall behind him.

He opened his arms wide, "It is good to see you up and well, Ezi. We all feared the gods meant to take you from us."

"It is nice to see you as well." The elderly shaman was the one sabertooth in this clan that she trusted. She hadn't even seen him shift into his sabertooth form, and wondered if he might be too old to shift properly.

"Bring her to me." He coaxed her forward, and Ezi did as he bid.

As she approached, she held out her bundled child until she was safely in Eron's arms.

"What a pretty baby," Eron said softly as he gazed down at the child.

It was well known Eron would have liked to have a mate and children, but the gods had never been kind enough to give him any of that. It was a shame. Ezi could easily see him making a fantastic father with his gentle but firm personality.

He spun around, bent over, and placed the baby into a small fur-lined basket that he must have brought when Aiyre had informed him that Ezi was coming to the caves. A baby basket wasn't normally inside the cave.

Then he faced her again. "Come." He guided her over to one of the small fires, "Now sit." He commanded her.

She did as he said and watched as Eron took a hold of a few bunches of dried leaves. He dipped them towards the flames until they began to release a white smoke that trickled upwards in the cold air of the cave. Then he walked over to her as he chanted and waved the smoking leaves around her head.

Ezi sucked in deep and even breathes. The smoke filled her lungs and helped to calm her racing memories.

Then Eron moved over to the baby, and he waved the burning leaves around the child who gurgled and laughed, raising its arms over its head.

"You are a lively one." Eron smiled down at the baby before placing the still smoldering leaves beside a small fire.

Then he grabbed a bowl and walked over to Ezi. He dipped a couple of fingers into the bone bowl and wiped the mixture over her face until her face was completely covered. Eron left her to walk over to the baby. He rubbed the mixture over the baby who just cooed and gurgled in delight to the sensation.

"Now," Eron said as he rose and took his own seat in front of the fire, "we will find out what name the gods will give to her."

He took a different bone bowl, raised the rim to his lips, and drank whatever was inside. She watched as his blue eyes grew hazy as the liquid took effect. His chanting grew louder until his voice echoed off the cave walls and filled her ears.

Slowly, Eron rocked back and forth as he

chanted, his eyes rolling back in his head. After what felt like a lifetime, Eron righted himself, looked her straight in the eyes and said, "Her name will be Flosa."

"Flosa," Ezi repeated as her eyes glanced across the fire and at her child. The name somehow made her feel closer and more connected to her child.

Chapter 5

Tor wasn't sure if he was alive or dead. He tried to open his eyelids, but they felt weighed down. The pain was there, but it felt distant like he'd somehow been removed from it. He growled in irritation to find himself in his human form. He could feel the separate fingers on his hands and his human toes. His sabertooth form had done its best to protect him, but even it ended up drained and needed a rest.

Then he felt hands begin to roam over his body. And there was something else… talking perhaps?

Fighting the darkness surrounding his mind, Tor ripped open his eyes and kicked out his feet while swinging his arms. If this was an animal hoping for an easy meal, then he was going to defend himself until his dying breath.

"Be calm." A soothing male voice reached his ears.

The voice sounded familiar to him. Glancing up, Tor's eyes landed on a face that he knew. "Darh." He froze in the middle of his thrashing about.

"Tor, we thought you were long dead and walking with our ancestors in the Eternal Hunting Grounds." Darh continued to run his hands over Tor's body as he searched for broken bones or other wounds… other than the one that had to be obvious on his leg.

"I thought I would be walking with them," Tor admitted. After the rhinoceros hunt, he hadn't thought he would see a member of his clan unless it was in the Eternal Hunting Grounds. He wanted to see his mother and father, but not this soon. Not if he had to die to see them.

"What happened?" Another person walked into his field of vision.

Shifting his head slightly, recognition lit up his face, "Jirk?"

"Yes." The other man bent down next to him. "What happened?" He repeated the same question as Darh as his brown eyes skimmed over Tor until he reached Tor's leg and then the other man visibly winced as he saw the wound there.

"A wholly rhinoceros." Tor croaked out of his sore throat. He had no idea how long he'd been laying on the ground without water, and his throat didn't like the prolonged speaking.

"It attacked you?" Darh's eyebrows rose in skepticism. They might be irritable creatures, but they weren't known for attacking without a reason. They were large enough to deter predators from attacking a healthy one.

"Not before I attacked it."

Darh snorted as he shook his head. "Why would you hunt a wholly rhinoceros by yourself. You were asking to be killed." He looked at Tor like he was some young cub who couldn't learn.

Tor just shrugged. "I needed the challenge to take my mind off troubling thoughts."

Darh pursed his lips as he shook his head. "We were supposed to be out checking traps for rabbits, but we will have to bring you back to the village instead. Eron and Tira will need to heal this gash before it becomes something more serious."

"How close are we?"

"A valley away."

"My sabertooth must have brought me back." Because Tor definitely didn't remember walking back towards the village. He wasn't even sure he would have known the way back.

"It knew you would be safer near the village then out there with all the predators lurking around." Jirk nodded his head, his shoulder-length brown hair waving over his shoulders. "The wound is scabbed over now, but I'm sure it was bleeding all over when you got it."

Tor relaxed against the ground, knowing his clan would take care of him. The pain was coming back to the forefront now that he was conscious.

"How should we get him back?"

"Hand me your shirt." Darh stripped off his own shirt as Jirk did the same. Once Darh had both of the shirts, he tied the arms together. "Now we can roll him onto the shirts and pull him back to the village."

Jirk nodded his head in approval. "Let's get him back then. Daerk isn't going to believe his eyes."

"I almost didn't believe my own eyes when I first spotted him."

The men gripped his shoulders and legs and quickly shifted Tor onto the shirts. A brief shot of pain rocked through him as his leg jostled, and he let out a grunt as he ground his teeth together.

"Sorry." Darh apologized. "But we have to get you back to the village, so Eron can take a look at your wound and get it healed."

Tor nodded his head as he gritted his teeth

until the pain slowly faded into the back of his mind as a darkness called him into the back of his mind. There was no need for him to suffer more than he'd already had. He was turning his life into Darh and Jirk's hands.

He felt them begin to drag him over the ground. Every once in a while, a bump would have him sucking in a pained breath. After several more bumps as they dragged him, the pain became too much, and once more the darkness pulled him down into a black abyss, and he feared it wouldn't be much longer until he was walking in the Eternal Hunting Grounds.

Daerk sat at a campfire, his eyes scanning over the village he'd seen through a harsh winter after kicking out the last leader, Brog. That man had been a disease in the village, but things were lighter and easier now that their meat hut was bursting at the seams. All Daerk had to do was keep it that way.

A couple of children ran past him as he sat there at the village fire. One corner of his lips crooked upwards as he watched them play a game of chase. Someday, when they were older, they'd be playing games of chase in their sabertooth forms to perfect their hunting skills, but for now, it was simply a game. They wouldn't be able to shift into their other form until they were slightly older.

Ezi had given birth a couple of moons ago, and there were some more babies on their way. The clan was prospering, but the land they lived in had a way of taking and giving happiness at the same rate, and he worried more trying times would be in store for them.

"Where does your mind wander to today?" Aiyre plopped down beside him, her brunette braid flopping around behind her back.

And once more, he had another reason to smile. "Hoping I am still the best person to lead this clan." He reached out and fingered a couple of beads on her shirt. "These are pretty."

She sent him a dazzling smile. "I sewed them on yesterday."

"I like them."

Aiyre cocked her head to the side as her gorgeous brown eyes scanned over his face. "I can't promise that there wouldn't be a better person somewhere out there to be a leader," she waved a hand vaguely around, "but when it comes to this clan, you are the perfect leader. Our clanmates can now breath without the worry of inciting Brog's wrath."

It was true. No one had to worry about him going into a rage and throwing clan mates into a fire like Brog had tried to do.

"I worry about our next winter," Daerk admitted as he absently rubbed one of her shoulders. He'd been reluctant to put all this pressure on his shoulders, and now that he had so many lives relying on him he didn't want to let them down. Everyone had confidence in him, and it made him worry he wouldn't live up to their expectations.

Aiyre shook her head as she leaned into his touch. "We have a summer to look forward to, and if we lead correctly, winter will be easier. It will never be easy, but the gods are so far smiling down on our clan."

"Still…"

She placed a gentle hand on one of his own. "What if I ask Eron to ask the gods?"

"Do you think they will answer such a question?" Daerk could remember several occasions where the gods had deemed no answer was necessary. The gods only spoke to Eron when they had something to say, and he worried that they would once again find their lips sealed tight. Or worse, they would confirm his fears that he wasn't the right leader for their people.

"I am sure they will give you whatever answer you need to give you confidence, whether it is through Eron or the actions of this world." Aiyre patted his hand.

Daerk cocked his head to the side as he examined the woman beside him. "Are you sure you are not a god? The wisdom you hold has me wondering." His eyes narrowed to slits as he examined her.

She tossed back her head with a thunderous chuckle that seemed to take a hold of her entire body. When she recovered, she slapped one of his hands playfully, "I am no god."

Aiyre leaned her head onto his shoulder, and her delicate scent wafted up to his nose. He stroked a hand over her hair, enjoying the comfort she brought him. Their meeting hadn't been an easy one, but it'd been worth the battle. He rested his own head against the top of hers.

A pronghorn shifter and a sabertooth shifter seemed like a funny match to him, but who was he to question the gods. They seemed to think she was the perfect woman for him, and he wasn't complaining.

He pulled her in close to his side. A feeling of contentment flowed through him. This moment was perfect.

"We need help!" A cry went up.

Daerk leaped to his feet, suddenly forcing Aiyre to catch herself as she too stood up next to him. They looked around frantically, their eyes searching out the source of the voice. For a brief second, he thought he might have heard something that wasn't there, but when he glanced over at Aiyre her eyes were just as frenzied.

"Over here!" The voice called out sounding strained.

"Come." Aiyre grabbed one of his hands and rushed them over to one side of the village. As they came around a hut, their eyes landed on a staggering sight. "It can't be," Aiyre uttered under her breath.

"Tor?" Daerk darted forward as the two men ceased dragging his friend across the ground. As he bent down on the ground next to Tor, he lifted the other man's head into his lap. He knew it was Tor, but he looked like he was either dead or about to join their ancestors in the Eternal Hunting Grounds. "Fetch Eron and my mother!"

"I'll go!"

He glanced up for a brief second and watched Aiyre sprint off in the direction of the caves, where Eron would be communing with the gods. Her fur-lined boots flew over the ground. He glanced back down at his friend. "What happened?"

"We were out checking traps for animals when we stumbled on him lying on the ground in his human form."

The other man stepped forward. "We couldn't believe our eyes at first."

Daerk looked up and finally recognized the faces of the men. It was Darh and Jirk who stood in front of him. "Where did you find him?"

"Not far from the village." Darh pointed off in the direction they'd come. "He was near one of the massive trees that mark our territory."

"This wound on his leg." Daerk brushed over it lightly with a few fingertips, and the first sign of life came from Tor's lips as he gasped in pain. But his eyes did not open, and the blue tinge to his lips caused Daerk's heart to tremble. This here was a dear friend, and it hurt him to see Tor in such a state. "Let's get him to his hut while we wait for Eron and Tira."

Despite the fact that Tor had been gone for many months, Daerk had kept his hut ready and waiting, because he'd always been sure that Tor would once more return to them. He just had hoped it would've been in a better state and not with a gruesome wound on his leg.

"What have you done to yourself, my friend?" Daerk shook his head as he gently placed Tor's head back down and took up one side of the fur shirts.

Jirk took the other side, and together they picked up Tor's torso using the fur shirts that were tied together and slowly eased him through the village until they arrived at the right hut. Jirk went in first, backward, and then Tor and Daerk entered the hut, which had a brightly burning fire. Daerk had never let that fire burn out. He'd never given up hope that Tor would once more rejoin their clan.

Rir, Tor, and Daerk were like brothers. They'd been close ever since they were cubs and nothing would separate them.

Gently, they placed Tor down on the bed of furs by the warm crackling fire. Pulling back, Daerk scrubbed a hand across his face. "I always knew he would come back to us at some point, but I was hoping I would see him walk into the village, not have to be carried."

Jirk nodded his head as Darh came into the tent after them. "Some of us wondered if we'd ever see him again."

Darh nodded his head in agreement. "Some of us thought we never would."

"Where's Eron?" Daerk turned to face the entrance of the hut feeling irritated that no one was here who could ease Tor's suffering. The wound was turning blue and black right before his eyes, and he wasn't sure his friend would make it through this. It oozed yellow pus and had Daerk's mouth turning up on one corner in disgust. But it also made him glad Tor appeared to be passed out due to the pain... he could only imagine what this nasty wound would feel like.

"I'm here!" Eron busted through the hut flaps, Aiyre hot on his heels.

Daerk watched on helplessly as Eron knelt down next to Tor. The clan shaman placed a small leather bag by his side and ripped open the lid exposing animal stomach bags that contained everything that he would require.

"I'm going to need some hot water," Eron stated.

"I'll grab it!" Aiyre left the hut in a rush, her braid swinging behind her until the hut flap closed behind her, and she was gone from sight.

Then Daerk glanced back down at Tor. "Will he live?"

"Only the gods can answer that question Daerk. You know that." Eron returned as he dug through his pack, pulling out herb after herb, some Daerk couldn't even name.

"Aiyre said hot water was needed?" Tira rushed into the hut, carrying a couple of animal skulls full of water. Trails of steam rose off the top.

"Place them down beside me." Eron motioned but never even turned to look at her.

Tira rushed over to Eron's side and placed the skulls on the ground beside him. "That wound looks nasty." She commented as she got a better look. "Anyone know what happened to him?"

Darh stepped forward. "He mumbled something about a wholly rhinoceros."

Tira shook her head. "He tried to hunt one?"

"I don't think he said." Darh looked over at Jirk who just shrugged in response.

Daerk rolled his eyes as he scrubbed his hand over his face again. "Attacking a rhinoceros while on his own sounds like something Tor would do. He's always been a bit overconfident."

Tira made tisking noises with her tongue. "He should know better."

"In his state of mind, he may not have known any better." Daerk shook his head. "He'd been rejected and was hurt, and it may have festered until he wasn't thinking about his actions. Just look at him. You barely see the man under all that grime and hair."

"And now he may die."

"I'm doing my best to prevent that from happening." Eron chimed in. "And with the blessing of the gods, I may just be able to do it." He finally turned to face the people in the hut. "Some of you should leave. Your presence is only stifling the hut."

"You stay, Daerk," Tira said, "we three will leave." And then she quickly ushered the other two men out of the tent, but not without giving Daerk a nod of support. And with that simple nod, she sent him all the courage he needed to stay. His mother knew Tor and Rir were like brothers to him.

Eron poured one skull of hot water over the wound, doing his best to cleanse it of dirt and disease. Then he threw a mixture of flowers and leaves into a stone bowl and began mashing them.

"May I?" Daerk approached and bent down, needing to do something for his friend rather than standing there uselessly.

"Here." Eron handed it over eagerly, his aging hands needing the opportunity for rest.

"He'll live."

It wasn't a question Daerk was asking, but a statement. After everything their clan had been through he needed Tor to be by his side. He couldn't lead without support and his friends.

Chapter 6

"What's going on?" Ezi asked Aiyre the moment she sat down around the village fire and noticed the buzz in the air. Everyone's had their heads pressed together as they whispered. When the child in her arms fussed, she bounced the child on her hip as she folded her legs under her butt.

Aiyre nibbled her lip a little as she studied Ezi.

Ezi's eyes narrowed on the small movement. "What?"

"Tor is back." Aiyre blurted in a rush.

Ezi sucked in a harsh breath as his image flashed in front of her. Those piercing blue eyes of his, eyes that seemed to engulf her until she was left gasping for air. Shaking herself, she glanced around the village, "Where is he?"

"In his hut."

"Maybe I should head back to mine." As Ezi made movements to get up, Aiyre held out a hand, stopping her.

"You don't have to worry about him trying to convince you to join him in matehood right now."

"Why not?" Ezi settled back down, trusting Aiyre's word that there was no reason for her to worry.

"He's gravely injured. Turns out he thought he could hunt a wholly rhinoceros on his own." Aiyre shook her head with a heavy sigh.

Ezi let it sink in for a few minutes. She may not have wanted to accept his mate hood, but she would never wish him ill because he had always been a nice man. He'd never pushed the mate hood on her.

"Will he die?" The baby reached up and pulled lightly at one of the strands of her hair. Ezi shifted her head away, so the child wouldn't be able to yank out a clump.

"Eron's doing his best for Tor."

"He is in his hut?" She had no idea why she was asking… it wasn't like she ever wanted to set eyes on him. If he died, it would take care of the only problem she had in this clan. Living with sabertooths was hard, but being a sabertooth's mate was impossible.

"He is." Aiyre looked over at her, studying her. Then her eyes shifted to the child in Ezi's arms. "How is Flosa?"

"Fussy as ever." Ezi sighed. "I don't think I've slept well in days." She was sure there were shadows under her eyes. If Drakk was still alive, she'd be able to share some of these duties with him, but instead she was all on her own…well, maybe not all on her own. She did have Aiyre, who adored Flosa.

"Would you like to hold her?" Ezi offered. "I could use some time to sleep and eat."

"I would." Aiyre all but lunged at her, yanking Flosa free and then cooing at the baby in her arms. "Maybe she will keep my mind off of Tor and what Daerk must be going through."

Flosa smiled up at Aiyre, and her arms came up as she tried to play with some leather strings hanging off Aiyre's shirt, but her clumsy baby hands found it hard to capture the moving strings.

Ezi felt a pinch of bitterness in her heart.

Aiyre was always better with Flosa than she was. Sometimes she wondered if the gods had blessed the wrong woman with a child. Aiyre and Daerk were trying everything they could think of, like having Eron ask the gods of fertility for their blessing, and drinking certain bitter brews of tea that Eron and Tira served them. Tira was skilled with her herb use, and she was Daerk's mother, so if anyone was going to help them succeed in their dreams, it would be her.

The baby gurgled in delight as Aiyre waved her braid near the child's hands.

With a frown, Ezi turned on a fur booted heel. She had some place she had to go, and she couldn't watch the way the two of them interacted.

Weaving her way away from the village fire, she passed several large huts where women in this clan stayed until they were married to a man who had his own hut for her to call her own. Unfortunately, Ezi hadn't been given her own hut, and she was currently living in one of the communal huts. When she'd first arrived, she hadn't been thrilled with staying so close to sabertooth shifters… not after they decimated her clan and her family.

Now, she could be around them. They had proven over and over again that without the fear of punishment from a deluded clan leader, they were all good people at heart. She still had trouble trusting them fully, but she was trying.

Then it came into sight.

Tor's hut.

Ezi stood stock still as she stared openly at the hut just a rock throws length away from her. With just a few steps, she could look inside and see for herself. Her tongue darted out of her mouth, curled, and her top teeth came down, pinching the piece of flesh as she debated with herself.

Then she took a few cautious steps towards the hut.

Laughter had her head snapping around to see two young sabertooth shifters headed her way, gabbing about something.

Ezi turned tail and darted away from the hut before she was seen near it. It was no secret in this clan that she was the reason Tor had left in the first place, and she was sure her presence would get people wondering.

Knowing her child was in good hands for a little while, Ezi raced towards the edge of the village, the huts and people streaked past her, and once she got to the edge, she stripped her clothes off, and shifted.

In a matter of seconds, she was in her pronghorn form. She stamped a hoofed foot in excitement. It'd been so long since she'd been in this form. The pregnancy had prevented it, and then she'd been too busy with Flosa.

Her long hears flickered back and forth, rubbing against the two horns on her head. The sounds of the village were a little more amplified, her prey senses always looking for sources of danger.

With a jump into the air to stretch all four of her long legs, she sprinted into the nearby forest, eager for a refreshing run to help clear her mind. Tor might be back, but she wasn't about to let him ruin the peace she'd created here for herself amongst the sabertooth shifters.

"Thank you for watching her for me." Ezi took the bundle of furs into her arms and saw a tiny face fast asleep.

"You know I am always here." Aiyre sent her a smile. "How was your rest?"

It was like her friend and fellow pronghorn shifter knew she hadn't gone and rested like she'd said. Aiyre was smiling like she could smell the shift and romp through the forest that Ezi had enjoyed.

"It helped." Because the run in her pronghorn form had helped her. It had relaxed her and helped her to see clearly. She'd been so close to letting her curiosity take control of her, and if she'd been caught snooping on Tor? She was positive it would have created some questions in the clan, like why she even cared in the first place.

Which she didn't care.

He could die, and she would never shed a single tear.

"Thank you again." Ezi sent Aiyre a smile as she turned to head back to her hut with Flosa fit snuggly in her arms. With night approaching and Flosa finally settling down, Ezi wanted to take her chance at a goodnight's rest. Something she rarely got with the baby and the nightmares.

"I'm always here for you," Aiyre called out.

Ezi slowly walked through the clan she now called home. It was a decent-sized clan, and probably one of the largest in this area, so it felt safe. Or as safe as a pronghorn could feel amongst so many sabertooths. It went against her every instinct, but strangely, her pronghorn side hadn't protested where she was living. Maybe because it knew there was nowhere else that would be safer for them.

Or for the child in her arms.

She glanced down at Flosa.

Aiyre had promised to help Ezi leave this clan once the spring melted the thick layer of snow on the ground, but now that she actually had the child in her arms, she realized she wouldn't be able to make such a journey. She wasn't even sure where the closest pronghorn clan lived.

She approached her hut. A communal hut. It was large and provided enough room for the women inside, but Ezi wished for her own hut. Large mammoth bones and tusks held the taunt furs up, and a trickle of grey smoke rose from the top where a hole had been cut in the top fur to let out the suffocating smoke.

Pushing through the hut entrance, she relaxed immediately. This hut was her sanctuary away from everyone else out there. She knew the women who lived in here well, and after a few restless nights had begun to trust them. Now it was just the baby and nightmares that bothered her.

Ezi walked over to a small mound of furs with a baby-sized dent in them, and placed Flosa in it. The child's eyes were already shut tight with sleep, and Ezi was eager to join her.

She plopped down in her own bed which was a mere foot away from Flosa's bed, and laid down. Her eyes watched the flames of the small fire in the hut, causing shadows to play across the animal skin walls.

It was peaceful, and if she forgot where she was, she could almost imagine herself back in her old village of pronghorn shifters.

A small smile creased her lips as her eyes sank closed. At least in her dreams, she could frolic with her old clanmates once more.

A cry tore through her pleasant dreams, dreams that showed Drakk's smiling face, and teasing remarks.

Bolting up in her bed, Ezi's eyes raced around the inside of the hut. Her heart thundered in her chest, but everything was quiet. Had she really been reliving the night of the attack again? It'd been weeks since she'd had a nightmare like that, and she'd been hoping it meant she never would again.

Every other woman in the hut was fast asleep, meaning she hadn't cried out in her sleep. She earned herself several glares when she did that, even if they understood what she'd gone through. Ezi understood their glares. It was never pleasant to be woken up with screams.

She stretched her arms above her head and yawned the nightmare away. When she looked down at Flosa, she found the child still fast asleep, but probably not for much longer. The child tended to pick the most inconvenient times for a feeding.

Quickly, Ezi glanced at the entrance to her hut.

Tor's hut wasn't far from hers. It would be a

simple jaunt over there and back, and then she could stop wondering about his condition. She didn't want to seem too interested by asking about him, so she wasn't sure exactly how bad it was.

She bit her top lip as she did her best to hold still.

Failing at restraining herself, she jumped to her feet, and she glanced down at Flosa to make sure she was still fast asleep. Satisfied that the baby wouldn't wake until she got back, Ezi quickly left the hut before her resolve faded.

The village was quiet at this time of night. The only people awake would be any guards that were posted around the perimeter of the village. Brog, the past clan leader, and his friends were still somewhere out there. Everyone figured it was only a matter of time before he came back for his revenge.

Ezi's skin prickled in fear. She could only pray everyone was wrong, and Brog would stay far away from them. Maybe he had fallen into a river and drowned, or found some other poor clan to terrify. As long as he didn't come back.

Despite knowing no one would be out and about at this hour, Ezi's eyes continued to scan the darkness. She didn't need anyone catching her looking in on Tor. All she was doing was satiating her curiosity. Nothing more.

The sky above her was a maze of tiny glistening lights. Every once in a while, a white light would streak across the sky above her before disappearing. It was magical, and something only the gods would be able to explain.

As she rounded a hut, she heard laughter

from within, and her feet paused as her ears perked up. There was some more giggling before throaty moans began to emanate from within the fur walls.

Ezi's heart broke at those sounds because it reminded her of the first and only time she and Drakk had shared furs together. He'd been a kind lover, showing her what to do and taking their sweet time to get to know each other. She'd been awkward and unsure of herself, but he'd been slow with her, talking her through everything.

Shaking her head, she left the hut behind her with some quick steps.

Then she was there. Standing in front of Tor's hut.

Sucking in a deep breath, she darted forward before any random clanmate could spot her, reached out a hand, brushed the fur flap aside, and walked inside. The warmth of his hearth fire wrapped around her in a tight embrace.

She stared at the flames for the longest time, before finally glancing over at the bundle of furs on the other side of the hut. Despite the flickering flames, Ezi found it hard to see the form on the other side of the hut he was so buried in the blankets.

Slowly, her feet drew her closer until she was standing right beside him.

Her eyes shot wide.

He looked nothing like the man she'd known for that brief period in time. He was a wild man. His black hair was long, and she could see the knots in it. Someone would need to take a knife to it to get those knots out because no bone comb would get those out. And then there was his beard. It was almost summer, and no other man in the clan was wearing such a long thick beard.

And despite the wild man look he had, she could still see how attractive he was under it all. The man had been born with a fantastic facial structure. His sharp nose cut down his face, and his beard had a hard time hiding the fierce structure of his jawline.

"What did you go and do?" Ezi shook her head. She still believed he was a gentle man, even if she didn't want to be his mate, and she hated to see him like this.

Then her eyes glanced down at the fur covering him. Reaching down, she gripped the edge of the fur and ripped it off of him, exposing a large bandage that Eron must have wrapped around his leg.

For one brief second, she felt a stab of pity pierce her heart. With the size of the bandage, it had to be a horrible wound. Other than his leg, he looked fine. More than fine.

Her eyes lazily moved over his naked expanse of skin. His honed body was that of a hunter. There wasn't a single piece of fat on this man. She could see the ropes of muscles in his arms and the temptation to reach out and stroke a finger down his arm was strong, but she resisted. Then her eyes dipped lower to between his thighs.

Ezi licked her lips.

Drakk had nothing on Tor when it came to his member. The long member hung between his legs and pulled at her feminine core. Would he grow like Drakk or not?

Ezi frowned and shook her head before whipping the fur cover back over his body. She'd been gone too long from her child, the person she should be worrying about. Spinning on a heel, she left his hut and made a vow to the gods that she wouldn't be back.

Chapter 7

Tor had never been so hot in his entire life, but it was strange. He was hot, but because of how much he was sweating, he was also shivering. Every time his eyes opened, he would glance over at the fire. All he could think about was jumping into those flames. Their flickering embrace would be sure to warm him.

He opened his mouth, but all that came out was a gurgle of nonsense. He'd been out for too long, and his throat was dry.

If he couldn't call for help, then he would do it on his own.

Tor slumped his torso over the edge of his bed of furs, and soon the rest of his body followed him. Pain seared through his leg as he landed on the ground. He ground his teeth as he rode through the pain, waiting for it to dissipate.

After what seemed like an eternity, the pain finally receded until he was able to open his eyes once more, and began crawling his way towards the fire. Once he felt it touch his skin, he knew he would finally be warm enough, and then, maybe then this pain would finally leave him alone.

He was so close. All that filled his vision were the orange and yellow flickers of the flames as they danced, coaxing him towards them.

"What are you doing Tor?" A cross voice hollered at him from behind.

Tor scooted faster over the ground, knowing

he was about to be interrupted from his mission. His hands hauled the rest of his body across the ground as his arms bulged with the movements.

Then there were hands clawing at his shoulders, clamping down around his shoulders until the fingers dug into his flesh.

Tor growled deep in his throat, warning the person behind him to his foul mood. He tried to summon his sabertooth, but the blasted thing wouldn't appear. Instead, it stayed hidden somewhere deep inside his body.

"Come Tor. Let's get you away from this fire and back into bed where your body can rest." He was finally able to recognize the voice of Daerk.

"I have to get," he tried to wiggle out of Daerk's grasp, "to the fire. It will warm me."

"Tor!" Daerk yanked him up by the scruff of his neck and dragged him back to his bed.

Pain rolled through him as his leg got trapped under his body before righting itself. Black dots filled his vision, but he forced the pain away, not wanting to blackout again. He was tired of spending most of the time unconscious.

"Try not to be too rough with him." Eron's stern voice broke through Tor's delusions. "I'd hate for you to reopen his wound after I spent so much time healing it."

"He wants to sit in the fire. Not beside the fire, but in it."

"He has a fire burning inside of him. It will cool in time, and in the meantime we will have to take turns watching him to make sure he doesn't do something to himself on accident." Eron bent down next to Tor. "The fire will do you no good Tor."

Tor couldn't believe it. These two people were supposed to be his friends, and yet they denied him the one thing that he wanted the most, to be one with the dancing flames. Their every wiggle enticed him as if rubbing his face in their warmth.

"I need to be in the fire."

Eron shook his head as he placed a hand on Tor's arm. "Hold in there. This fever will break in no time, and you'll regret having jumped into a fire. Burns are no fun."

"It will warm me."

"We will warm you," Eron promised. "Quick Daerk, build up that fire." He waved a hand at the fire and the spare wood sitting nearby.

Daerk dashed towards the fire and began stirring it up until a heatwave washed through the inside of the hut. Then he watched as Daerk threw a couple of logs onto the fire, the flames quickly licking at the edges and catching the dry bark on fire.

Tor's eyes sank shut.

"Are you still here?" Eron patted his arm, and Tor's eyes shot wide. "Don't fall asleep on me now. I came here to find out how you are and treat your wound."

"Am I in the village?" His voice surprised even his own ears. It was rough from all the time he'd spent passed out. "Water?" He croaked.

"I've got some." Daerk came back into view as he poured some water from an animal skin hanging on his waist into a bone cup. "Here." He handed it down to Eron, but Tor reached up and snatched it.

"I can." He winced as his words scraped up

his dry throat. Then he raised himself on an elbow and took a sip of the cool water that gently soothed his throat. Within minutes, he'd sucked down the whole cup of water. He handed the cup back to Daerk and slowly laid back down on the bed of furs.

"It's good to see you awake and able to do some things for yourself." Eron smiled down at him, and he returned the smile that he'd known since he'd been born. Eron was like a second father to almost everyone in the clan.

"I'm glad I'm not with our ancestors."

"You're lucky you aren't." Daerk folded his arms in front of his chest. "You're an idiot."

Tor smirked as he chuckled, and then began coughing as his sore throat complained about the sudden laughter.

"Here," Eron held another bone cup up to Tor's lips, "this will help with any pain while I tend to your wound."

Tor leaned forward, and the moment the liquid hit the tip of his tongue, he pulled back and spat it out, nearly hitting Eron. "What is that?" He croaked.

Eron's lips pursed as he grumbled and made a new batch. "It's juice from herbs mixed into water, and I need you to drink it."

"It tastes like piss."

Daerk let out a bellow of a laugh. "Because you know what piss tastes like?"

Tor chuckled. "I could imagine what it tastes like."

"Uh huh." Daerk wiped a tear away from the corner of his eye. "I believe you."

"Shouldn't you remove him from my hut if

he isn't helping me feel better?" Tor asked as he hitched a thumb over at Daerk.

"Someone needs to watch you." Eron handed him another cup of the bitter liquid. "You tried to jump into your hut fire. Until you prove you aren't going to harm yourself, then you will be watched."

Tor held his breath, scrunched his nose, and downed the liquid in the cup before swallowing it with a curse and handing it back to Eron. "It was the fever, but now that the hut is warmer, I don't have that urge."

"You'll have to forgive me if I'm still worried about you harming yourself. This wound will only get worse before it gets better."

Daerk walked over to the other side of his bed and bent down. "Don't worry, I'll be here to bother you back to health."

"Great." Tor rolled his eyes and let his head roll to one side, and then he caught it. It was just a brief scent on the wind, but it was there. Something floral and delicate. A scent he hadn't smelled in many moons. It was so strong he wondered if she'd maybe even been inside his hut recently. "How is Ezi?"

Silence greeted his ears.

He turned his head so he could look at both of the men bent down around him. "How is she?" He sniffed the air again, but in his human form he couldn't be sure it really had been her scent. What if she was dead? This silence that was greeting his questions was beginning to cause his heart to pitter-patter inside his chest.

"She had a rough birth," Eron said as he glanced up from Tor's wound.

"Is she...?" He couldn't even say the word

out loud.

"She's alive." Daerk rushed to fill him in.

"And the baby?" Tor hoped they both were fine. The child might not be his, but he knew how much it would mean to Ezi. It was one of the last things she had from her clan and from a man she'd loved. He wanted to hate the other man, but she had known her partner before Tor came into her life, and he was now dead, and no threat to Tor.

"The baby is fine as well. Very healthy."

Relief washed through him.

"And she is here? In this clan still?" That hint of her scent could have been his traumatized mind imagining things.

"She is." Daerk nodded his head. "She hasn't asked to leave, probably because of her newborn and because Aiyre is here. They are like sisters."

"Has she asked about me?" Was that his heart hitching in his chest?

Daerk glanced over at Eron who just shrugged in return. His leather shirt bunching up around the shoulders with the movement.

"It's fine if the answer is no." It wouldn't surprise him terribly if Ezi didn't care about him. He was nothing more than another sabertooth shifter to her.

Eron bent further over his wound. "I think I may have overheard a conversation or two between Ezi and Aiyre about your health."

A little hope soared into his chest, sending his heart racing in his chest.

"Maybe she just wondered how long she had until you were better and she had to leave."

And then his hope was dashed.

Tor glared up at Daerk. "I prefer to think my mate won't run from me." Deny him over and over again, sure, but not run from him.

His sabertooth purred in agreement.

He rolled his eyes. The stupid thing was finally making its presence known. It'd been quiet for so long, but one whiff of Ezi and it was eager to come back.

"Do you think you could ask if she'd come visit?"

Daerk rubbed a hand across his chin, playing with the stubble that was growing there. "I'm not sure she will agree."

"All you have to do is ask." Tor glanced down at where Eron was working on his wound. Whatever he'd drunk was working well, and he couldn't feel a single thing as Eron poked and prodded his leg. He glanced back up at Daerk. "All I'm asking is that you ask her."

"I will ask her," Daerk promised, "but I can't promise that she will agree."

"That's fine." Tor's eyes sank closed as he relaxed on the bed of furs beneath him. It felt good to be home again. It'd been too long. Perhaps his wound had been a blessing from the gods. It'd gotten him back home, some place he needed to be. All these months alone had been hard on him.

He heard the entrance to his hut rustle as Daerk left.

"Almost done," Eron said.

"Take your time. It feels good to be back here and surrounded by my clan mates."

"I hope your time away from the clan helped you find whatever you sought." Eron said as he continued to work.

Tor frowned. "I'm not sure what I sought by running away."

"Is that what you did? Run away?"

Talking to Eron was never easy. The old man saw too much, but maybe that should be expected when he was always communing with the gods. This man was the wisest person Tor had ever known.

A sharp piercing cry penetrated the air around them, and Tor's eyes shot wide.

"Is that…?"

"Ezi's the only woman with such a young child at the moment, so it must be," Eron confirmed, not even looking up from his work.

Flashes of Ezi passed through his mind as the baby continued to cry out, and then silence fell. She must have given the hungry child what it'd been crying out for, but her image never left him. Those jade eyes of hers could never be forgotten. They'd penetrated his very soul, and now that he was back, he wanted to have his mate by his side once more.

After a week of listening to the sounds of the clan right outside his walls and Ezi's crying baby, Tor couldn't take it anymore. He needed to be a part of this world that was carrying on around him instead of being bedridden.

He wanted to be a part of the clan, and he

was hoping for a glimpse of Ezi. Daerk had yet to convince her to come by for a visit. So, if she wouldn't come to him then he had no other option than to go to her. He'd given her as much time as he could by leaving, but now that he was back he had an itch to take his mate as his own.

If Eron caught him sneaking out of his hut, the old man would have his head, but it was a risk he was willing to take. Just one glance to make sure Ezi was fine, and it would be worth it.

His sabertooth purred in agreement. The stupid thing only liked showing itself when he was thinking of his mate… it had a one-track mind. Otherwise, it was completely useless.

Even with the encouraging words of others, Tor wanted to see for himself that Ezi and her child were fine. Childbirth could be tricky, and there was a small part of his mind that was worried that people might be lying to him. He'd been near death's door, and he worried Ezi hadn't visited him because she'd been unable.

Rising up from his bed, Tor wobbled a bit. His legs weren't quite stable yet, but he wouldn't be deterred. Eron himself had said how well his thigh was healing and had even mentioned that walking around might be good for it, but he'd never said when. Tor felt like a naughty child going behind his mother's back. He just hoped he wasn't caught.

When he reached the hut entrance, he raised his hand and then paused. Maybe he was being silly. If he saw Ezi, it would only bring back all the hurt of her rejection and leave him wanting something he might never be allowed to have.

He raised his other hand to his chest and rubbed the area over his heart. It felt like it might be cracking inside his chest, and he hoped that couldn't truly happen.

His sabertooth growled in frustration, pushing him forward. It wanted to lay eyes on their mate.

Shoving his hand against the hut flap, Tor walked outside into a warm day. The sunshine streamed down, highlighting everything around him, and he wondered how he'd been gone for so long.

A couple of children ran past him, and a smile creased his lips. It felt good to be back in his clan. He missed having all this life surrounding him. His days away from the clan had been lonely and quiet.

He wasn't sure if it was just him or not, but there seemed to be a few more huts in the clan, meaning he'd missed the joyous occasion of a couple of mates joining together. He was curious to find out who had joined, but that could wait until later.

Tor began walking around the huts, stretching his legs out, and feeling like his normal self. There was a bit of a limp to his walk, but it was so much better than being cooped up in his hut. There was still some pain in his leg, but it wasn't searing pain, it was just a bother more than anything else.

As he neared the middle of the village, he leaned up against the outside of a hut allowing his leg some rest. He didn't want to overdo it and end up back in bedrest with Eron always watching.

And then he saw her.

The breath left Tor's chest in a rush as his eyes scanned over her eager to see how she was doing. Was it possible that she'd gotten more beautiful while he'd been gone? If he hadn't been leaning against a hut, he might have fallen to the ground with her overwhelming beauty.

She was wearing her brunette hair loose, and he loved how it flowed around her shoulders. Her gaze was focused on a bundle in her arms, and his eyes slowly dropped to that bundle. Little arms reached up out of the furs, trying to grip her swaying hair.

A smile spread across his lips as he forgot about his leg completely. She looked happy and in love with the child in her arms, and he felt his heart pinch a little more. He wanted to be there next to her, supporting her and the child.

But there… there was something awkward about the image in front of him.

The smile slowly faded from his lips as Tor realized what he was seeing. It looked like Ezi wasn't comfortable with her own child. Every touch looked strange and cautious, and it caused him to worry about her.

He'd always known she'd make a great mother, but every movement of hers was stiff and uncertain like she wasn't sure how to interact with her child.

Or maybe he saw something that wasn't there. It had been several months since he last saw her, and it was like he was relearning her movements all over again. It had to be in his head. Ezi would love any child of hers unconditionally.

The child cooed in her arms as the loose hair dangled above its face.

As Tor continued to watch their interactions, he felt longing creep into his heart. He wanted nothing more than to join them, to be a part of that loving interaction.

Forgetting himself, he placed his full weight on his injured leg, and dots swam across his vision as pain seared up his spine and into the base of his skull. Tor reached out, trying to catch himself, but missed and plummeted to the ground with a grunt as his leg gave way under him.

As he glanced up, he caught sight of Ezi's face. She was facing him, and her lips had gone round with her shock to find him so close. He reached out a hand, wanting to speak with her, but it wasn't long before his clan mates rushed to his side to give him aide and she spun around on a heel and left the area in a rush.

It was then that his heart shattered inside his chest as he watched her back recede.

Chapter 8

Ezi felt her head reel as she hastily put distance between herself and Tor. He was back up on his feet and moving around the village, and it worried her. Last time she'd asked Aiyre about Tor she'd gotten the impression he wouldn't be up on his feet any time soon.

She was putting distance between them not because she feared him, but because it was only a matter of time before he pressed her for this mate hood that burned under the sabertooths' skins. It was instinct.

When she'd heard the grunt of pain, she hadn't dreamed it would be Tor. The look on his face. The agony. And she wasn't entirely sure if it was because of his wound or the sight of her flinching away from him.

Now that she knew he was getting back on his feet, she would spend more time in the hut she shared with other single women in the clan. Despite having a child, she was unmated, which meant she didn't get her own hut.

Once she dashed through the entrance of the communal hut, she felt some panic slide off her shoulders. Tor wouldn't be welcomed in this hut. It was a place only for the women of the tribe. A place that would offer her shelter from those piercing sky-blue eyes of his.

Ezi plopped down on her bed of furs and placed the cooing child in its own bed.

"There you are."

Ezi glanced up to see Aiyre headed straight for her. "Where else might I be now that Tor is walking around the village?"

Aiyre shrugged and then turned her attention to Flosa. "How's the child?"

"She's doing well." Ezi picked up a leather strap near her bed and began to braid her hair. "She has an appetite, and I swear she's more active than any other child I've seen."

Aiyre wiggled her fingers near the baby, and Flosa made a grab at them, but her chubby little baby fingers weren't quite quick enough.

"I saw you run away from Tor."

"I didn't run away from him." Ezi was quick to correct her friend as she tied off her braid and flung it over her shoulder. "I was startled, and my reaction was to run, but it wasn't because of him."

"I know I've mentioned this before, but," Aiyre placed her hands in her lap as she faced Ezi, "I still want you to know I will find another pronghorn clan for you to join if you wish. Now that Tor is back and healing, it might not be long before you find yourself running in any direction you can find. His sabertooth instinct will drive him towards you."

Aiyre was right. With Tor on the mend, it meant her peaceful time in this clan was coming to an end.

"I wish you knew where Girk had gone." Ezi referenced the only other pronghorn shifter who'd made it out alive the night their clan had been attacked. Unlike them, he had decided to venture away from this land to find another pronghorn clan to join. If Ezi hadn't been hurt in the attack, then she and Aiyre may have decided to join him. She still had the scars from that night to show exactly how dangerous a sabertooth could be.

"Sadly, I'm not sure I can find him again," Aiyre smirked. "Although, knowing Girk, he'll be sure to leave some sort of sign at any clan gatherings in the area. Would you like me to reach out and find out where he's gone?"

Ezi glanced at Flosa, who'd finally closed her eyes. "If I run, Tor will follow. Maybe not closely, but he'll be there."

"He left when you pushed him away." Aiyre placed her hands behind her back and leaned back. "He might not follow after you."

Ezi rolled her eyes as she leaned back against one of the bone supports of the hut. "Do you think he left the village thinking I would leave? He knew where I was. If there's one thing I know, it's that these sabertooths always know where their mate is."

"True." Aiyre laughed. "Daerk always knows where to find me. You know, I think it's that nose of theirs." She tapped her nose with a finger as she chuckled, and Ezi joined in.

"It's much better than ours."

They sat there in the hut in silence, watching other women in the clan go about their own business. Some sat weaving near a fire while chatting about something, and others came and went as they went about daily tasks.

Perhaps she should find something in the clan to do that would occupy her time and her hands. Flosa mainly napped, fussed, ate, and entertained herself, so there was some time on Ezi's hands.

Then again… Aiyre's offer was still spinning around her head, tempting her.

"I haven't decided on leaving the clan or not."

"No need to rush to a decision." Aiyre smiled at her. "The offer will always be there."

"Does Daerk know?" Ezi couldn't see it going over well with their sabertooth leader, but then again, he should know he'd mated a strong-willed woman who'd do anything for those that she loved. And that was why Ezi loved Aiyre so much. She was dependable and loyal.

Aiyre snorted, and Ezi had her answer.

"You're so brave among these sabertooths." Ezi marveled. "It's like that night never even happened with you."

Aiyre shook her head as the light in her brown eyes slowly dimmed. "I will never forget what happened to our clan, but I have chosen to forgive the people in this village. It was Brog who wanted us dead, not Daerk or any of the remaining sabertooths."

"They still helped."

"I know, and sometimes I find myself wondering if any of them truly regret what they did." Aiyre sucked in an unsteady breath, "Then I remember I can't do anything about the past. I don't want to waste what I have here, thinking of what I could have had back in our clan."

Ezi wished she could push the attack from her mind, but every time she closed her eyes, those horrible memories kept flashing back. All that blood and death. It'd been the first time she'd ever been hunted down by a predator.

"Well," Aiyre perked back up, "I came to tell you something that might help with getting your mind off Tor."

Ezi raised an eyebrow.

"Mammoths have been spotted not far away, and the clan will soon be preparing for a mammoth hunt." Aiyre wiggled her eyebrows over at Ezi like this news should tempt or excite her.

"I'm not a hunter."

"No," Aiyre raised a finger into the air, "but you would be helpful in gutting the mammoths and assisting us in getting the meat back here to the village. Think on it. There's no need for an answer right now." Aiyre rose from her seat, brushed the dirt off her palms, and waved a few fingers at the baby who was still fast asleep and then left the hut.

Ezi wasn't sure a mammoth hunt would be right for her, but then again Tor most likely wouldn't be going with his injured leg. It could be a good time for her to get away from him while she tried to collect her thoughts on what to do.

Every day since the mammoths had been spotted, there was a hum of excitement buzzing through the clan. The massive beasts had come back to their land. The gods had blessed them once more, and Eron was eager to send thanks to them while performing a hunting ritual.

Ezi had to admit there was a buzz of excitement in her chest at the thought of the hunt. It was hard to remain aloof when there were so many smiles floating around her. A mammoth hunt was definitely a sight to be seen.

Gathering Flosa in her arms, she walked out of the communal hut and into the clan that was preparing for the hunt. She wanted to do something, and this was her chance to assist the clan that'd been kind enough to take them in and see to their safety.

She weaved her way through the village until she spotted some women near the village fire. The red-hot coals glowed from last night's fire.

"How can I help?" Ezi took a seat beside several sabertooth women and Aiyre. The task they were performing looked easy enough.

"We always need more hands," Aiyre confirmed with a smile as her eyes briefly left the spear in front of her.

"Here," another woman in the group pushed some supplies towards her.

Ezi placed Flosa down beside her on the ground, and the child smiled up at her.

"How is she?" Aiyre asked as she finished building a spear and placed it in a small pile next to her.

"Hungry. Nothing has changed." Ezi picked up a wooden staff, placed a sharpened stone into the slit at the end, and then began wrapping a long length of leather cord around the spear. "Is this correct?"

The sabertooth woman next to her leaned in and examined the weapon. "It looks perfect."

"Good." Ezi tied off the end of the leather strip and placed the spear by her side. "I'd been hoping there would be a task for me."

"This should help us greatly during the hunt," Aiyre confirmed. "It takes a lot of spears to bring down a mammoth. Those beasts are protected by a thick layer of fat and hair."

"Us?" Ezi wrapped another spear tip, making sure the stone was held tightly in place. She didn't need it falling apart the moment a hunter launched the spear at a mammoth.

"I plan on joining the hunting party."

Ezi nodded her head, not too surprised by this. Aiyre had always been a great hunter in their clan, and she would be an asset on the mammoth hunt. "You've always been an exceptional hunter. Will the sabertooths be hunting in their human form?"

A couple of the women in the group shook their heads, while a couple of women nodded theirs.

"Some will be in their human form and some in their sabertooth forms." One of the women explained.

"Do they need you then? Surely, a group of sabertooths can kill a mammoth without you."

"Worried about me?" Aiyre reached out and patted one of Ezi's hands. "There's no need to worry about my safety. I'll be safe with Daerk by my side."

"I do worry about you. Without you, I will be alone in this clan." Ezi whispered the last sentence, not wishing to offend any of the women here. No one had been cruel, but it still didn't feel like her clan, and she would have trouble staying without Aiyre.

"Isn't that your own fault for being lonely?"

Ezi's head snapped back at the bitter tone in Aiyre's voice.

"I don't mean to hurt you," Aiyre rushed to reassure her, "but isn't it your fault?" Aiyre leaned closer to make sure none of the other women would hear her. "You've never tried to be a part of the clan, and as far as I know, I'm still your only friend here. If you tried, there are several women who would love to befriend you."

Ezi knew Aiyre didn't mean to be hurtful, but her words still stung like a well-placed insect bite.

"They took so much from us," Ezi uttered under her breath.

"I can't argue with that, but it was Brog and his men that were responsible for the deaths of our clanmates. The rest of them," Aiyre waved her hand at the village around them, "had nothing to do with it or were frightened into their actions. They are as much victims as we are."

Ezi glanced at the women around them who were making spears and arrows and happily chatting away with each other. "I'm not even sure where to start when it comes to making friends."

"That's okay." Aiyre rubbed a hand across Ezi's back. "Perhaps you should consider coming with all of us to the mammoth hunt," Aiyre said the last part louder to include the other women in the discussion.

"Yes, you should join us." The woman right beside Ezi sent her an encouraging smile. "A mammoth hunt can be quite the experience, something you'll never forget. I can still remember my first mammoth hunt, and even though I didn't hunt, just being near those beasts was invigorating."

"Yes," another woman pitched in, and Ezi knew her name as Afri, "I still remember how their feet cause the ground to tremble and the branches in the trees to shake."

"I'd love to join, but..." Ezi glanced down at Flosa, who was happily watching the women around them.

"We can have another woman take care of her while you're away."

The baby smiled up at her. Her little eyes dancing with delighted glee as she watched a woman nearby building a spear.

"A sabertooth?" Ezi whispered on a single breath.

"Your trust in these people has to start somewhere." Aiyre raised her eyebrows while a corner of her mouth lifted up as she sighed. "It has to start somewhere."

"I haven't been the best mother, but leaving her in someone else's care?"

"She'll be fine, and she'll be even better if her mother gets a chance to be a part of this clan." Aiyre finished another spear. "If you belong to the clan, Flosa will learn to trust the people here."

It made sense to Ezi. If she was afraid of the sabertooths around them, then how could she teach her daughter to befriend the children here. Children learned from the behaviors of their parents.

"Think this was the gods' plans all along?" Ezi teased Aiyre.

Her friend cocked her head to the side as she finished yet another spear. "What do you mean?"

"They gave me Flosa to push me into finding a place here in this clan."

Aiyre shrugged her shoulders. "Could be, but I couldn't possibly speak for the gods."

"If you decide to join us," another of the woman leaned in, "you could also join the hunting ceremony Eron will hold in the caves. It'll be in a couple of days."

Ezi smiled at the woman. "Thank you. I think I will attend." Joining in the ceremony wouldn't be for long, and Aiyre was right. At some point, she had to start trusting these sabertooths and becoming a part of the clan.

Out of the corner of her eye, she saw Aiyre nodding her head, clearly happy Ezi was finally giving the people in this clan a chance. She figured time would only tell what kind of people they were, and in the meantime, befriending some of them would make her life a happier one.

Drakk definitely wouldn't have wanted her to be living her life in misery. He was the kind of man who took every opportunity to enjoy life, and if she wanted to honor his memory, then she figured she should do the same and find a way to enjoy the rest of her life.

Chapter 9

"Now, she likes it best when you give her a small jiggle while she feeds, and when she sleeps make sure she stays covered, she likes to kick off her furs, and then I wake to find her shivering." Ezi handed Flosa over to the sabertooth woman in front of her. "Oh, and–"

"Ezi!" Aiyre grabbed one of her arms and tugged her away from the woman. "Inde knows what she is doing. This isn't the first time she has taken in an orphan or looked after another clan mate's child."

"Sorry." Ezi ducked her head as a blush flushed across her cheeks. "I don't mean to question your ability."

"You're a first-time mother." Inde smiled kindly, and her eyes were filled with nothing but love when she glanced down at Flosa. "You aren't the first protective mother, but I assure you she is in good hands." Then she turned and disappeared through the flaps of her hut. She was the only woman who had her own hut since she usually had so many children under her care.

"She'll be fine."

"I wasn't worrying." Ezi shook her head. "Just startled that she would say I was protective."

"Why would that startle you?" Aiyre hooked an arm through Ezi's and guided her towards the caves. It was nearing the time for the hunting ceremony.

Ezi hated to admit this, but if she couldn't

confide her secrets in Aiyre, then who could she turn to? "I feel as though I haven't been the best mother."

Aiyre scoffed as they passed a few clan mates. "You are worrying for no reason. You've kept her fed and happy, and yes you had a rough start, but I think it's understandable. She reminds you of Drakk, and I can only imagine the hurt you feel every time you look at her face."

"Thank you." It felt good to hear Aiyre reassuring her.

"I'm here for you." Aiyre squeezed one of Ezi's hands. "I keep saying it."

"It does feel good to have someone else looking after her," Ezi admitted. She felt horrible for saying it, but Flosa was a demanding child, and now that she had some time to herself, she looked forward to it.

"I'm sure I'd feel the same in your position, but still, I can't wait for my first." Aiyre's eyes took on a distant look as she glanced away, almost looking like she was blinking away unshed tears.

She and Daerk still hadn't been blessed with any children, and Ezi knew it wasn't for lack of trying. Those two were inseparable. Ezi would bet Daerk was somewhere close, ready to come to his mate's side in a moment's notice.

Her eyes scanned the village around them, wondering if she'd see Daerk close by, but she couldn't see him. It didn't mean he wouldn't be nearby though. He could be inside a nearby hut or around the next tree.

"What will the ceremony be like?" Ezi had yet to go to a hunting ceremony. She'd never been interested in being a part of any hunt back in her pronghorn clan, and then it had been the same when she came to the sabertooth clan.

"I'm not sure it will be the same as ours." Aiyre skirted past a pile of furs laying outside someone's hut. "If it is similar, then I expect a pipe to be passed around, some markings to be drawn on the warriors, maybe a drink, and some chanting from Eron as he calls upon the gods to aide us."

"It doesn't sound too different than some other ceremonies." Ezi agreed.

"I suppose not."

They broke out of the village and joined a group of sabertooth shifters on their way to the caves. She found herself eager for the upcoming night.

Tomorrow some of the clan would be leaving for the mammoth hunt. She hadn't been sure she would join, but it would be the perfect opportunity for her to be a part of the clan and get far away from Tor and his intense eyes.

Several men pranced by wearing sabertooth pelts, and her jaw dropped.

"They kill their spirit animal?"

"Different clan, different rituals."

Their pronghorn clan would never hunt pronghorns. To them, they were sacred, possibly even ancestors living a permanent life in their pronghorn form. It was a strange difference. One she had a hard time understanding after a life of thinking one certain way.

The men continued to prance past the women, and Ezi's eyes dipped across their bodies, which were completely naked. All of them were well-toned, and with the pelts flapping in the wind and the movements of the mens' bodies there was little left to her imagination.

A few of the men playfully grabbed at some of the sabertooth women, earning themselves squeals of delight and lighthearted smacks from the women as the men grabbed at their clothing.

Ezi glanced over at her friend to see Aiyre's eyes filled to the brim with excitement. And as she looked around at the faces near her, she found several people with the same look in their eyes, but she doubted she looked thrilled. Her heart skittered in her chest. She was making the conscious choice to be a part of the sabertooth clan, and she prayed to the gods Drakk would understand.

The path they were taking had been trampled down to dirt after several generations traveling the same path so many times a year. She and Aiyre had to be some of the few if not only pronghorn shifters who had traveled this path with this clan.

Just on the outside of the path was tall, greenish yellow grass waving in the light wind. By the time they came out of the caves, the sun would be asleep, and the moon would be shining down on the land below. Already the sun was disappearing on the horizon in a brilliant display of searing oranges and reds with a hint of pink hiding among the white puffy clouds.

When Ezi focused once more on where they were headed, she saw the mouth of the cave system looming ahead. It looked like a giant mouth waiting to swallow them up. It even looked as though it had a few teeth because of the rocks jutting down from the ceiling. Strange that she hadn't noticed how intimidating the caves looked before.

A shiver spread over her skin, but she shoved the fear down.

It was her time to trust the sabertooths and become one of them, while they called on the gods for assistance with the upcoming hunt.

"Here," a clan mate walked up beside her and presented a small lit branch. It'd been dipped in animal fat to help it burn longer.

Ezi took the offered branch and watched as the clan mate dropped back to the back of the group.

"Thankfully, the cave floor is pretty much rubbed smooth, so there shouldn't be much to trip us up." Aiyre supplied right before they walked straight into the mouth of the cave.

"It was still nice of them to give us a lit branch."

Even with the torch right next to Ezi's face, her eyes took a second to adjust to the sudden darkness of the cave. The chill of the rock reached out and prickled her sensitive skin. Her leather dress ended at her knees, and the sleeves were cut short at her shoulders, leaving plenty of skin bare to the air.

"How far?" Ezi asked when the journey seemed to be continuing for an eternity. They were going a lot deeper than when she introduced Flosa to the gods. That ceremony had taken place in a closer cavern.

"We're headed to the hunting cave, and it's further in." A clan mate leaned in and answered from behind before Aiyre could utter a single word.

The only sound were their groups' footsteps

until she saw an orange light flickering in front of them and distant chanting rang down the corridor. The light grew brighter, and she felt her heart skitter away in her chest. It was a strange feeling, but she actually felt some excitement for the upcoming night.

Then their group broke into a large chamber.

Right in the middle of the chamber, a fire burned brightly. The smoke trickled up towards a small hole in the ceiling. The rock wall around the vent had been stained black with all the fires the clan and their ancestors had burned in here.

When she turned her eyes back to everyone inside the cave, she figured almost the entire clan of sabertooths was here for the hunting ceremony.

Eron stood near the fire with Daerk not too far away. Both of them had the top half of a sabertooth skull on their heads, and the long canines framed both of their faces, giving each a fearsome look. They also only had on sabertooth pelts, leaving the rest of their bodies exposed.

Even though Eron was an elder, his body still bore the signs of a hunter. And Daerk… there was a reason Aiyre was so in love with her sabertooth. Not only was he a man who was gentle, but he had a body that would appeal to any female. Their sabertooth leader looked ready to take on the whole land with that skull atop his head.

Glancing around at the clan around her, Ezi wondered if any of them would change into their sabertooth forms, and whether or not she'd be able to handle the sight without screaming like a madwoman.

Eron raised a bone pipe to his lips, took a puff, and then passed it over to Daerk. Daerk's cheeks puffed outward as he took a draw on the pipe, and then his lips moved out in a kissing gesture before releasing a long line of grey smoke.

Slowly, the bone pipe made its way around the chamber until it finally reached her. Ezi took it with two hands, raised it to her lips, and puffed on the end of the pipe before passing it on to the person on her other side.

As she breathed out, a stream of white smoke left her nostrils.

The herbs or whatever Eron had put in the pipe began to work within a few minutes of her first puff on the pipe. Everything around her took on a hazy dream-like quality. Immediately, she felt her muscles relax, and her mind ease.

Then she froze as she felt eyes watching her. Looking over her shoulder, Ezi spotted the source of those stares.

Tor.

He was here.

The pipe smoke that was now floating through the air, and her lungs calmed her response, but she still felt a surge of apprehension. She hadn't known he was doing well enough to come here. It hadn't even crossed her mind.

He also had a skull atop his head. His beard had been trimmed down, and his hair cut shorter. His chest was bare to her view, and she took in her fill as the area in her core warmed at the sight of him. She may not be keen on his sabertooth side, but he was still good looking, and it was hard for her to look away.

Tor sent her a smile, his blue eyes dancing with the light of the fire between those long canines that framed his face. He shoved a shoulder off the wall and began walking around the outside of the chamber, but there was a limp to his movements now. His wound may be well on its way to healing, but it looked like there would be lasting effects. Unfortunately, the limp only gave him a more feral look as he prowled around the edge of the group.

Her heart tripped over itself until his intense eyes finally glanced away.

Ezi raised a hand to her chest as she walked further into the crowd, trying to disappear in the throng of people. She was alarmed by her reaction to him. Her body was hot, and she felt flustered.

It wasn't long before the air filled with Eron's chanting, the words echoing off the stone walls. She couldn't make out the words he was speaking because of all the echoes bouncing off the walls. The thumping of a drum began to beat a rhythm, and the people around her began dancing wildly like the spirits had taken over their bodies.

It was hard to keep the smile off her lips as she watched the life-celebrating around her. Aiyre had been right in insisting she come here. She'd been alone for too long and being a part of this ceremony warmed her to her core.

Slowly, the cavern filled with a hazy smoke as a couple of more bone and wooden pipes joined the first. It appeared Eron wasn't the only one with a pipe at the ready.

Ezi sucked in deep breaths of the sweet and delightfully alluring smoke. Her nerves calmed, allowing her shoulders to finally slump in relaxation as the music thumbed through the cave. It bounced off the walls and vibrated through the rock floors under her feet.

Hesitantly, she stomped a beat with one foot as she joined in the dancing around her. She wasn't as carefree as the rest of the clan around her.

A sabertooth woman stepped up beside Ezi, dipped a hand into a bowl she was carrying, and then swiped a line across Ezi's face, starting at her temple and curving around her face and ending at her chin. Then the woman danced over to the next person.

She blinked in confusion. She knew it was a part of the ceremony, but the woman had been so quick, and the mark had been placed on her in a matter of seconds.

With the intense heat from the fire and all the bodies dancing around the chamber, Ezi felt the mark on her face dry and tighten quickly.

Ezi picked up her torch as she walked over to the fire and then placed her torch on the ground by the fire. With all the dancing feet, this would be the safest place for the torch to lay.

When she refaced the crowd of people, she felt eyes watching her once more. Glancing over to the side, she saw Tor dancing with his clanmates, but every once in a while, he would look over at her, like he knew exactly where she'd be in the cave. It had to be the heightened senses of a sabertooth shifter.

Her silly heart skipped a beat. Not in fear but in anticipation.

Now that he was back on his feet, she worried about his intentions. It was only a matter of time before he came sniffing around.

Ezi worked her way back into the crowd, letting the thumping of the drums enter her soul. Someday, Flosa would know the joy of clan ceremonies, and she was eager to share it with her daughter.

Tor was doing his best to keep his distance, but it was hard to ignore being in the same cave as Ezi. Her scent was easy to pick up and had his nose zeroing in on her. Despite glaring at him, he could tell she was enjoying herself, and it relieved him. He worried about her.

There'd been several rumors drifting around the village about Ezi being distant with her child and trying to separate herself from the village. He knew it must be hard on her living with the same people who'd taken so much, but they were doing their best to make it up.

Glancing back up from where he danced, he saw Ezi eyeing him from across the chamber. He could feel all the questions racing through her mind.

Clearly, his presence was throwing her for a loop. She'd got used to him being gone, and he would have stayed away longer, but his wound had brought him back sooner.

After being gone for so many months, it must be a shock to her.

He snorted as he shook his head as he continued to stomp a beat with the drums that echoed through the cave.

Ezi must have believed she'd gotten rid of him. And now he was back to haunt her.

Last time, he'd been too eager for his mate. Now that he'd had time to cool down and see it from her eyes, he realized he'd rushed her. This time though, would be different. He was ready to win her over, slowly. There'd be no rushing her. He would restrain his sabertooth side as best as he could.

Tor would have loved to stay away from the clan for longer, to give her more time, but his injury had prevented that, and now that he was back, he wasn't so sure he could leave for a second time.

A woman danced up to him, and he stopped briefly, allowing her to paint a stripe down his face. Then she danced away to continue painting stripes on other people.

Working his way through the crowd, Tor sought the wall of the cavern. There was a limp to his step, despite the efforts of Eron and Tira. They'd done their best with healing his leg, but the damage from the rhinoceros's horn had been too much for them.

It was his own stupidity that'd gotten him into this situation, and he blamed no one but himself.

Once he got to the wall, he rested a shoulder against the rough rock and lifted his bare foot off the ground, shifting his weight back onto his good leg. He was only here because Eron wanted him to use his leg, but he wasn't supposed to overdo it.

He'd always have the limp and the nasty scar to remind him of how stupid he could be, and hopefully, it would remind him not to be that stupid again.

"I'm glad you were able to join us!"

Tor spun around to find Daerk coming up behind him. Daerk presented the ideal image of a clan leader. The sabertooth skull over his head made him look dangerous, and his whole body was exposed to everyone's view. There was a reason he was leader. He was strong and intelligent. Brog had no chance against him.

"It's good to be off my furs and walking around." Tor laughed as he kept his weight off his injured leg. "I can only look at the inside of my hut for so long before I go crazy."

Daerk shivered. "I can only imagine what you've gone through as you've healed. Have you tried shifting?"

"Not yet." Tor shook his head. "Eron doesn't think there would be any problems caused by my wound."

"That's good." Daerk looked relieved. "Not being able to shift would drive you crazier than sitting in your hut all day."

"I feel bad for worrying everyone."

"We are just happy you are better. Maybe even good enough to join us on the mammoth hunt?" Daerk smiled at him hopefully.

"It's tempting." Tor could use the mammoth hunt to get his mind off his leg, and off of Ezi. Her scent was everywhere, and it called to his inner sabertooth.

"Think you can still hunt?" Daerk teased him.

"Still hunt?" Tor snorted. "I'm insulted you would even think I wouldn't be able to because if my memory is correct, I'm even better at hunting than you." He stuck a finger against Daerk's bare chest, prodding him back.

Daerk laughed, the sound loud, but even it was swallowed up with the festivities nearby. "Whatever you want to think, my friend."

"I'll think about joining." And most likely he would end up going. It would give him and Ezi some more distance. She already had so much to handle with her child, and he wasn't keen on causing her any discomfort.

Tor's eyes sought out her familiar form in the throng of moving bodies, and it didn't take him long to spot her amongst the crowd. Her jade eyes were dancing with wary joy as she joined in with the clan in asking the gods to assist them on their mammoth hunt. From what he'd heard, she hadn't blended in well with the clan while he'd been gone, but now, it appeared that she was trying to befriend everyone.

"What will you do about Ezi?"

Tor looked back to Daerk, who was also watching Ezi, and he shrugged. "I'm not sure."

"Just be sure you don't cause her any distress," Daerk warned with a stern glint to his eyes. "Aiyre will have my head if you do, and none of us will be pleased if that happens."

"I don't plan on anything." Tor looked back over at Ezi. "I don't intend to cause her any distress, but I do wish to convince her that I am the man for her."

"I hope you the best."

"Thank you." He just had to continue believing that he wouldn't have been given a mate who he couldn't win over.

Daerk placed a hand on Tor's shoulder, squeezed lightly, and then walked off. Tor watched as his longtime friend, who he considered to be a brother, walk over to Aiyre and wrap his arms around her, drawing her into his chest. Aiyre rested her head against his shoulder as she gazed up at him, and even from this distance, Tor could feel the love radiating off both of them.

Tor's heart pinched under his ribcage. He wished he could do that with Ezi. Hold her tight. Take away all her fears. Promise to be by her side no matter what. His lips fell flat as longing turned his celebratory mood sour. He needed some air.

Spinning on a heel, Tor pushed his way through his dancing clanmates until he broke free. Then he quickly walked through the dark cave system until he walked out of the mouth of the cave. The cool night air wrapped around him, and he sucked in several deep breathes as he did his best to clean his lungs of Ezi's intoxicating scent.

His sabertooth growled in disagreement. It wanted to continue to bask in her delicious scent. To bring the scent into their lungs and make it a part of their body.

"Not now," Tor growled at himself as he stalked away from the entrance of the cave, looking for a secluded spot to rest his leg.

Chapter 10

Sweat beaded on Ezi's brow and she found the air in the cave stale and unbearable. The thumping of the drum and the chanting of all the people in the cave had her head throbbing. Glancing around, she did her best to spot Aiyre, but with all the shifting bodies, it was hard to find anyone.

With one last glance around, she headed for the entrance of the cave. Slowly, she walked through the dark cave system, hoping she wasn't about to get herself lost. Then again, the sabertooths had good enough noses to seek her out when they found her missing.

Her slippered feet scooted over the smooth stone as she kept her arms stretched out to her sides to keep her from falling if she bumped into something. She should have grabbed a torch from near the fire, but she was well on her way, and she wasn't interested in going back to the craziness of the ritual.

Then she broke out of the cave system and found the outside just as dark. The bright lights flickered high above her head, and the moon provided the only significant amount of light. She felt like she'd been in the caves for only a few minutes, but clearly, she'd been in there for a lot longer.

Ezi began walking back to the village but stopped in the worn path. She glanced towards the village and then looked around the murky night. Flosa was with another woman, probably fast asleep, and if she went back to the village, she would have to once more continue caring for Flosa.

With a small nibble to her bottom lip, Ezi made her decision and walked away from the village, straying from the well-worn path and into the tall grass nearby.

If she went back, she'd retrieve Flosa and go back to the communal hut, which would have plenty of women still there. Not everyone in the clan had left for the ritual since there were still things that needed to be done; watching children, maintaining fires, and so many other tasks.

Ezi didn't want to go back quite yet. Inde wouldn't expect her back until much later anyway.

She was beyond ready for her own hut… but there wasn't a single man in the clan she wanted to mate with to get a hut.

No one in her communal hut appeared to mind that Flosa would cry out several times in the night, demanding sustenance, but it would make Ezi feel better if she wasn't bothering anyone. It would also provide her with some much-needed alone time. There were always a pair of eyes watching her, even if they didn't mean to be.

A rabbit froze in front of her in the dark. Its long grey ears went down along the length of its body as it attempted to blend in with the environment. They stared at each other in the dark. Then she pressed onwards. The rabbit stayed frozen until it decided she'd encroached far enough into its space, and then its long back legs propelled it forward until it disappeared into the long grass nearby with a small rustle.

Ezi lost track of time as she pressed further into the dark night. She wouldn't venture too far out of the village, due to the fact she was still scared about Brog being somewhere out there.

That thought had her pausing.

Maybe she should head back...

"Wandering around?"

Ezi whipped around nearly tripping over her own feet as the male voice wrapped around her like a tight embrace. "Tor?" The name left her mouth on a rushed breath.

"It's me."

She watched him melt out of the shadows of some trees as he walked towards her. The sabertooth skull was still on his head, and his chest was bare. The moonlight glinted over him, shadowing parts of his face and body. If she didn't know better, she would have thought he was a sabertooth god.

"You followed me?" Ezi bristled as she finally regained her voice.

Tor snorted. "You followed me."

She cocked her head to the side as confusion replaced the irritation.

"I was already out here, resting my leg," he waved a hand in the air, "when you strode past me."

Her haunches fell as she realized he was speaking the truth. Tor may be a sabertooth, but he'd never lied to her, and his story was believable.

"Why are you out here and not celebrating with the clan?" He took a couple more steps closer to her. "You looked like you were enjoying the ritual."

His scent wrapped around her, warm and inviting with a hint of trampled grass. If she didn't know better, she would have thought he might have shifted into his sabertooth form and rolled around in the grass.

"I needed some fresh air. All the smoke was getting to me." She raised a hand to her temple, rubbing it with a couple of her fingers.

"I will join you."

Ezi glanced over at him to find his well-toned chest puffed out slightly, hope shining bright in his eyes. "I would like some peace and quiet. With Flosa, I don't get much time to myself."

Some of that hope disappeared from his eyes, but determination soon filled its place. "You shouldn't be out on your own in the dark, even if we are closer to the village. You never know what might be lurking in the dark… or who might be lurking in the dark."

Clearly, she wasn't the only one who worried about Brog's return.

She pursed her lips. She could just go back to the village… then she wouldn't have any need for Tor joining her.

"You can join me." Ezi relented, and when he took another step closer to her, she added with a raised finger, "But you will not touch me."

Tor immediately raised his hands in a surrendering gesture as he took a small step back. "You may lead." He waved a hand in front of him in a sweeping motion. "And I will stay back a few paces."

Ezi didn't hesitate. With a few quick steps, she had them moving through the inky darkness of the night. Her senses weren't as good at night, but they were still better than a non-shifter.

A light wind shifted some nearby tree branches, and she found the shuffling of the leaves soothing. This was the kind of peace she needed. Flosa was a good child, but she could be fussy. Another rabbit hopped away as they surprised it in the tall grass.

Then Ezi felt him staring at her.

Turning her head slightly over her shoulder, Ezi caught his eyes moving over her like he was assessing prey. He was most likely trying to figure out his plan of attack on how to win her over. She hated to reject him because she was sure he was a fine man, but she wasn't wanting what he offered.

"It is hard to enjoy a walk with you staring at me." She grumped and caught him shrugging beside her in response.

"It's hard not to stare when such a lovely creature is standing beside me."

Heat crept up her neck and cheeks, and she was glad for the cover of night. She didn't need him knowing she was flattered by his compliment. She'd never thought of herself as lovely. No one had said that to her, not even Drakk. He'd been a caring and gentle man, but the praises had been few and far between.

Instead of answering, Ezi just kept walking as she did her best to ignore his presence. Animals scurried out of their path in a panic as they made their way through the dark landscape. For the most part, they were the hunters out here, and the animals knew it.

"Stop." Tor held out a hand in front of her, and she jerked to a stop, not wanting to make contact with the offending arm.

"What is it?" She looked over at him as he surveyed the land around them. His eyesight must be a lot better than hers because when she gave the area a cursory glance, she saw nothing out of the ordinary.

"Over there," he pointed with his other hand, and she followed the long finger, "there is a sabertooth stalking through those bushes."

It took Ezi several seconds and a brief moment of squinting to finally spot what he'd seen with ease. There was indeed a sabertooth crouched low to the ground. Its paws made no sound as it eased over the grass, probably stalking a rabbit or some other prey.

"I'm surprised you spotted him." Ezi felt a small bit of apprehension spread through her, but she was standing right beside a man who would protect her. Whether or not she'd rejected him, she knew Tor wouldn't let anything bad befall her. It just wasn't in his nature.

"I smelled him long before I saw him."

"You must have smelled the trail of blood and death that all sabertooths leave in their wake." It was out before she thought about it.

Silence greeted her answer, and she cringed inwardly.

Peering through the darkness, Ezi caught a brief moment of pain flash across his face, and for the first time in her life, she regretted her words. She wasn't a cruel person by nature, and she hadn't meant to cause him harm.

"I didn't–"

Tor waved a hand dismissively. "Your words rang with conviction. After everything you went through, I can't blame you for how you feel about my people. I only hope we can make it up to you somehow."

His words had her feeling even worse because she could hear the truth ringing loud and clear in every word.

"Still, I didn't mean to imply you are just as mindless as an animal."

"Maybe we should continue our walk this way." Tor redirected her away from the sabertooth that was prowling through the area with a hand to her back. A gentle touch that wasn't intended to cross any boundaries with her. "I'm glad I ran into you."

She cocked her head to the side as she stepped over a few larger stones on the ground. "Why?"

"I had an idea I wanted to speak with you about." His voice trembled a bit, like he wasn't sure he should say what he was thinking, but was doing it anyway.

"Yes?" Ezi had no idea what he was about to say to her, and she felt some tension enter her shoulders as she braced herself for what might come out of his mouth. She figured he was about to ask her about being his mate again. So much for a peaceful walk through the night.

"You and Flosa can't be very comfortable in the communal women's hut."

He wasn't wrong with that assumption.

Ezi scooted past a small sapling before they entered the nearby forest. The branches overhead reached out like bony fingers in the night, and they sent shivers of fright racing down her spine. One moment the world she lived in could be nothing but good things, and then the next it would rain terror down over her head, and she found it hard to trust.

"Some privacy from the other women in the hut might be nice." She agreed warily. She still wasn't sure where he was going with this.

Tor cleared his throat, and she got the impression he might be a bit nervous. Carefully, she watched him out of the corner of her eyes as she readied herself to refuse him.

Tor felt a couple of beads of sweat run down the length of his spine. Once more, he was about to place himself in a position to be rejected, but here he was.

"I was thinking… you could use my hut to get some privacy."

Silence greeted him, and some more sweat ran down the sides of his face. Raising a trembling hand, he attempted to wipe the beads of sweat off his brow, but his hand knocked against the teeth of the sabertooth skull. Whipping it off his head, he wiped his brow as he waited impatiently for her answer. He had no clue as to what was going through her mind.

"With you?" Her voice barely a squeak.

This was his moment. Right now, he could push her away even more, or he could bring her slightly closer. Unfortunately, there was no way for him to know what answer might scare her away.

"I had hoped we would both be sleeping in my hut," when she turned wide, alarmed eyes on him he rushed to say the next part before she darted away, "but I am willing to let you have the hut to yourself."

Silence once more entered the forest, but she was now faced away from him, and he wasn't able to read her face to see what might be going through her mind.

"You would do that?" Ezi sounded puzzled by his generosity.

"I want you and Flosa to be happy, and I'm sure it is stressful being in the communal hut with all the women coming and going at all hours of the day and night." Not only that, but it would relieve some of the stress on Ezi. She had to sleep in a hut full of sabertooths, and he was sure she didn't sleep well with that knowledge.

"Thank you." Ezi turned and dazzled him with a brief smile.

His heart stopped in his chest, and before he knew what he was doing, he stepped forward, wrapped an arm around her waist, and leaned in, planting a kiss on her delicate lips. She trembled in his arms like she was fighting herself, but then she gave in and returned the kiss.

Her lips were soft and sweet, yet when he pressed into them, they turned defiant and kissed back. Joy spread through him at this wonderful taste of her. Tor's sabertooth rose inside his chest and purred in delight.

Then the magic was gone.

"Stop!" Ezi ducked, pulling out of his arms and darted away into the dark night.

Tor sighed. He'd just ruined tonight. His eyelids slid closed as he rested his forehead against the prickly bark of a tree.

"How stupid can you be?" He muttered. He'd known better than to kiss her. He'd known better! She wasn't ready for him.

Tor couldn't trust himself around his mate. Every time he proved to her, he was a sweet man, he ruined it with his eagerness to claim his mate. It was like he was taking one step forward and two steps back.

Pushing away from the tree, he slowly followed after her scent, which still drifted around in the night air. He wasn't planning on catching up to her, but just trailing after to make sure she made it back to the village in one piece. There were plenty of dangers hiding around the forest.

There was still the strong scent of a wild sabertooth roaming the area, and Tor could also smell a badger or two in the area. Although small, those little beasts could be a curse to deal with. Tor would rather take on another wholly rhinoceros than a badger.

Within minutes, the village came into view, and he knew she was safe and sound. Now he could only hope that she would still take his offer of his hut. The morning would only tell if he'd completely scared her away.

Tonight, Tor would enjoy sleeping in his hut in case it was the last time because if she did take his offer, he would be sleeping under the stars once more. His sabertooth growled at him. It wasn't thrilled with the idea of being homeless once more, but if it pleased their mate, then who was it to argue with his decision.

Chapter 11

"Did I just spot Ezi walking into your hut?" Daerk strode over to Tor as he stretched out his injured leg.

Tor grunted a yes and continued to stretch out his leg. One of his hands was braced against the trunk of a tree, and his other hand was reached behind his back, hooked onto his foot.

"You convinced her to sleep in your hut?" Daerk sounded mystified, maybe even a little proud at Tor's skill in wooing his mate.

"It's not what you think," Tor confessed. He wished he could brag that he'd won her over, but it was far from the truth. His mate was still scared of his touch, which hurt him even worse than a wholly rhinoceros horn piercing his flesh.

"Hmmm?"

Daerk was going to laugh at him. Tor was sure about it. He almost didn't want to say anything else, but this was his clan leader, and he had to hope his longtime friend would be able to give him some advice on how to handle Ezi.

"I gave her the use of my hut. She will use it, but I will not be sleeping there with her." Tor released his foot and let it fall back onto the ground. Eron had told him some stretching might help him to heal while keeping most of the mobility of his leg. He was willing to do anything to keep the use of his leg. There was no way he could be a hunter if he couldn't stand or run.

"Where will you sleep?" Daerk's arms

folded in front of his chest as he raised a dark eyebrow. "I hope you aren't thinking of leaving the village again."

"No," Tor was quick to toss out, "I'm not thinking of leaving. I learned my lesson. Running from Ezi won't make anything better if anything, it just makes it worse." He pointed to his leg with a smirk.

"Good." Daerk unfolded his arms, looking more at ease now.

"I figure since it's spring, I can enjoy sleeping out under the stars so she can get out of the communal hut."

"Still," Daerk shook his head, his golden eyes never leaving Tor, "I worry about the two of you."

"There's nothing to worry about," Tor reassured him.

Daerk let out a long breath through his nose, and Tor knew he had yet to convince his friend that things were going in the right direction. Daerk had it easier with Aiyre, and their relationship was different. She was a strong hunter, and she'd been able to handle the attack better than Ezi.

"Enough talk about your mate. We need to talk about this mammoth hunt coming up." Daerk's eyes brightened at the thought of a hunt.

Excitement built in Tor's chest. A mammoth hunt was just what this clan needed. It would show everyone that the gods had been cruel during the winter, but generous during the spring.

"The women were kind enough to stock us up on spears and arrows for our hunt."

Tor nodded his head.

"We will want to figure out which men

should stay behind in the village and which should join us on the hunt." Daerk glanced around to make sure no one was close to them before he said, "I still fear Brog coming back for revenge, and I don't want the village to be left unguarded."

"I'll think on it."

"Some of the women will be coming with us as well, so they can help with the butchering and hauling back the meat, bones, and fat."

Tor wanted to share this with Ezi, but he wasn't about to ask her to join him on the hunt. She had Flosa, and he figured she would want to stay here in the village instead of traipsing all over the place.

"Will Aiyre be joining us on the hunt?"

Daerk snorted. "You think I can stop her? Or want to stop her?"

Tor chuckled. "I suppose she wouldn't want to stay here if there's a hunt she can join."

"She's a fierce hunter." Daerk agreed, as a wide smile spread across his lips and love entered his eyes.

It was good to see Daerk enjoying the gift of a mate. She'd been good for him and given him the push he'd needed when it came to challenging Brog for the leadership of the clan.

"I don't doubt it." Tor chuckled again. Aiyre had surprised them all. When Daerk had first mentioned that his mate was a pronghorn shifter, Tor hadn't been sure how it would work out. But it'd worked out better than he could have ever imagined. She was strong and capable and led the clan just as well as Daerk.

"Is Rir coming?" Tor asked. He hadn't seen

his other friend since arriving and was beginning to wonder where his other friend was.

"Rir and some other men have been watching the mammoth herds. You won't see him until we go hunting, but I'm sure he's heard you're back. We were worried about you, and when you arrived, word spread like a fire through dry grass."

"I can't wait to see him." And find out what he'd been up to since Tor left the clan.

"He won't have much to tell you since his life is the same as you left."

That didn't surprise him all that much. Three people finding their mates in a year would be a tremendous but splendid thing. At least, Tor had found his mate, even if he didn't have her by his side.

"Come with me, and we can figure out which men to bring with us. We need the best hunters, because we need a mammoth or two for our meat hut."

Daerk led them through the village, and Tor felt his eyes drift over to his hut as they passed nearby. Ezi would be inside, sleeping in his furs tonight. Even if he wasn't in there with her to enjoy her being in his hut, he felt a sense of calm come over his sabertooth. The animal enjoyed knowing exactly where she was and that she was happy and safe.

A small smile spread over his lips as he watched a trickle of smoke leave the hole in the top of his hut. She was inside.

His sabertooth purred and tried to push him towards the hut, but he resisted the urge. He'd already startled her once with a kiss, he wasn't about to scare her out of his hut. This was the step in the right direction that he needed.

Ripping his gaze off his hut, Tor continued to follow after Daerk until his eyes landed on Darh and Jirk.

"Hello!" He raised a hand and waved at them, hoping they would see him and come over.

And they did just that as they raised their hands in greeting and walked over.

"It's good to see you on your feet and doing so well." Darh greeted him. "How is the leg?" The other man's eyes slid down Tor's leg.

"It is stiff, and I still have a limp, but it works." Tor flexed his leg in front of all three men.

"Good." Jirk slapped him on the back, nearly toppling him with the unexpected movement. "We worked hard to get you back to the village, and I would hate to see our efforts were for nothing."

All the men chuckled as Darh playfully swung an arm at Jirk, that Jirk was forced to dodge or get walloped in the face.

"Be quiet, you." Darh hushed Jirk.

"What?" Jirk looked between all the men. "Tor understands me."

Tor rolled his eyes. "I do, my friend." Then another smile creased his lips. "Are you two planning on joining the hunting party?"

Jirk shrugged, causing his tanned leather shirt to bunch up around his neck. "I wasn't sure who was staying and who was going."

"We should bring them." Tor looked over at Daerk who quickly nodded his head. "They would be better suited to helping with the hunt than sitting here guarding the village."

"You will come with the hunting party

then," Daerk confirmed with a solid nod of his head.

The two men smiled like they'd lost their minds with excitement.

"Then we have some packing to do." Darh's eyes sparkled with eagerness at the idea of joining a mammoth hunt. Then he guided Jirk away as they discussed what to bring with them.

Tor had missed this. There was no way he would ever leave this village again.

"We still need several more men." Daerk frowned as a crease formed between his eyes. "I worry about leaving too few warriors here in the village though."

"Worried about Brog?" No one had seen the old clan leader or his followers since he'd been kicked out. Tor wasn't sure they ever would see that man again. He was probably long gone, tail tucked between his legs. He was most likely taking over another clan and running them into the dirt.

"Brog, another nearby clan, or an animal attack. All are possibilities."

"I'm sure we will figure it out." It was the best Tor could do. He wasn't too concerned, but he knew the role of leadership weighed heavily on Daerk's shoulders. This hadn't been his friend's goal, to become leader of the clan, he'd only sought to get rid of Brog.

With a pat on Daerk's back, Tor led them through the village as they sought out more men.

Chapter 12

Ezi glanced around the inside of Tor's hut with interest. She had been inside briefly, but now she had time to look around. There was nothing special, just the normal things every other hut had like a fire pit, some weapons, and a bed of furs. It was sparse.

A reed basket on the other side of the hut caught her attention. With Flosa in her arms, Ezi walked over to the basket, flipped up the lid, and her breath caught at the sight of the beautiful dress within. Bone and wood beads as well as seeds and dyes decorated the dress in a mesmerizing pattern.

Knowing he hadn't had a mate before her meant that this must be from his mother... and after living in this clan for many moons, she knew his parents were long dead, like hers. A fond smile curved her lips. It was sweet that Tor had saved something so special.

Placing the lid back into place, she left it alone, not wanting to disturb his things, especially something with so much emotion connected with it.

She placed Flosa down on Tor's furs and then went about the task of getting Flosa's bed of furs set up for her small body. She still couldn't believe Tor had been willing to give up his hut to her. She did feel a small bit of guilt creep into her chest. He was still recovering from the wound on his leg, and now he would be sleeping with the stars as his only cover.

Ezi frowned.

Then again, he had been the one to offer the

hut, so there was no reason for her to feel bad about accepting the offer. It wasn't like she'd forced him into it.

Once she had the furs in the proper arrangement, she grabbed a hold of Flosa and then placed her into the fur basket. Flosa's eyes were closed, her face scrunching up every once in a while, as she dreamed.

"Ezi?"

Spinning around, Ezi found Aiyre's head popped in through the hut flap.

"Aiyre?"

"You are in Tor's hut?" Aiyre stepped fully into the hut, her eyes scanning over the inside. "Why are you in here?" She asked when Ezi didn't reply fast enough.

"He offered it to me."

"Offered?"

Ezi shrugged. "He thought it might be better than the communal hut. Allow me some space and give me a place where Flosa couldn't bother anyone with her crying."

"Where will he sleep?"

Ezi shrugged again, as the guilt crept back into her heart. If it rained, he would get soaked to the bone… then again, he had lived on his own for many moons. He should know where to seek shelter from the weather.

"Well, I'm sure he will find somewhere to sleep." Aiyre smiled at Flosa and then turned her attention back to Ezi. "Have you decided if you are coming to the hunt?"

Ezi bit her bottom lip as she tilted her head

side to side. "I thought about it, and I think it might be good for me. Inde was wonderful with Flosa when I went to the ritual. I'm just nervous about leaving her for a longer time, but I still believe it would be good to be a part of the hunt." It was time for her to be a part of the clan and show interest in their welfare.

Aiyre beamed as her brown eyes lit up with glee. "I'm glad you found at least one sabertooth you can trust. Now, we just have to get you to trust the rest of them."

"I trust Daerk." Ezi said defensively. Their fierce leader had done nothing but protect them. He was the sabertooth who had found them wandering around during a snowstorm after the attack, and he'd brought them to a cave to save their lives. It was the first time she thought a sabertooth shifter might actually be more than a brutal animal.

"It's hard not to trust him." Aiyre agreed. "He speaks the truth and tries to do his best for everyone in this clan."

Ezi supposed she trusted Tor as well. She might not like the thought of being his mate, but he was a nice man who'd done nothing to her. Except for that kiss. Her eyes stared blankly as her mind revisited that kiss that he'd planted on her lips. It'd been unexpected, and at first, she hadn't known how to react, but then she'd fled. Absently, she raised a hand and rubbed a finger across her bottom lip. She feared that scolding kiss would never leave her mind.

"What are you thinking about?"

Ezi shook her head as she remembered she had company. "Just remembering the hunting ceremony, and how much fun I had being a part of the clan." It was sort of the truth because she wasn't about to tell Aiyre about that kiss. There would be too many questions, and Ezi had no answers.

"It was fun." Aiyre plopped down on a fur that was near the fire pit and quickly got to work on building up the fire until there was a great plume of smoke lazily swirling up to the hole in the top of the hut.

"Maybe I could bring Flosa with me to the mammoth hunt." Ezi said absently as she took a seat between Flosa and the fire. She was getting better with Flosa, and she figured with enough time, she would be the loving mother that she wanted to be for Flosa. She might not have Drakk around to help her, but she did have this clan.

Aiyre frowned as she shook her head, her braid swinging behind her head. "I don't think so. Flosa will be happier here, and the hunting ground could be dangerous for a baby, and it would prevent you from shifting and fleeing the area if you needed."

Aiyre had some good points.

Ezi sighed, "You're right."

"I'm glad you want to bring her, and I want to say yes, but it's better for her to stay here."

Ezi glanced at Flosa.

"But… I can see if there is a way to bring her. We will have a camp a little way from the hunting ground, a place that would be safer."

"Thank you."

"I make no promises."

"I understand." Ezi smiled. "I won't miss this hunt. She either can come or will stay here with Inde. Should I bring anything with me?"

Aiyre's lips pursed as she thought about Ezi's question. "A small pack would be good, but make sure it is light. We have a distance to walk, and we don't need anyone getting tired. The men will bring dried meat for us, and there will be plenty of berry bushes at this time of year."

Ezi's stomach flipped in excitement. She'd never been to a mammoth hunt, and she was nervous. Sometimes the mammoths could stampede and trample hunters. She'd heard terrifying stories at the clan gatherings. They were a time when all the nearby clans would get together for trade or finding mates. A shiver ran down her spine, causing the fine hairs on her neck stand up. Those stories always horrified her because it sounded like a terrible way to die.

A hand landed on her thigh, and she looked up to see Aiyre smiling at her encouragingly. "All will go fine."

"What are you talking about?"

"I saw the line creasing your forehead." Aiyre pointed to Ezi's face.

Ezi smacked her hand away and rolled her eyes. "I've heard the stories about these hunts. How can you be sure nothing will go wrong?"

"Only experienced hunters will be coming since we need to bring down at least one mammoth. Younger hunters will have their chance later."

"Still, I've heard stories about these beasts, and they might be even more protective since they'll have offspring at this time."

Aiyre grabbed a long stick sitting near her and stirred the fire. "We will be safe."

"You will be one of the hunters?"

Aiyre smiled over at her, her eyes filled to the brim with her excitement. "Yes."

A little envy entered Ezi's heart. She loved Aiyre, but sometimes the other woman made her feel weak and useless. Aiyre could do anything. She could hunt, build spears and arrows, lead a clan of sabertooths and so many other things, while Ezi was still struggling to get past the death of their clan.

"The light in your eyes has dimmed." Aiyre placed a hand on Ezi's thigh and gave her a light squeeze through her tanned animal skin pants.

Ezi quickly turned the corners of her mouth up in a fake smile. "I'm fine, just thinking about the upcoming hunt."

"As much as I want to stay here with you, Daerk wants all the hunters to meet up and discuss our plan on hunting the mammoths." Aiyre rose to her feet and brushed off some dirt that had stuck to her pants as she'd sat on the ground.

"I'll see you later then." Ezi smiled up at her.

Aiyre gave a small wave and disappeared through the hut flap.

The fire crackled in front of her, and Flosa mewed softly in her sleep, but other than that it was quiet in the hut. It was strange, but now that Aiyre was gone, Ezi was feeling a bit lonely. After living in the communal hut for unmated women since they'd arrived, it was weird for her to finally have some quiet and space.

She sat there for a few more moments, hoping this sense of loneliness would leave her alone, but it didn't. Even her pronghorn side shifted inside uncomfortably. She was born to be a herd animal, and sitting alone caused some anxiety to prickle at her skin.

"Sorry," Ezi apologized to Flosa as she stood and scooped up Flosa who's face scrunched up in protest, but the baby never once woke up.

Then she darted out of Tor's hut and into the sunshine. It felt good to enjoy the warm rays after such a long winter. The air was still fairly brisk, but it didn't require layers upon layers of furs to stay marginally warm.

With Flosa pressed up to her bosom, Ezi strode through the village, enjoying the life around her. Children ran around wildly as they chased each other in a game that one of them had conjured. She passed a group of women weaving some baskets from long green grass. All this life caused her to miss her pronghorn clan, and a bit of sadness crept into her heart.

As Ezi rounded a hut, her eyes landed on Tor.

She paused, frozen in place.

He was facing away from her, and she decided to take a moment to watch him. He was handsome. His face was well cut like it had been chiseled from rock, and his long black hair was loose around his shoulders except for a couple of braids that she could see framing his face. Now that he'd cut his hair and tended to the strands, it looked much better. Then her eyes shifted to his shoulders. Those shoulders of his were wide, and for a second, she could imagine what it would be like to be wrapped in them.

Again, the kiss floated through her mind, and her lips tingled in happiness. They wanted nothing more than to experience it once more.

One taste and she couldn't wait for more.

Tor was trouble. Not only because he was a sabertooth shifter, but because there was a small part of her that wanted to explore this matehood he'd suggested. Maybe it was good she was going on this mammoth hunt. It would give her some much-needed space from him because she couldn't see him going with his limp.

Relief washed through Ezi at that thought. The limp would prevent him from going… or Eron would prevent him. That old shaman was strict when it came to healing. He would never let Tor reopen or cause worse damage to that leg.

Tor was speaking with another man, and she found herself interested. Sneaking off to one side where she'd be able to overhear the conversation better, she listened in.

"This looks good." Tor tested a spear in one hand. He motioned with it, sticking the tip forward as if he were throwing it at prey. Then he pulled it close to his face before examining the sharp stone point.

The young man in front of him perked up, his eyes shining with light. "This will be my first mammoth hunt."

"You're a skilled hunter and proven yourself against larger beasts. There's a reason Daerk chose you to come." Tor continued to praise the man.

Ezi raised an eyebrow. Hadn't Aiyre told her there would only be experienced hunters? She shrugged. Aiyre hadn't said they would be experienced hunting mammoths, but Ezi had assumed.

The young man took back his spear. "Thank you. I won't let you down." Adoration shown bright in the man's eyes as he eagerly looked to Tor. Tor was someone the members of this clan looked up to, and it for some reason, it warmed her heart a bit to see this.

"I know you won't." Tor slapped a hand against the man's back, earning himself another smile of adoration from the young man.

Ezi cocked her head to the side as they continued to talk. Tor was so good with the man. Everything he said was kind, and if he had a piece of advice, he made sure it wasn't a harsh criticism but a suggestion.

Then she saw Tor's nose lift into the air as he gave a couple of noticeable sniffs. The sides of his nostrils flared out, and then his head turned and their eyes collided, pinning her to the spot. A smile crooked one side of his mouth up as his dark eyes scanned over her.

Ezi swallowed hard. She wanted to move her feet, but she couldn't seem to get them to work.

"I'll speak more with you later." Tor dismissed the younger man. His eyes never left her, like she wasn't the only one who couldn't break this connection.

The man looked between them, and with a smile he turned to leave.

"Ezi." Tor purred as he prowled closer, his limp adding a dark but irresistible allure. His dark eyes never left her as if he couldn't get enough of her.

A shiver spread through her, and she hugged Flosa slightly closer to her chest like the baby would somehow keep her from trembling in delight and collapsing into a puddle.

With a few long strides, he was standing right in front of her. His gaze bored right into her eyes, and when his head descended, she prepared herself for another one of his stunning kisses. Her heart hitched in her chest, and she held her breath… but it never came.

"I've never seen Flosa yet, but Aiyre has told me about her." His eyes were now focused on the bundle in her arms, his head bent low as he smiled at the child.

A small flutter of regret flickered through her. She'd been hoping for one of those searing kisses. Last night was still fresh in her mind, which had to be the reason she was still thinking about it.

A smile tugged on his lips as he glanced up at her as if he knew the direction of her thoughts.

Glancing away, Ezi felt a hot blush creep up her neck and cheeks. This man could read her too well, and she feared he might just win her over if she was still thinking about such a simple kiss.

Flosa giggled up at Tor as he bopped her on the nose with a finger.

"May I hold her?" Tor straightened and reached out his hands.

Ezi wanted to scream no and run away, but when she turned her head up and looked into his blue eyes, she saw a flash of something… longing perhaps? She turned her gaze back to Flosa, who appeared to be in love with Tor. Her little eyes danced with glee every time he wiggled a finger at her.

She was here to live in the village for the foreseeable future. She couldn't avoid him forever, and at some point, she had to hope being his friend would be fine. She couldn't promise anything other than being his clanmate.

"Here," Ezi offered Flosa. Aiyre's words rang in her head. She had to befriend the people of this clan.

Tor took the baby into his arms, cradling her in the crook of his arm. Tender. Such a strong man, yet he was treating Flosa like a delicate flower.

"She's beautiful, like her mother." He glanced up and sent her a charming smile.

Ezi's heart melted in her chest. Not at his words, but the image he presented in front of her. Something inside her couldn't resist him when he had Flosa in his arms. She had no idea why, but it was there pulling her towards him. The baby was so small, and he was so large, and her feminine side went crazy.

"That's enough." Ezi snapped as she rushed forward, snatched Flosa out of his arms and darted away. She didn't stop walking until he was left in the dust.

Pausing beside a tent, she relaxed against one of the bone supports, doing her best to rebuild the ice around her heart. The sabertooth was wearing down her defenses, and she couldn't let him do that. For a brief second, Tor's image had been replaced by Drakk, and she'd lost her nerve. Tor shouldn't be the man holding Flosa. It should be Drakk.

"You shouldn't like that man." Ezi frowned down at Flosa as she scolded the baby. "You're a pronghorn shifter, and he is a sabertooth. We are prey, and he is a predator. Such things go against nature."

"Against nature?"

Ezi's head shot around to find Aiyre standing beside her.

"Daerk and I have found a way to make it work, and though the gods haven't blessed us with a child, I wouldn't say it's against nature."

"I… I…" Ezi had no idea what to say. She'd just be annoyed with her reactions to Tor. Her body responded to his very presence, and it irked her.

Aiyre's face scrunched up as she frowned and shook her head. "I thought you were trying to be a part of the clan."

"I am."

"You can't be a part of the clan if you can't learn to trust people." Aiyre's eyes turned thoughtful. "Perhaps you should continue to think about whether staying here will be what you want. I fear Tor, and you will drive each other insane."

"Leave?"

Aiyre shrugged. "There has to be a pronghorn clan somewhere. I like thinking that Girk found another clan to join after he left us, and if I could find him, you could join a clan where you knew another."

Ezi's heart throbbed in her chest as she thought about the possibility of leaving Aiyre behind. "I don't wish to leave."

Aiyre's brown eyes softened. "Tor won't leave you alone, even if he wanted to leave you alone. His sabertooth needs to win you over."

Ezi chuffed. "You think he wouldn't follow me if I left?" Because she had her doubts, she could ever escape Tor. Now that he was back, she was sure he would always be nearby. If she left for another clan, he would leave with her.

Aiyre shrugged, causing her fur shirt to bunch up around the shoulders. "We could try to sneak you away."

With a sigh, Ezi shook her head. "Don't give up on me, Aiyre. I just need more time. His sudden appearance surprised me, and I need to grow used to seeing him around."

"I want to make sure you don't stay here for me." Aiyre pointed her hand to her chest. "I want you to be happy, and if Tor sniffing around your hut makes you nervous, you won't have time to enjoy the village."

Ezi sent Aiyre a thankful smile. "Thank you. I will be sure to let you know if I need to find a new clan." And Aiyre needed to stop worrying about her. She was a grown woman with a child. She could handle Tor's presence, no matter how much he annoyed her.

Aiyre grabbed one of Ezi's hands and lightly squeezed it. "Don't let anyone over here you. They might think you don't like being around this village." She sent Ezi a smile before going on her way.

Ezi heaved a sigh. Leaving the clan wouldn't get rid of all her problems. There were still the nightmares that plagued her. It was like the attack on her clan just happened yesterday. All the details were still so vivid and fresh in her mind, and she was beginning to wonder if those images would ever leave her alone.

Ezi stretched out by the large village fire. Inde had done such a great job with looking after Flosa the first time that Ezi had given her baby over to the sabertooth once more. Now, she could eat with the clan before sneaking away and shifting into her pronghorn form in the forest.

The itch to shift was driving her insane. Her pronghorn was a restless creature. After so many months of carrying the child inside her body and not being able to shift meant her pronghorn wanted to be out more than normal.

Several clan members were gathered around the fire as fresh meat was cooked next to the fire on spits. A couple of men took turns spinning the spits because standing right next to the enormous fire could get a bit too warm.

Ezi watched sweat roll down both of the mens' faces as they worked the spits. Their arms tensed with muscle as they spun the wooden spits. She'd feel bad for them if they didn't have giant grins plastered to their sweat-soaked faces. They'd made a game out of spinning the meat, seeing who could stand by the fire the longest before needing to switch out.

A smile crept across her face as she watched them.

"Men."

Glancing over to her side, she saw a sabertooth shifter roll her eyes as she laughed.

"As long as they are having fun," Ezi commented in return.

The woman next to her laughed. "True. I'm Fina."

Ezi returned the smile. "Ezi."

"It's good to see you out here with the clan. Let me know if I can help you with anything." Fina's smile was genuine and warm.

"I will," Ezi promised, feeling a part of her icy heart melt some more. It was amazing to realize she knew very few names in the village. Even after so many moons, she could barely name half the people in the village.

"Here."

She started as a hand popped into her field of vision. It belonged to one of the men that'd been turning the roasting animal on the wooden spit. His smile was addicting as it stretched over his bearded face, and she found herself smiling back as she raised a hand to accept his offer.

"Thank you." Ezi's hand took the offered bone plate that had a slab of meat resting on it.

"Let me know if you need more." The man's

brown eyes danced with excitement as he turned and raced back over to the fire to cut another slab and bring it to another person sitting around the fire.

"Looks good." The woman beside her leaned in and sniffed loudly. "May I?"

"Have some." Ezi wasn't above sharing, especially since the man had brought her way too much meat. She held out the bone plate, and Fina ripped a chunk off the meat with her teeth before placing it back on the bone plate.

Ezi watched as Fina chewed her bite of the meat. Her eyelids closed slowly as she let out a moan of appreciation.

Licking her fingers, Fina said, "With the meat hut full, I can finally enjoy eating. Before now, every time we ate something, we worried about how much meat was left."

"It must have been scary." Ezi could only imagine a village full of hungry sabertooth shifters. They must have been slobbering at the mouth with their need to sink their teeth into hot bloody flesh. Another shiver spread up her spine. Shaking herself mentally, she scolded herself. She had to stop imagining these sabertooth shifters as monsters, or they would stay that way in her mind.

The sparse winter had driven them to attack the pronghorn clan. It was no excuse, but Ezi could understand the fear of starvation. If they hadn't turned on the pronghorns, then they may have turned on each other.

Daerk had driven Brog out, after all.

Ezi balanced the bone plate on her lap as she ripped off a piece of meat with her hands. She slipped the meat into her mouth, and saliva built up in her mouth as she began chewing. The fat dissolved quickly in her mouth.

"Good?"

She nodded her head in answer to Fina's question.

Yanking off another piece, she used two fingers to slide it into her mouth. She wasn't quite sure what the meat was from, but it was something she would eat again eagerly. The roasting meat on the spit was just a piece of whatever large animal they'd taken down recently.

After a few more minutes of eating and talking with Fina, Ezi found her pronghorn side begging for the shift. It wanted to stretch its long legs out in the forest.

"Leaving for your hut?" Fina asked the moment Ezi stood up beside her spot by the fire.

"Yes." Ezi lied, not wanting anyone to know she was about to go frolicking in the forest. She was afraid someone would stop her since it was night, and there might be predators lurking about. And there was also the worry that Brog was lying in wait to strike. Or they'd want to join her, and she couldn't be around a sabertooth while it was shifted. It was too soon for that. Way too soon.

Fina sent her a smile before turning back to the merrymaking near the fire. Her curiosity about where Ezi was headed satisfied.

Good.

Breathing a sigh of relief, Ezi disappeared easily amongst all the smiling clan members who stood or sat around the fire. With the mammoths on their way, there was a lot to celebrate. Aiyre wanted her to use tonight to befriend everyone, but that would mean she'd have more people watching her. Right now, she had a good balance of being a part of the clan and being able to disappear without too many people wondering where she'd gone.

Slinking between the huts with quiet footsteps, Ezi quickly strode to the edge of the village with a slight bounce to her steps. Then she walked into the nearby forest. The old trees towered over her offering protection under their green leafy boughs. The night air was crisper away from the smoke of the village fire, and she sucked it in with greedy breaths.

Glancing around to make sure no one was around to spot her, Ezi ripped off her tanned animal skin shirt. The cool night air rushed up to brush against her skin, pebbling her nipples. Her hands gripped the waistband of her animal skin pants, and she slid them down her legs, pulling her moccasins off in the same swift motion.

She grabbed her clothes and placed them near the base of a tree trunk. She would need them when she got back, or someone would know she'd gone off for a run. If she was caught, she knew Aiyre would scold her like a naughty child.

Stretching, Ezi let a smile slip across her face as her pronghorn jumped inside her for joy.

Her shift came over her quickly. Her skin stretched, her arms turned into long furred hooved legs, her neck cracked as it stretched out and large ears sprang from her head. There was a bit of pain when she shifted, but over the years it'd become normal, barely an inconvenience.

Stamping a hoof against the ground, Ezi lifted her head, her ears flipping back and forth as she took in all the night time sounds around her. She could hear her clanmates talking and laughing within the village. She couldn't make out any of the words, but she could hear the voices. The scratching of a rabbit in the underbrush had her ears pricking forward once more.

With a leap high into the air, she pranced off into the forest.

Chapter 13

Tor felt like he should look away, but he was curious about his mate. If he was going to win her over, then he needed to know her. Which was the same reason why he'd followed her the moment she'd tried to sneak away from the village fire.

It was hard to resist following her when his inner sabertooth saw the nerves causing her eyes to flicker around. He'd known she was up to something.

When Ezi pulled off her beaded animal skin shirt, it took all his strength not to pounce on her, and his sabertooth growled in frustration at his restraint. Unfortunately, it would just have to be patient. Tor was determined not to push her away more than he already had… assuming he could keep his sabertooth in place.

Tor's eyes zeroed in on her nipples as they puckered up in the night air like they were begging for a man to caress them. His tongue darted out of his mouth to lick his suddenly dry lips. The sight of her in the moonlight had his cock stirring and his sabertooth growling with pent up desire. Then she shed her pants, and he watched her ass in the moonlight. Those pale orbs were just begging him to pounce on them, maybe even give them a slight bite.

As she stayed bent and moved the clothes to the base of a tree, he could see the plump folds of her sex in the dark. His cat eyes didn't need to be in sabertooth form to see every perfect inch of her body. He wanted to kiss his way up the inside of her thighs until he reached her hot apex.

His pants grew tight as a bulge formed within. Shoving a hand against his cock, he willed the thing under control, but it was like it had a mind of its own. Both it and his sabertooth wanted him to storm towards her, push her down until her butt was high in the air, and take her from behind.

He threw his head back as he stifled a groan. The images that flashed through his mind had him nearly spilling his desire into his pants.

Then Ezi straightened back up, and his eyes roamed over her small form. She was perfection. As he watched on, she began her shift. It took no more than a few seconds before she was standing in the forest in her pronghorn form.

She was stunning.

Tor never thought he'd stare at a pronghorn with lust, but here he was. All four of her legs were slender and well built. The belly of her pronghorn was a cream color while her head, back, and legs were a fawn brown. And the dainty horns on her head were adorable, although he wasn't sure he should ever say that to her. There was no telling if those observations would insult her.

In a flash of movement, Ezi bounded off into the night.

Tor frowned. Disappointment soared through him once she was out of sight. He'd been hoping to watch her some more, to learn more about her. He couldn't be expected to win over his mate without the proper information. A hunter needed to know his prey before he could be sure of the kill.

As he turned to walk back to the village, a thought entered his mind.

He could easily shift and follow after her. She was a lone pronghorn in the night. How could he just go back to the village without making sure she didn't get herself eaten. It would destroy him if anything happened to her when he could have prevented it.

His sabertooth purred in agreement.

Tor didn't give it a second thought. Whipping off his clothes, he threw them haphazardly, and let the shift overtake him. Once the transformation was complete, he stretched his paws in the dirt, his claws digging into the soft ground under his feet. He loved being in his sabertooth form. Sometimes, it felt more right than being in his human form.

Raising his pink nose into the air, he quickly picked up on her lingering scent. Leaping into action, his sabertooth form ate up the ground as he caught up to Ezi. When she finally came into sight, he slowed down, keeping right outside her field of vision and sense of smell.

Tor didn't plan on interrupting her nighttime run. He just wanted to be close enough to help her in case she ran into trouble.

Ezi's nighttime run was perfect. Her pronghorn had calmed, and after an hour or so of running around, she found a spot to shift back into her human form. Once she was back in her other form, she rotated her head side to side to crack her neck and stretched her arms high above her head.

She would take a small break, and then shift back into her pronghorn form and go back to find her clothes.

"You're far from the village."

Whipping around, her jaw nearly hit the ground under her feet. "Tor?" Her eyes raked over him, barely able to process what she was seeing.

He strode towards her, completely naked. Her eyes bugged out of her head. She tried to rip her eyes of his tanned skin that glowed in the rays of moonlight. When her gaze fell even lower, she felt her mouth go dry. His huge cock was hard and straining for her attention.

It had it. Her heart thudded in her chest as her body responded to the sight in front of her. Her mind screamed at her to shift and run. They were both naked and alone... there were no eyes to see them. There were no eyes to stop them.

"It is me." His dark voice purred in the night as he no doubt sensed the confusion rolling off her.

Ezi's heart thudded to a stop in her chest as her mind lost itself. She couldn't move off her spot. It was like she was frozen to the soft grass under her feet.

Tor prowled closer. "Hello, mate."

There was that word again. Mate. It scared her... but a small part of her found it thrilling as well. His dark voice made it sound like a seductive secret that only they shared.

"You followed me?" She found her voice as she accused him. A spark of outrage found its way through her stunned state.

Tor had the audacity to shrug. "I noticed

you leaving the clan on your own. There are many dangers lurking about." He waved a hand around the shadowy night. "If I let something happen to you, I would never be the same man."

She smothered the spark of happiness that he'd be bothered by her death.

He stalked even closer. Her pronghorn yelled at her to run from this predator that was hunting her. Taking a step back, she attempted to put some space between their naked bodies. Them being together here in the night while naked was courting danger.

Before Ezi could get far, his hand whipped out and snatched her upper arm, yanking her back towards him. Throwing her hands up, she bumped into his chest, her hands landing on his hard muscles.

Ezi's mouth popped open as she turned her head up to gaze into his blue eyes, which looked several shades darker in the night. Flecks of gold danced around in the depths, flecks that she'd never noticed before.

Her fingers played with the fine dark hairs on his chest, twirling in them as she waited for his next move. She wasn't sure she trusted herself to move. Her breasts were so close to touching his bare skin, and she could feel the heat pouring off of him in waves.

"Scared?" His spare hand came up to caress a thumb across the racing pulse on her neck.

Her eyes narrowed up at him. "I'm not scared." Not of him, but maybe she was scared of the intensity in his dark eyes and the heat coursing through her blood at his simple touch.

A small smile curved one side of his mouth up. "You smell good."

Ezi frowned. If she wasn't his mate, she would think he was implying he wouldn't mind a bite of her delicate flesh.

Tor chuckled.

"What is funny?" Ezi asked bristling a bit more, as her hands continued to play in the dark hairs of his chest. She should pull back and leave, but here she was standing within his embrace.

One of his fingers skimmed over her lips. "I prefer seeing a smile on your lips rather than a frown."

"I haven't had much to smile about." Ezi's eyes glared up at him.

"Let me give you something to smile about then."

Before she had time to process his words, Tor's head dipped down, and he captured her lips with his. Her eyes widened in shock before sliding closed in bliss. The kiss was light, not demanding, more like an invitation to something greater.

Ezi pulled back. There was an emotion rising inside her, and she wasn't sure she was ready to face it. As her eyes scanned over him, trying to read him, she caught sight of his expression. It looked like he'd gone to the Eternal Hunting Grounds. His eyes were hooded, and there was a confident smile plastered on his face.

"I need more." Tor leaned back in and recaptured her lips, and this time, he demanded her surrender. He was asking her to give in and give him what he longed for.

Ezi melted as she let the hand on her arm, pull her in closer. He smashed her breasts between them and the intimate contact sent a thrill piercing through her. Tor didn't kiss like Drakk. He was more forceful, and Ezi found it intoxicating. He was demanding what he thought was his.

Her eyes popped open when she felt his tongue slide across the seam of her lips.

Pulling back slightly, he whispered, "Open for me, mate. Let me taste you."

Then his lips were back on hers. Hesitantly, she opened her mouth, curious what he would do. His tongue slid between her lips and lightly touched the tip of her tongue. A smile curved her lips as she touched him back.

A growl rumbled through Tor's chest in approval, and some of her fear rolled away.

One of his hands roamed over the naked flesh of her body, curving around her hip and giving it a brief squeeze before moving to the small of her back. Everywhere his hand traveled left a line of warmth, causing her to press into his chest more, soaking up his warmth.

Ezi was surprised by the pleasure coursing through her. His kisses were addicting, and not unpleasant like she thought they would be. Drakk had never kissed her like this like she was the only one who could quench his thirst.

Groaning, Tor's wandering hand made its way into her hair, gripping it in a hard fist that tilted her head back, giving him better access to her mouth.

Tor could scarcely believe he was holding his mate. Kissing his mate. His sabertooth wouldn't stop purring in joy. It wanted to shift in front of her, to impress his mate with his size and strength, but Tor held it back. Shifting in front of Ezi would do nothing but ruin the moment.

A pronghorn shifter, especially in her delicate state of mind, wouldn't enjoy seeing a sabertooth shifter in his animal form.

Ezi's soft body molded against his front, and his cock twitched. Then she rotated her hips, and her abdomen rubbed his cock, and it throbbed, pressing into her as it begged for her attention.

One of her hands broke free from between their hot bodies, and she began exploring his body in return. Her small hand brushed her fingertips over his chest and down his abdomen before dipping lower to the head of his cock.

Her strokes were hesitant, but it felt so good to feel his hot length in her hand. Little pulses of pleasure shot through his cock, tightening his balls with anticipation.

His sabertooth growled inside him, and a growl rumbled out of his chest and into her mouth. His tongue continued to tease her as it went in and out of her mouth, drawing her into his own. The hairs of his beard pricked her skin with delightful tickles.

Gods how he needed her. Under him. Above him. All around him.

He was so close to having his mate.

That's when he felt it.

His fingernails were elongating into sharp claws. No! No! Tor screamed at his sabertooth to restrain itself, but the beast was beyond listening to him. It wanted to take his mate and show her his power.

It was too soon!

A feral growl rolled out of his mouth, and Ezi shot back, severing their kiss. Her jade eyes went wide in the moonlight, and he saw the fear spread through them.

"Don't fear me." But the words came out muffled as he tried talking around his growing canines.

"Let go of me!" Ezi screamed as she began beating him with her fists.

Tor held on to her waist, not wanting to let her go, but also not wanting to tear into her delicate flesh with his sharp nails. One of her fists flew through the air and connected with his nose.

Thankfully, he didn't hear a snap, but the pain rocked his head back as he let go of her waist. She didn't wait for him to recover.

In a flash, she'd shifted into her pronghorn form.

"Ezi. Wait. I can control myself." He held out a hand, but she was gone. Her hooves kicked up patches of dirt and grass before she disappeared into the night.

Tor roared at the blinking stars above him. If he wasn't a sabertooth, he'd have his mate by now. He was sure of that. Every time he got close to her, his other side would push her away.

Running a clawed hand through his hair, he sucked in several deep breaths trying to calm himself, but the predator inside wasn't about to let his prey get away, not when he could smell her need in the air. She'd been just aroused as himself.

Ezi fled. Her heart thundered inside her massive pronghorn ribcage, and she wasn't sure it was because she was running or because of how close she'd been to opening her thighs to a sabertooth shifter. So close.

A roar ripped through the night air, and she stumbled over her long hooved legs, caught herself before she went down and continued to tearing through the woods. It would take her several minutes of running before she got back to the village and the safety of his hut… assuming he wouldn't follow her right inside.

Twisting her head side to side, she searched for a place to escape. Blood roared in her ears as her hooves pounded over the ground. Tor was a fierce hunter and her mate, and she had no doubt he would find her no matter where she fled.

With every hoof beat a whiff of crushed grass would drift up to her pronghorn nose. It was the one scent that stayed with her as she flew through the forest. Every other scent zipped past her as the wind whipped through her short fur.

Another loud roar from behind had her heart skittering in her chest as it seemed to cause the branches above her tremble in fear.

Tor was hunting.

Hunting her.

A thrill sped through her. She did her best to quell the anticipation coursing through her veins. This should scare her, not cause her body to heat. Even her pronghorn was quivering in need and expectancy. They were both crazy. This was a sabertooth shifter chasing them down.

In a split-second decision that she knew she would regret, she zigged, veering away from the village. She was about to play a tricky game with a dangerous adversary. He would want more, and she… she was just looking for a way to release some pent-up emotions.

Then Ezi heard the snap of a twig behind her. Her ears flicked back, and then she flew through the air as a large paw landed against her flank, sending her reeling, she shifted mid-air into her human form and prepared herself to hit the ground… but she landed against a bare chest as Tor took the brunt of the fall.

"Mate." He growled, the words guttural and barely understandable.

Before she could utter a word, he flipped over her until he was above her, and then he stood up on his knees. His blue eyes flashed with the speckles of gold she'd noticed earlier. She almost wanted to say the gold glowed like a hot coal. Then her eyes noticed the tips of his canines peeping out from behind his upper lips.

His sabertooth was sitting right under his skin.

A thrill pierced her, and she wasn't sure whether it was fear or exhilaration that flowed through her veins.

His chest moved in and out as he sucked in deep breaths, and she did the same as they both recovered after the wild dash through the forest.

"Tor."

"Stop." He growled.

Ezi snapped her mouth shut as she waited in silence. He looked like he was warring with his inner sabertooth, trying to regain control of the beast within. She should end this, end this now before it went any further.

"Touch me," Tor commanded her.

Ezi hesitated. She could end this… but they were hidden in the darkness of the night, and she did find Tor to be an attractive man who could ease the itch within her.

Decision made.

Ezi's hand grabbed a firm hold of his cock. Her eyes never left his as she slowly stroked his length, before rubbing her thumb across the head where she encountered a bead of wetness. She spread it around in lazy circles as she explored his length.

Then her hand ventured lower to his balls. She cupped them, feeling their weight in her palm. Lightly, she played with them, exploring them to her heart's content.

"Stroke my member," Tor growled above her.

Her gaze dipped to his erect member as she wrapped her fingers around it. It pulsed and a slow smile curved her lips as she pumped it. When she heard Tor suck in a deep breath, the smile on her lips grew even larger. Glancing up, she noticed his eyelids had sunk closed, and his lips had parted in pleasure.

His hips bucked eagerly under her ministrations, and soon they were both pumping his cock in her hand.

Tor abruptly yanked back, and her hand slid away from his cock, but she didn't have to wait long to find out what he wanted to do next. Tor reached between them and knocked her thighs apart with his hands.

The cool night air rushed up to brush her sex, and then Tor's hot mouth covered her. Ezi startled as she pushed at Tor's head. "Tor!" What was he doing? Drakk had never done this. Did anyone do this?

Pulling away slightly, he growled at her, "Let me taste you. Let me pleasure you."

"I don't think–"

Tor sucked against her flesh as his teeth scraped her nub. Sensation rolled through her, and her hips bucked, shoving her sex into Tor's face. Ezi's head rolled on her shoulders as she moaned in ecstasy.

His tongue leisurely licked from her nub down to her entrance, where he stuck the tip in her. Then he trailed his way back up to her nub, where he rubbed with the tip of his tongue. Sizzles of pleasure coursed through her, and her hands fisted in the grass next to her body.

Tor's hands pressed against the soft flesh of her thighs, opening her up to him more fully. He pressed a couple of fingers into her entrance, spreading her as he thrust them inside. His tongue danced across her nub as his fingers hit every sensitive spot within her. Her hips bucked wildly as the pressure built inside her frame.

Glancing down her abdomen, she saw his dark head of hair between her legs, which were raised around him like a couple of mountains. His beard tickled her skin, but it only added to the pleasure racing through her.

Ezi's hips jerked as the pressure inside her built to an unbearable amount. She was going to crash.

"Tor." She pleaded as she thrashed around on the ground.

"I want to hear you." He growled against her sensitive flesh, and it was all she needed to push her over the cliff. "Scream my name."

"Tor! Yes!" Ezi's eyes slid shut as her hips bucked. His hand pressed into her flesh as he drove his fingers in and out of her in a harsh rhythm. She hissed in much needed air as her body heated. And then she crashed. Her entrance clamped down around his fingers, and her legs pressed against his head.

As the pleasure dimmed, her body spasmed as he slowly stopped thrusting his fingers into her.

Opening her eyes, she watched him lean back up onto his knees, a smile plastered all over his face, his canines still showing, but they'd receded a bit.

"You're beautiful, Ezi."

She flushed at the compliment. What they were doing was scratching an itch. After tonight, she planned on things going back to the same, her avoiding eye contact with him and Tor pursuing her relentlessly.

One of his rough-skinned hands ran over her soft thigh in a gentle caress. Then his eyes fell to her leg, and he bent closer.

"From your wound?" A finger ran over the scar she'd forgotten.

Glancing down, she nodded her head. "From the injury, I suffered when the sabertooth shifters attacked."

"One of them bit you?"

Glancing up, Ezi saw the spark of rage exploding in his blue eyes. Before his fury consumed him, she rushed to say, "I haven't seen or scented the same sabertooth here. He either died that night or left with Brog."

The fury slowly eased out of his eyes. "Good." And then he laid down over her. His chest pressed her back against the ground as his lips found hers. She melted under his tender caresses. Raising her hands, she dug them into his black hair and pressed him against her.

Tor chuckled.

She felt him reach between their hot bodies, and then the head of his cock prodded her soaking wet entrance.

Tor broke the kiss and grinned down at her. "Feels so good."

Ezi's hips bucked, thrusting his cock into her slick entrance. With a groan above her, Tor took over. His hands gripped her hips, his claws digging into her skin as he pumped into her. His thrusts were wild and deep.

"Feels so good." He groaned above her. The muscles in his arms strained in the flickering moonlight.

Tor was huge, and he stretched her to the point that she thought he might break her. It was like nothing she'd ever experienced before. They fit perfectly.

Their moans of pleasure mixed together in the night air as he stroked in and out of her tight entrance. Her hips bucked against him until she felt his balls bouncing against her. He wasn't able to get any further into her body.

Ezi felt like she was soaring through the night sky among the glittering lights high above. Her breasts bounced wildly, and the scent of crushed grass assaulted her nose. When they were done, she would have grass stains all across her back, she was sure.

"Oh gods! Tor!" Her hands gripped his arms, her nails digging into his flesh as her body began to clamp down around him. Then Tor's roar joined her moans as he shot deep inside her.

Chapter 14

Since Ezi's night in the woods with Tor, she'd hidden herself away until the mammoth hunt. There was no way she'd be able to face him after such a passionate night of kissing... and... she shook her head driving the memories away.

What had she been thinking? The answer was, she hadn't been thinking. She should have run straight into the village and into her hut, but instead, she'd veered off course. She was insane! Tor was causing her to lose her mind.

A shiver spread through her... but she wasn't sure whether it was a shiver of excitement or disgust.

Flosa cried out in a piercing shriek that had Ezi wincing as the baby demanded food.

"Here I am." Ezi strode over to the small fur bed that held her child, bent down, and picked up Flosa. Peeling back one side of her shirt, she guided Flosa's small head to her nipple, and without any help, the baby latched on eagerly.

A shuffling noise at the other side of the hut had Ezi spinning around. Her heart rate spiked as she expected to see Tor coming for her, but when she finished spinning around, she found Aiyre standing just inside the hut.

"How is Flosa?" Aiyre stepped closer. Her eyes focused on the baby in Ezi's arms. Longing shone bright in the other woman's eyes.

Ezi sighed. "She's been restless and cranky."

She rotated her head, stretching out the muscles in her neck. "I'm not sure I can leave her with Inde and go on the mammoth hunt."

Aiyre smiled kindly as she shrugged. "It's your decision, but you might regret missing it. From what I've heard, the herd is one of the largest any of the hunters have seen."

"I haven't decided. I'm just not sure." Ezi glanced down at Flosa's brown hair that covered her head. She still didn't feel as close to her child as she wanted. There was still a barrier that she hadn't been able to push past. Every time she glanced down at Flosa, she saw streaks of Drakk… and it hurt.

"The hunters and women who are coming to the hunt are gathering in the center of the village." Aiyre walked towards the entrance of the hut. "If you don't come, we will leave without you, so make sure you decide quickly. The women will leave before the men, so we can get a camp set up."

And then her friend and clanmate left. The hut flap waved behind Aiyre.

"You won't hate me if I go, will you?"

Flosa fussed as she pulled away from Ezi's breast. Her small little eyes looked up at her and then a smile spread across Flosa's face like she was beginning to realize Ezi was her mother.

Something warm and fuzzy entered Ezi's heart, and she smiled down at Flosa. "You won't even notice I'm gone. I'll be back for you in no time, and you seemed to enjoy being with Inde. Just don't her crazy with your fussing."

Flosa cooed, as she raised her tiny chubby hands into the air.

Smiling, Ezi gave Flosa a finger to clutch in her tiny hand. It wasn't a firm grip, she was still too young for that, but her hand did curl around Ezi's finger. Another spark of warmth entered her heart.

Perhaps all Ezi needed was some patience and then this motherly love would come to her.

With hope blossoming inside her chest, Ezi tucked her breast back into her shirt, hugged Flosa close and pushed through the flap of the hut. The outside world greeted her with bright rays of sunshine.

She felt as though the gods were giving her the push she needed to go on the mammoth hunt. Nothing could go wrong when the world around her was so cheery and bright.

As Ezi weaved her way through the village, she caught sight of a large group gathering in the middle of the village. That must be a part of the women and men who would go on the mammoth hunt.

Quickening her footsteps, Ezi approached Inde's hut. Shoving a shoulder against the entrance flap, she entered the hut, her eyes needing to adjust to the darker light levels inside. The thick furs they used on the huts weren't good at letting light, but they did keep the cold of the winter and night out.

Children of all ages were gathered inside, amusing themselves with games or wooden toys, and younger ones were sitting in fur-lined beds. It looked like several of her clanmates were taking advantage of Inde's services.

"Ezi!" Inde looked up from where she was breastfeeding another child, who would soon not need breastfeeding. Pulling the child off her teat, she placed the baby in a fur-lined bed and then walked over to Ezi.

Her top half was bared to the world, but that was common place in their world. Clothing was more than optional. It wasn't needed sometimes, especially with shifters when it would only get torn to shreds.

"I'm here to give you Flosa. I've decided to join the women in the mammoth hunt." Ezi held out Flosa who was smiling and watching the world around her with interest.

"She's a joyful little baby, and I'm happy to have her in my hut."

Ezi snorted as she rolled her eyes. "Then she hasn't woken you up in the middle of the night too many times."

Inde gave a bark of laughter. "You're right. I'm sure she will show her fussy side if I have her for long enough. You will be gone for a few days, so maybe I'll see her at her worst."

Inde reached out, put a hand under Flosa's head and another under her tiny body, and lifted the child into her arms. Then she lightly jiggled the baby a little in her arms. Turning, she placed Flosa near another baby and then walked back over to Ezi.

"It's good I don't have a mate." Inde smiled. "What man could stay sane while living here with all this noise?"

Ezi hadn't noticed the noise until Inde pointed it out. There was crying, laughing, gurgling, and a whole assortment of other noises coming from the children within the hut. She raised an eyebrow. "You're right. It might be a little too much."

And that had her thinking of Tor. Could he tolerate the noises Flosa made when it wasn't his own child? Some of the child's screams could annoy Ezi, and it was her child. It wouldn't surprise her if he demanded she get rid of the child. Humans did that all the time, from what she'd heard. Sabertooths could be the same way. Why would he want to waste his time on a child that wasn't his own?

"Do sabertooths accept another's child as their own?" The words were out of Ezi's mouth before she could halt herself. Inde wasn't a friend, just a sabertooth clan mate, and this question held a lot of implications.

Inde cocked her head to the side, her ear nearly touching the shoulder of her shirt as she studied Ezi, and Ezi shifted her moccasin feet over the ground uncomfortably.

"Each man is different," Inde started slowly, "but if you're speaking about Tor?" Inde sent her a kind smile. "You couldn't find a nicer man. I think he would be happy to take any child into his hut."

Ezi would be the judge of that, but it was a relief to hear Inde didn't think he would ever try to get rid of Flosa. When he'd been showering her with kisses the other night, his thoughts hadn't been of nice things. He'd wanted to win her over, but it wasn't just her she had to consider. She also had to think about Flosa.

She was still displeased with her pronghorn form. Wasn't it supposed to flee from danger? Sense danger? How could a sabertooth shifter not be dangerous?

"There you are."

Ezi and Inde both turned to find Ake standing in the open entrance of the hut. One of her arms was held out straight as she kept the flap entrance open.

"Ake. What brings you to my hut?" Inde asked.

"Aiyre asked me to come with the women, so Ezi can bring her baby." Ake walked forward, her arms outstretched for Flosa.

Inde bent down, picked up the child, and handed her over after seeing Ezi nod.

"I would love to bring her with me." Ezi smiled, and relief consumed her. She'd been leaving Flosa in anyone's hands but her own. "I'm glad Aiyre thought of you."

"As am I. It gives me a reason to join the women. I would hate to miss a mammoth hunt." Ake handed Flosa over to Ezi when she motioned for her child.

"Thank you." Ezi bowed her head slightly before turning on a heel, with Flosa clasped tightly against her chest, and left the hut with Ake following close behind. It didn't matter if Tor was the nicest sabertooth shifter in the land, he was still a predator who could kill her at a moment's notice. She and Flosa needed time away from him.

Ezi needed time away so her body could cool.

She weaved her way through the village of huts until she arrived back at Tor's hut, she pushed through the hut entrance and stared down at her small pack that she'd left on the ground. "Can you take Flosa?"

Ake was right next to her in a second, her arms outstretched. Ezi relinquished her baby into the other woman's arms, bent, grabbed her small pack and then went in search of the group of women who were preparing to leave the village. She could get used to Ake being nearby. She might even use the other woman to get some more sleep while they were gone, then she would be able to resist Tor's charm when she got back.

"You're coming?" Aiyre's voice rang out with happiness when she noticed Ezi approaching. "I'm glad Ake found you. With Flosa being still so young, I figured you would like to have her nearby."

Ezi nodded as her fellow pronghorn shifter walked towards her, with a pack slung over her own back. "I am coming, and it does settle my mind to have her with me."

"I thought you might have changed your mind again. You seemed so uncertain, and I didn't want you to stay here and miss this opportunity."

Ezi shrugged. "It was a difficult decision to leave Flosa, but now that I can have her come with, it made the decision easier." Especially since it would get her further away from Tor for longer if she didn't have to worry about Flosa. After their passionate night together, Ezi and Tor both needed some space.

Right as she had that thought, she felt his presence lurking nearby. Slyly, she glanced over to her side, not moving her head, and spotted Tor leaning against a hut studying her from a distance. His blue eyes almost appeared black from her angle, and she wondered what he could possibly be thinking about.

Perhaps he was angry with her for abruptly leaving him back in the forest and forcing him to chase her down. Their passionate kissing and coupling had gotten quite heated… maybe more than just heated. He'd sought her pleasure several times.

A shiver spread through her as Ezi remembered the way he'd begun to shift into a half-beast half-human. It wasn't something a pronghorn could do, and she was surprised to find that Tor could do something so... horrible. Those claws that'd been gripping her waist. Another shiver raced down her spine in horror. And she'd let him enter her.

"Come," Aiyre placed a hand on Ezi's arm, distracting her from her thoughts, "the women are setting up over here, and we should be gone soon."

Ezi shook off any thoughts about Tor and followed Aiyre over to the other women with Ake trailing behind them. Soon she would be far away from Tor. Far away from his delectable lips that sent tingles straight to her toes and those wandering caresses.

Aiyre stopped by Daerk, rose up on her toes, and planted a kiss on his mouth. "I will see you in a day or two." She reached up and patted the side of his bearded face.

Daerk nodded his head, his nose close to hers as one of his hands worked its way into Aiyre's brunette braid. "I will see you soon, mate." He growled down at her before he placed a loving kiss to the tip of her nose.

Ezi glanced away as she walked over to the rest of the women. She wanted to give Aiyre and Daerk their privacy. Ever since Aiyre had accepted him, they'd been inseparable. Even with Ezi's mistrust of sabertooths, she was glad something so wonderful had come from that night of terror.

"Ezi." One of the women greeted her with a warm smile, but she couldn't seem to remember her name.

"Hello." Ezi returned the smile, still trying to ignore the pair of blue eyes that were focused in on her. Tor was still standing off to the side, watching her, assessing her. He was probably trying to read how she felt about the other night.

"Are you ready for the mammoth hunt?" Fina came up beside them, a glow in her brown eyes.

Ezi nodded. "I'm hoping it will take my mind off things."

Fina sent her a sympathetic look. "We all know you still suffer from your memories of that night. Let us know if we can do anything."

Not liking all the eyes suddenly on her, Ezi smiled broadly and waved their concern away with a dismissive hand. "I don't need anything. All I need is some time to figure out my place in this clan." Which should be easier now that she wasn't cloistering herself away inside a hut.

The women started discussing how and where they should set up the camp as they began walking away from the village. Aiyre was in the lead with a few other female hunters, and the rest trailed behind.

Glancing over her shoulder, Ezi cast one last glance back at the sabertooth village and caught sight of Tor. Those intense eyes of his were still watching her as he continued to lean against a hut looking relaxed, and she wasn't sure they would ever stop their watching.

Aiyre's words floated through her mind. Maybe she should try to find another pronghorn clan to join, and the best place to find them would be at a clan gathering. She'd just have to wait until the first clan gathering happened, which wouldn't happen any time soon.

Chapter 15

A couple of days later, the women had set up the camp near the hunting ground. There were a few fur tents for when the men arrived, other than that there were furs set up around the immediate area for the women.

Ezi stepped out of some nearby bushes with some berries clutched lightly in her hand to find the men arriving. Women stood up from where they sat, and if they had a mate, they ran into that man's arms. Unmated women simply greeted the arriving men with smiles and waves of their hands.

Her eyes landed on Ake, who was in love with Flosa. The baby was bundled up in some tanned furs in Ake's arms. It was nice to have them both here with her, and she was glad Aiyre had been kind enough to think up the idea.

Even though she knew he wouldn't be here, her eyes still searched the crowd of faces to see if Tor would be there among the men. When her search came up empty, she sighed in relief. She'd been right. His limp had prevented him from coming on the hunt, and she would finally get some time without him watching her.

"Hello, mate." A deep voice said from behind her.

With a gasp that parted her lips, Ezi spun around nearly losing her balance as she let go of her fistful of berries.

Tor's hands shot out and caught her around

the waist before bringing her firmly against his hard chest. "Thought you could escape me?" He raised a dark eyebrow as his blue eyes read her.

Ezi's mouth hung open in shock. "You came." She almost didn't believe her eyes.

"I did." He smiled down at her, his blue eyes darkening as his eyes zeroed in on her lips.

He was going to kiss her again. The intensity of his eyes told her that much. Would she let him? There were two sides warring inside her. There was one side that wanted nothing more than to sink into his embrace and let him take the worries of the world away for her. She was tired of running. But then there was another side of her, a side that wanted to run screaming in the opposite direction of this sabertooth shifter who refused to give up on her.

Out of nowhere, Tor raised a hand and ran a thumb across her chin and up to one corner of her mouth. "Juice from a berry." He held up his thumb, which was now stained blue.

A blush crept up her neck and face. "Oh." So, he hadn't been thinking about kissing her. He'd just been focusing on her messy eating habits.

He raised his thumb to his mouth and licked off the juice in one fluid movement of his tongue. Her eyes followed his every moment, and the area between her thighs heated as she imagined that tongue on parts of her body… what that tongue had done to parts of her body.

Tor dipped his head lower until his lips were almost touching hers. "I can smell your arousal, mate. You want me, yet you restrain yourself." His last words were barely audible as they sank into his chest as a deep growl.

A tremor thrummed through Ezi as her two sides warred inside. She did want him, and it scared her.

"I can't want you." She finally uttered in a single breath.

"Why?" Tor leaned back, his eyes scanning over her face as he waited patiently for her answer.

"It will be a betrayal." At his confused look, Ezi continued, "Your clan destroyed mine. If we are together…" she shook her head, "It would be wrong. I would be disgracing their memory."

"I had nothing to do with their deaths." Tor's eyes bored into hers.

"You're a sabertooth."

He shook his head. "You would push me away, simply because I am a sabertooth?"

When she said nothing, Tor released her like she'd burned him, and she stared at him in shock all over again. Before he marched away, she thought she saw a flash of hurt streak through his eyes, and a sliver of guilt entered her chest as she watched his back recede.

She was simply being honest with him. The night they'd shared was fantastic, but it didn't mean she intended to share his furs for the rest of their lives.

Tor stalked away from her, leaving her to stand there blinking in confusion. He shook his head as his sabertooth growled at him to go back to his mate and satisfy the need that he could smell pulsing through her.

His sabertooth began forcing the shift, and he felt his canines elongate. Groaning, he forced the beast back where it belonged. His beast was getting harder to control the more he denied it their mate. They'd had a taste of Ezi the other night, but he couldn't seem to win her heart, and her body wasn't enough for him.

Wishing he could look back her, Tor ground his teeth together. He couldn't do that. He couldn't give her the satisfaction of getting to him. Her rejection hurt him more than he could put into words. She was from a mateless shifter species, and she would never understand the pain he was experiencing.

"Did I spot Ezi in your arms?"

Tor spun to find Rir beside him. A smile cracked across his face, shattering the frown that'd been adorning his face and brightening his foul mood. "Rir. It is so good to see you again." He hadn't seen Rir since he left the clan.

"We all thought you were dead." Rir wrapped an arm around Tor's shoulders and brought him in for a brief hug. "I would've come back to the village to see you, but someone had to scout the movement of the mammoths."

"I understand." He clapped Rir on the back with an open hand and brought him in for another hug. Daerk and Rir were like brothers. Ever since they were children, they'd been close, and he could trust them to always have his back.

"You and Ezi?" Rir asked again as he pulled back. "She's accepted you?"

Tor shook his head sadly as he played with his beard with one hand. "She still won't accept me."

"Sorry." A pained expression crumpled Rir's face. "I have no idea how this rejection must hurt, but don't give up on her. Her eyes still haven't left you since you walked away."

"I'm doing my best with her. I can smell her desire, but she resists me." Tor didn't plan on giving up on Ezi, but it was still hard on him. All he wanted was to shower her in happiness and give her everything she wanted… and right now, she wanted him to leave her alone. Unfortunately, he wasn't sure he could give that to her.

"Sometimes I wish I had my mate, and then I look at you and Daerk and rejoice that I don't have one." Rir shook his head of brunette hair that had streaks of gold. "Daerk and Aiyre haven't been able to have a child yet, even with the help of Eron and the gods, and you…" he waved a hand in Tor's direction, "found a mate too traumatized by pain to accept you."

Tor cringed. He and Daerk hadn't been blessed by the gods yet, but there was still hope. "One day, we will both get past our troubles, and you will be jealous of what we have." He promised.

Rir chuckled. "I hope you are right. I would gladly be the jealous friend as long as you and Daerk can find your happiness."

Tor glanced back at the camp and finally spotted Ezi among the other women. When he'd walked into the hunting camp earlier, he'd wanted to surprise her. His sense of smell had told him to walk around the women, and he would find his mate among the berry bushes on the other side. He'd been right.

Unfortunately, it hadn't been the warm welcome he'd prayed for.

A smile curved his lips as his eyes fell to her lips. Even from this distance, he could see the berry stains around her mouth. She liked the sweet taste of those blue berries that grew nearby. He would have to make a note of that.

"Good luck." Rir slapped him on the back, forcing him to throw out a foot on his good leg to catch himself.

"I don't need luck. I need the gods to help me. To direct me." Tor growled in frustration as he watched Ezi speaking with some of the women.

"The gods will give you what you need when you need it. That is what Eron has taught us since we were children."

"Rir! Tor!"

They both turned to find Daerk heading straight for them, his strides filled with the purpose of a leader.

"Aren't we glad to have Tor returned to us with only a limp?" Daerk asked.

Rir's gaze turned to Tor's injured leg. "I did notice something strange about the way you walked." Then he glanced up at Tor's face. "I heard rumor from some men that you were injured while hunting on your own."

"Tor was stupid and hunted a wholly rhinoceros on his own." Daerk's eyes fell on Tor, and Tor got the feeling his leader was trying to figure out if he would be a problem during the hunt.

But Tor had learned his lesson. There would be no more solo hunting when it came to big or dangerous prey.

Rir shook his head as one corner of his mouth turned down in a frown. "What were you thinking? Rhinoceroses are ill-tempered beasts and thick hides."

"He wasn't thinking," Daerk replied before Tor could even open his mouth to defend himself.

"I thought I could take it on my own." Tor folded his arms in front of his chest as he got defensive.

"When has any hunter taken a wholly rhinoceros down on his or her own?" Rir scoffed. "You're lucky the gods didn't bring you to the Eternal Hunting Grounds."

"The gods wouldn't want someone so stupid in their land of perfection."

Both men bellowed in laughter, and Tor frowned at both of them.

"I'm not sure why I came back," Tor grumbled.

Rir wiped a tear away from one corner of his eye and flicked the droplet. "We are happy you're alive and well. We are only teasing you." Rir pointed to Tor's leg and changed the course of their discussion. "Think you can hunt with that limp the rhinoceros gave you?"

This time it was Tor's chance to chuckle at them as if it was the silliest question he'd ever been asked. "I may suffer from a limp, but I can still hunt. Hunt better than you."

Rir looked over to Daerk.

"Don't look at him," Tor growled as his eyes darted between the two men standing before him. "I can hunt. I know I can."

"He'll hunt with us," Daerk confirmed with a firm nod of his head. "But," he held up a finger, "if you hinder the hunt, you will be asked to step aside. There will be no arguing with me."

Tor nodded his head. "I understand."

As much as he might want, and need, to join the hunt, he wasn't about to let his limp ruin it. If it got in the way, he would step back and do something else, but he really hoped it wouldn't ruin his ability to hunt. Hunting was something he enjoyed. A way to free the mind from all other worries.

The stars glistened up in the dark sky as Tor made his way back to the camp the women had kindly set up earlier in the day. He'd been out stretching his leg, preparing himself for the hunt. The moment the mammoths came to their hunting grounds, he wanted to be ready.

After so much time on his own, he enjoyed the peace and quiet that came with the night, and the walk had helped to bolster his mood. The only sounds to keep him company had been the animals and the bugs, and they'd never bothered him. Very few things would want to bother a sabertooth shifter.

Tor strode towards the flickering campfire, where most of the hunters and women were gathered. He may have grown used to living on his own, but he still enjoyed being near his clan. He could now sleep with both eyes closed, with no worry about stumbling upon an enemy stronger than himself.

As he approached, he caught snippets of conversations, but there was one voice he wasn't hearing. His eyes searched the group, wanting to see her. It was hard for him not to seek her out. It was instinct for him to check on her.

But there was no sign of Ezi. He turned his gaze to the darkness of the night outside the circle of light the fire provided. He couldn't see her.

A piercing cry floated through the night air, and a smile spread across his face.

At least Flosa was on his side. She was giving her mother away because he saw Ake sitting by the fire, which meant all he had to do was follow the noise of the baby, and he would find Ezi.

First, he needed some food. He strode into the group of clanmates.

"Want some meat?" A man beside the fire asked as he noticed Tor.

Tor nodded. "Give me some extra."

The man standing over the fire nodded as he used a bone knife to cut slices of the meat off whatever animal one of them had caught nearby. Placing it on a large piece of bark, the man handed it over to Tor.

Now he could go in search of his mate, who was most likely trying to hide from him. His one worry was that she might be skipping her dinner to avoid him, and his sabertooth couldn't stand the idea of her being in discomfort as her stomach growled in hunger. If she thought hiding away would prevent him from looking out for her, then she was wrong.

As he left his clan mates around the fire, he passed by a pile of moving furs. A woman's giggles could be heard underneath as she begged whoever was with her to do more. A small smile curled his lips as he imagined Ezi and himself in a similar position.

The one small taste he'd had of her a few nights before was still plaguing his mind. He would give one of his arms to have another chance to see her naked and wanting before him.

Flosa pierced the night with another displeased cry.

Tor shook his head. Like mother like daughter.

It seemed Flosa was taking on her mother's stubborn traits, because as he neared he could hear Ezi pleading with Flosa to shush, but the child insisted on revealing her mother's location to anyone with ears.

"Flosa…" Ezi's voice was exasperated, and she sounded close to the end of her patience.

"I've brought you food," Tor called at as he neared. He was finally able to make out her form in the dark, sitting alone on a pile of furs, slightly removed from the group.

Silence greeted him. It was like she thought she could blend into the night. Then Flosa let out another wail.

"Here," he held out the food he'd brought as he came to stand next to her.

"No, thank you."

"Take it Ezi," he waved the bark under her face, "unless you can say that you have eaten tonight."

His eyes went wide as she let out a growl and snatched the meat-laden piece of bark from his hands. She placed it by her side as she sat, and looked confused how to hold Flosa while eating.

"Let me take her." Tor held out his arms. He would be more than happy to hold Flosa, not only because it'd help Ezi eat, but because he was fond of the child. Flosa looked so similar to her mother, and it played with his heartstrings.

Flosa shrieked some more, and Ezi winced. A line formed in between her eyes as she waited for Flosa to quiet down.

"I don't know." She finally said when Flosa petered out.

"You can trust me." Tor prayed to the gods above that she would relinquish her child to him. It would be a step in the right direction, and give him a much-needed boost of hope. If she could trust him with Flosa, then he hoped it would convince her he could be trusted with her heart.

Her lips pursed in the dark as she studied him.

After what felt like an eternity, she said, "Here." She raised her arms, and he quickly scooped up Flosa, pulling her close to his chest before Ezi changed her mind.

"Now eat." He commanded as he folded his long legs and sat across from her.

When he turned his gaze down to the child in his arms, his sabertooth purred in contentment. The purr vibrated through him, and Flosa's little eyelids began to sink down in tiredness. A smile spread over his face. It may not be a child he'd had with Ezi, but he still felt a pulse of happiness soar into his heart that Flosa was comfortable with him. Even if her mother had a hard time seeing his good side, at least her daughter could see it.

"She's quiet for you," Ezi said in awe over a mouthful of meat.

Tor shook his head. "I'm sure she was already growing tired. Her shrieking could be heard all the way from the fire." He chuckled at the last part.

"I hope I'm not bothering anyone." Ezi glanced back at the camp and all the people who still sat around the leaping flames.

Tor shrugged. "There's nothing you can do about her crying out. Sometimes, she'll have something to fuss over, and none of us will be able to figure it out or fix it. She isn't the first child in this clan."

Ezi chewed on some of the meat in silence, but he could feel her eyes running over him in the dark, and he wondered what she was thinking. What she was thinking about him.

"I would've thought you'd have no interest in Flosa."

He cocked his head to the side. "Why wouldn't I?"

"She isn't yours, and I have heard stories about men turning children away that aren't theirs."

Tor nodded his head, knowing where she was going with this. "You thought I might reject or even ask for you to get rid of her?" It wasn't uncommon for a man to refuse to raise a child that wasn't his own. In a world as cruel and fickle as theirs, it could become a burden, and some men would rather see their own blood survive.

"I feared you might even… kill her."

Tor's head snapped back liked she'd reached out and slapped him. "I would never."

"I can see that now." Ezi raced to say. "When you look at her…" Her voice trailed off.

"She is a part of you, and she makes you happy. I would never do anything to cause you unhappiness." Tor frowned. "I can't hurt you."

"I wasn't sure what to expect from a sabertooth shifter." Ezi glanced away, looking embarrassed that she even thought he could do something so cruel as killing a child.

He wasn't going to take offense though. She and Aiyre had been through so much after his clan had slaughter theirs. It would make complete sense that she didn't trust sabertooths. He just hoped he could win her trust.

Glancing back down at Flosa, he found her sound asleep. Her small lips were parted slightly, and the fingers on her hand would give little twitches in her sleep as she dreamed. Raising a hand, he stuck a finger through her slightly curled fingers, and when she clutched it, his heart nearly shattered in his chest.

This felt perfect.

Tor's sabertooth purred in agreement. They would eagerly take more moments like this. Away from the group, it was peaceful. It also allowed them to be with each other without watchful eyes, wondering if they could make it work. He was tired of everyone worrying about what was going on with him and his mate. Ezi and he would figure it out.

Chapter 16

Ezi couldn't believe Flosa was now asleep in Tor's arms. She could hear the purr coming from his chest from where she sat, and she wondered if that had lulled Flosa to sleep. She'd been worried Flosa wouldn't want to be near him. That she would sense he was something to be feared.

No. There was no need for her to have worried.

If she didn't know better, she would say Tor had won her child over. And that realization should irritate her more than it did.

He stuck a finger into Flosa's hand as she slept, and Ezi's heart pinched as her eyes took in the image the two of them presented. Tor looked huge compared to the tiny bundle in his arms. His well-toned muscles from years of hunting held Flosa gently like he was always meant to be a father.

Then her eyes traveled up to his face and the beard he had growing. It wasn't bushy like other men in the clan, more of a deep stubble. And those lips. Those lips that had showered her in pleasure like she'd never experienced before.

Heat rushed to the area between her legs as her thoughts continued in their passionate direction.

Tor's head shot up when a light wind blew towards him. Even in the dark, she saw his nostrils flare out as he sniffed the air. His blue eyes went darker.

"Ezi."

"Tor." She uttered, not sure where this was about to go but finding herself eager to see.

Lifting Flosa in his arms, he placed her into her basket of furs.

"Ezi." He growled as his inner beast began to show as it scented the need coming off her.

She knew he was asking her a question, so in response, she leaned back on her pile of furs. Inviting him.

With a growl, Tor leaped for her. He landed on top of her, his hands landing on either side of her head as he pressed his weight down over her. "Mate." He growled low before dipping his head into the crook of her neck and shoulder. His breath fanned out over her sensitive skin sending thrills of eagerness rolling through her.

Ezi's mind screamed at her to stop this, but her body had other ideas. It warmed, and a pool of heat gathered between her legs. An ache of need built inside her, an ache she knew only Tor could satiate.

"Gods, you smell wonderful." Then he spread hot kisses up and down her neck until he had her smiling and giggling.

"Tor!" She squealed as he sucked a piece of her flesh into his hot mouth, his tongue swirling around it.

Raising her hands, she pushed against his chest as his kissing continued to tickle her. "Tor!"

He broke away from her neck with a loud pop. When his head came up, there was a large smile plastered over his lips that she could see in the moonlight. "Ezi." He murmured down at her.

The night sky with glistening stars framed

Tor's face above her. And as a cloud moved above them, it shrouded his face in darkness not allowing her to read his eyes or see any expressions on his face. Her heart skittered into her chest, beating a frantic rhythm.

"I can hear your pulse running away." Tor planted a gentle kiss to her lips. "There's no need to fear me."

Ezi wasn't sure she feared anything about him. Her heart was pounding because of the desire coursing through her body. Even his inner sabertooth seemed a little less scary when she was this aroused.

Leaning back on his knees, Tor placed his hands at her waist and slowly undid the leather strings on her animal skin pants. Swallowing harshly, she glanced down to see his strong fingers working quickly and efficiently on the strings.

A blush of desire spread across her skin as her body readied itself for whatever he planned. She'd only ever been intimate with one other man, but it'd been fleeting and tarnished with copious amounts of bloodshed. She barely remembered what her night with Drakk had been like. All she could remember was what Tor had done to her last time.

"Slow?"

Tor's hands paused as he began to tug down her leather pants. "You can always stop this." He reassured her. "I told you I would never hurt you."

She nodded her head.

His hands resumed pulling her leather pants off until they were down around her ankles and she was able to kick them off with a flick of her ankles. Then his hands trailed up over her thighs until he reached the hem of her leather shirt.

"Sit up." He commanded.

Ezi placed her hands behind her back and pushed herself up, and he whipped the garment up and over her head once she raised her arms above her head. With a flick of his wrist, he sent the shirt flying through the air. It landed with a soft thump in the grass.

Tor's blue eyes were barely visible in the minimal light, but she felt them rake over her now naked body. His eyes stopped on her breasts, and the animal instinct inside her caused her back to arch, inviting him in.

Reaching out his hands, he took a hold of the firm orbs of flesh, kneading them in his palms. His hands warmed her flesh, and her mouth popped open as her breathing increased, and her heart thundered in her ears. He pulled lightly on her nipples, and she felt the area between her thighs moisten with her desire.

She had no idea what she was doing. She wished they had just smoked something from a pipe because then she could blame it on the smoke. This was all her and what she wanted.

Whimpering, Ezi's hips arched on their own, inviting him to do more.

"You are eager." He sounded surprised but pleased by this bit of information.

Ezi wasn't sure what to say to his statement. She wanted to protest by saying she wasn't eager, but another side feared he would put an end to this. And she didn't want it to end. It was hard to admit but true.

Not wanting to wait any longer, her shaky hands grabbed at the leather strings on his pants. Her nervous fingers fumbled with the knot. She sucked in a calming breath, but her fingers still wouldn't work properly.

"Let me." Tor purred. His hands wrapped around hers, pulling them away before untying the knot at his waist. With one long shove, he had his pants down around his knees.

"Your shirt." Her voice sounded breathless even to her own ears. She remembered the feel of his bare chest under her fingertips, and she wanted to run her hands over the muscle once again.

With a yank, he had the shirt pulled up and over his head and flying through the night air.

Immediately, her hands landed on his abs. Her fingertips ran up over the hard ridges and then landed on the planes of his solid chest. Her fingertips rolled in the fine hairs on his chest.

"I've never felt the urge to touch a man like this before." Not even Drakk. There hadn't been the same draw between herself and Drakk that she and Tor had. Drakk had been the first man to ask for her hand, and he was well known as one of the best hunters in her clan. It hadn't been a joining based on love, but she'd hoped for love to come in time.

Tor groaned above her at her words, pulling her out of her thoughts. "You tempt me woman."

Ezi shifted her hips under him, and he let out a hiss as one of her soft thighs brushed his rigid cock. Her gaze widened as she glanced down between his legs where his cock stood proudly among the black hairs covering his groin.

The area between her legs tingled in anticipation of the pleasure his straining cock could bring her. She loved how the broad head stretched her wide and hit every pleasurable spot inside her. It confused how a sabertooth shifter could bring her this much satisfaction.

A sliver of doubt entered her mind as she stared up at this predator poised above her. Maybe this was a mistake. Reality started to rush back to her, suppressing her rushing desire.

Tor slid down her legs until he was at her feet, and then his hands dove between her thighs. He applied a little pressure and tried to knock her legs open, but she resisted.

"I don't know," Ezi whispered up at him.

"About me?" His head lifted, and his eyes met hers.

She shrugged in the darkness, hoping he would see it.

"What can I say to relieve your fears?" His hands were frozen in place on her thighs.

Ezi swallowed. What was she doing? The rest of the hunters and women were far away, enjoying a meal around the fire. There were no eyes to watch her. To judge her. If she wanted to experience another night with Tor, this was her chance.

Tor knocked her thighs apart with ease as she made her choice and the cool air of the night caressed her inner lips.

"Gorgeous." Tor breathed as his blue eyes glittered in the moonlight.

Her pronghorn side was pleased with his comment. This strong male who could have most any female at his beck and call thought she was gorgeous. She wasn't sure how much of him appreciating her was due to her being his mate or due to the fact that he just liked her, but she wasn't completely sure she cared.

In a split second, Tor pounced, diving between her legs. "You smell so good." He purred before his tongue shot out and licked her. His eyes were centered on her hot, slick flesh.

"Tor!" She gasped. Drakk had never done this, and she wasn't sure what to make of it. Tor seemed to enjoy this wicked position as this was his second time doing it with her. Before she could decide whether or not to shove him away in scandalized horror like she should have the other night, his tongue shot out and licked her. Hot. Wet. And then his mouth closed around the nub between her plump lips, and he sucked it into his mouth.

Her hips bucked, and all thought left her mind. Raising her hands, she dug them into Tor's thick head of hair and clung on as he continued to suckle on her nub like his life depended on it.

Biting her tongue, Ezi held back moans that threatened to come up her throat. She didn't want to alert the people sitting by the fire to her moment of blissful surrender to the man between her thighs.

The pressure built as his tongue worked back and forth on her nub. Small, sucking noises came from his mouth as he worked her up into a lather. She quivered with the desire pumping through her, and her hands pulled his face more deeply between her thighs as her eyes sunk closed.

"Toooor." She moaned, forgetting about the people who might overhear if she was too loud.

"Tell me what you want." He murmured against her wet flesh.

"More. I want more." She begged. She wasn't sure what she wanted, just that she wanted to know where this pleasure could go. "I ache." It was the best she could come up with.

Ezi felt him smile against her.

Before she could blink, he pulled back until he was leaning on his ankles. His hands shot out and wrapped around her waist, flipping her onto her hands and knees.

"Tor?" Her voice quivered.

"You wanted more?"

"Yes."

Again, he knocked her thighs apart, leaving her open to him.

Tor wanted to stare into his mate's eyes as she came, but the night was already so dark that his sabertooth begged him to take her from behind. He was reluctant to deny the beast, knowing it had remained more patient than he would've ever expected. It was time to reward his sabertooth side with what it desired.

Her delicate floral scent wafted up to his nostrils, and they widened as he took a moment to let it wash over his senses and fill his lungs. He suppressed his worries. For all he knew, this would be one of the only nights he got with his mate. He wasn't entirely sure why she'd agreed to join with him these last two times, but he wasn't going to waste them.

Tor reached out and cupped one orb of her ass, enjoying the feel of her flesh in his hand. She was well trimmed, but there was still a bit of cushion on her that he enjoyed fondling.

From behind, he swiped a finger over her exposed sex. She was wet and ready, but he wasn't quite ready to sink into her. His exploring finger slid between her plump folds as he sought her nub. When he found it, he circled the tip of his finger around it.

Ezi threw her hips back in eagerness as her body searched for something only he would be able to provide her. With one last flick through her wetness, he pulled his hand back and gripped her waist with one hand.

Seizing his rock-hard cock in one hand, he guided it over to her slick sex. He felt her body tense as the large head contacted her wet entrance.

"Relax, Ezi." His voice went soft as he tried to calm his mate.

Reaching a hand under her abdomen, he played with her nub until she melted once more, and then he guided the tip of his cock to her warm entrance. Slowly, he pressed into her, her warm sheath providing a delicious resistance.

His hands gripped her waist, and he felt the fingernails on his fingers slowly shift into claws. His sabertooth wanted to be a part of this joining. Easing into her, he leaned over her back until his chest was pressed against her and he could reach around her body. He grabbed a hold of each breast, playing with her nipples.

"You are so tight." He groaned as his cock slid all the way into her welcoming body.

Ezi panted underneath him. "I want more."

Tor chuckled. "I plan on giving you much more." He promised with a kiss to her exposed neck.

Releasing her breasts, he placed a hand on the base of her neck and pushed her towards the ground, so her ass was higher in the air. Now he had better access, and he slid to the hilt, his balls smacking against her soft flesh.

"Gods help me." He groaned as her wetness surrounded him. "You're so tight and perfect." He worried he would spill his seed into her before bringing her to completion. There was already a tightness in his balls as his body readied itself.

Using his hands on her hips, he slowly pumped in and out of her, drawing moan after moan out of her mouth. One of his hands couldn't stop wandering over her soft skin. He slid a hand down the curve of her ass and reveled in the feel of it as his cock pumped into her.

Ezi bucked back against him. After a brief moment of shock at her body's demand, he increased the rhythm with a smile.

"Yes. Faster." Ezi bucked against him again, pounding herself on his member.

Tor felt her walls pulse around his cock as she grew slicker, and he began sliding in and out of her with ease. Her back arched, sticking her ass even higher into the air as she panted under him. Her hips were now moving on her own, so he let one hand find her nub and rubbed it vigorously with one finger.

"Ezi." He loved the sound of her name on his tongue.

Her moans grew into small whimpers, and he knew she was close. Satisfaction had his sabertooth purring in delight as he pleasured his mate.

Ezi couldn't get enough of these sensations that Tor sent racing threw her. She felt like her body was going to shatter into a million pieces. Pleasure rocked through her, as Tor's cock rubbed every delicious spot inside her. Her body responded eagerly by clamping down around his member in response to his demands.

Tor pumped into her, his fingers digging into one side of her ass. His other hand worked on her nub. Closing her eyes, she let the stars explode behind her eyelids.

With one last pump, Ezi plummeted over the edge as her body shuddered around him. Tor groaned above her, pumping wildly until she felt his hot cum spurt inside her. Her body responded by pulsing around his length some more.

A roar left his throat, and her animalistic side basked in the sound of pure pleasure. His finger came off her nub, but he continued to pump into her until her body relaxed against his and her front slumped against the fur.

Tor leaned over her back, and she felt him place hot kisses to her back as he pulled away, trailing the kisses down her spine.

Once his cock left her, she felt a moment of sadness as emptiness swam over her. She wanted his member back inside her, but she rolled over onto her back and gazed up at him.

"May I?" Tor motioned to the empty side of the furs next to her.

"Yes." Ezi rolled onto her side, leaving plenty of room for him.

Tor slid down beside her, bracing himself on his elbow as he laid down next to her. He reached out a hand and twirled a finger in her brunette hair. "Thank you."

She glanced down, unsure of herself now that the pleasure had washed away. "You should leave for your own furs."

"I'd rather stay here by your side."

Ezi's eyes shifted to the fire that glowed in the distance. The flames danced high into the sky, and she could hear the soft chatter of voices. The silhouettes of the clan could be seen sitting and standing around the fire, but no one appeared to have noticed their joining. Then again, with how many couples were out here, no one would know it had been them coupling.

"You will leave before first light." Ezi managed her most stern voice as she pointed a finger behind her. In the dark, no one would know who was in or not in her furs, but the moment the sun woke and shone down on them, people might see… and she'd rather keep this to themselves. Especially when she wasn't entirely sure what she was doing.

In the light of the stars, she saw him raise his hand to his chest. "I will be gone before the first person wakes in the morning, but let us enjoy this after bliss."

That satisfied her. Flipping over, she presented him with her back before reaching down and grabbing a hold of a fur and bringing it up her body. Ezi was tucked away snuggly in her basket within reaching distance.

Tor's hands wrapped around her waist drew her across the pile of furs and tightly into his chest. Then he slipped an arm under her head. "I'll give you distance," he whispered into her ear, his breath tickling the fine hairs on her neck, "but in the dark, you will be mine. In my arms."

Ezi's breath caught in her chest. She could hear the promise in his voice. "Fine." She murmured under her breath. She could do that as long as no one knew how she'd succumbed to his good looks and tender caresses.

Chapter 17

"Should we go back to my hut and continue this in my furs?" Drakk's deep voice whispered past her ear.

Turning around, Ezi smiled up at Drakk. They were currently in the clan caves as they joined under the watchful eyes of the gods. "I would love to go back to your hut." Ezi couldn't help the small flutter of her heart. She was joined with Drakk for the rest of their lives, and she had hopes for a family and perhaps some love.

As her eyes watched him as he stood, she realized that there wasn't love between them. They had joined because it was a good match that the gods had blessed. If there was love, wouldn't he be softly caressing her hair after their lovemaking?

"Are you coming?" Drakk turned and glanced over at her in the dim flickering light of the coals.

Ezi bounced to her feet, grabbed her clothes, slipped them on, and then followed after Drakk as he left the caves. Cold wind hit her smack in the face as they broke free of the cave system. Snow-covered the world in which they lived. The white crystals flickered under the moonlight, and everything seemed absolutely peaceful.

"Come." Drakk reached out and grasped her hand as he pulled her forward.

She followed after him, using his larger footsteps to help her get through the thick layer of snow. Their footsteps crunching over the snow were some of the only sounds in the dark night. Every once in a while, a branch overhead would creak under the weight of the recent snowfall.

When she glanced up, she saw the village coming

into sight. The village fire had died down, and there were only a couple of clanmates still out. The rest had gone inside their huts to get some sleep, make love to their partners, or just escape the cold night.

Her breath fanned out in front of her in small white puffs, as she kept up with Drakk's longer strides. He guided them past the village fire and over to his hut.

Her breath hitched in her chest as he held open the hut flap, and waved her inside. Her steps faltered as she stared at the entrance with a bit of terror. This would now be her life. Tied to Drakk until one of them died.

"Ezi." Drakk's voice dripped with exasperation. "Let's get inside before we freeze."

Ezi kicked herself. She was only scared because this was her first time with a man, but soon, this night would feel normal. She just needed to be patient and get herself inside his hut.

Walking forward, she sent him a thankful smile and reveled in the warmth inside the hut. A fire was built up in the middle of the hut, and she knew one of her family members, or Drakk's, had made sure it didn't die down while they were gone.

"Now," Drakk's hands wrapped around her waist as his head descended towards her ear, "should we continue where we left off in the caves?"

Her heart skipped into her throat as she nodded her head. "Yes."

He flipped her around in his arms, crushing her chest against his as one of his hands tilted her head back, and his lips molded over hers. Her eyes sank closed, and then… a piercing scream entered the night air.

Ezi pulled back with a gasp.

When she looked up, she found Drakk's eyes looking towards the entrance of his hut. The scream was joined by another and then another.

"Drakk?" Her voice trembled as the air around them seemed to fill with screams.

"Stay here." Drakk untangled himself from her, grabbed a spear sitting nearby, and strode towards the hut entrance.

"Drakk?" Her hand whipped out and caught one of his arms before he could leave the hut. "What is going on?" Her voice raised at the end of her question.

"Stay here!" He shook her off and then he was gone... right out the entrance of the hut.

Fear caused her heart to pound away in her chest as she stood there, listening to the horrible sounds outside. There were screams, growls, and gurgling sound that she didn't even want to process.

Then flight took hold of her, and she dashed to the entrance of the hut, shoving the flap aside, she gazed out in horror.

Sabertooths were tearing through the village. One sabertooth sprinted past where she stood, jumped high into the air, and then landed on the back of a clanmate. The beast sank its large canines into the man's neck, there was a cracking sound, and then the man went silent beneath the sabertooth.

Ripping her gaze off the sight in front of her, Ezi spun in place to see several more sabertooths tearing through the village. Her people were armed and trying to defeat the sabertooths, but the predators had caught them all by surprise, and she knew these were sabertooth shifters... probably from the clan nearby that'd been causing them problems.

Flight took hold of her once more, and she sprinted across the snow-covered ground within the village. She had to get out of here before the sabertooths came after *her. Her breathed puffed out in front of her, and her lungs burned as she sucked in the freezing air. She had to get out of here!*

The moment she broke free of the village, she felt a little anxiety leave her. Now she just had to find a hunting cave, a place where their hunters would stay while hunting away from the village or go if bad weather rolled into the area and they couldn't make it back to the village.

The further she got from the village, the higher the snow got until she felt like she was swimming through the thick fluff.

A growl ripped through the air behind her, and her heart skittered around in her chest as she tried to run faster… but it was too late. Teeth sank into her leg, and she screamed.

Gentle caresses over her head and through her hair, woke her from her restless slumber.

"Shh, Ezi. You were only having a nightmare, nothing more. I am here, and I will keep you safe." Tor's deep voice rolled over her, and her heart rate slowed as her pronghorn calmed.

Keeping her eyes closed, Ezi let the joy of the caresses course through her body. It was hard for her mind to think that a sabertooth shifter could be so gentle… so kind after such a terrifying nightmare. It seemed like it should be impossible, yet he was calming her and soothing her pronghorn side.

"Good morning, mate." Tor's lips pressed against one side of her cheek in a gentle kiss.

"Morning?" Her eyes popped wide to find

the area still cast in darkness. She calmed as she realized it was early morning before anyone else would be up.

"The sun will come up soon." Ezi shifted in his arms while he spoke so she could look up at him. "I will return to my furs." One of his fingers ran over the side of her face. Then he leaned down and placed a small peck of a kiss to the tip of her nose.

Ezi raised her hands and pushed him away. "Last night was my mistake. Please leave." Both nights that they'd been together had been her mistake. She lost her mind when he was around.

Shock and hurt flashed through his blue eyes as his head whipped back like she'd smacked him. A frown marred his face, but he rose up to his feet... and her face blushed.

He was butt naked.

And his cock was hard and stood proudly from between his legs.

Ezi couldn't stop herself from staring openly. His cock was something that had brought her more pleasure than she could have dreamed of last night. The head of his cock was broad, and in the rising light, she spotted a glistening drop at the tip. She followed the shaft down to where it met with his balls. They were tight with their excitement.

"Deny me, mate. It won't matter." He raised a hand and pointed a long finger at her. "I can see the desire pulsing through your eyes when you look at me." Tor strode away, his shoulders straight and his head held high.

With a grump, she flipped over on her furs and grumbled to herself. That man was infuriating, and it didn't help that every word he spoke was the truth.

Last night had been a success with Ezi. His sabertooth purred in agreement. A roaring success. Slowly Tor planned to slip past her defenses until he won her over and she couldn't get enough of him. He knew he only reminded her of what she'd lost. Before him, she'd had a mate, and it couldn't be easy on her, but if she gave him a chance he could give her something to be happy about. He could promise that.

Tor stretched as he watched his clan mates wake to the morning sun. After leaving Ezi's bed, he'd found his clothes, and patrolled the immediate area. The scent of a sabertooth shifter would keep most animals away from their camp.

Rir stood, spotted him and waved a hand as he strode over, his long legs eating up the ground between them. "Already awake?"

"Felt the need to walk around the area to help keep animals away from our camp." Tor nodded his head to the forest. "Soon, most the men will be going to the hunt, and I want to make sure Ezi and Flosa are safe from any wandering predators."

"Any sign of the mammoths while you were out?"

Tor shrugged. "I didn't go out that far."

"Last I heard, it would be a few more days before the mammoths show." Rir rubbed his hands together. "It's been so long since we've hunted mammoths, and I'm excited for the challenge."

Rir wasn't the only one. Tor felt anticipation surging through his system as well. His sabertooth itched to go hunting, but he wasn't sure which form he would hunt the mammoths in… assuming he did join the hunt.

"I'm not sure I should join the hunt." He unconsciously rubbed his injured leg with a hand.

Rir's eyes widened as if he thought he hadn't heard Tor correctly.

"I worry about my limp." Tor motioned to his injured leg, which was healed, but not without leaving him with a permanent limp. Eron had done his best to heal it properly, but there was only so much he'd been able to do after the wholly rhinoceros had shredded it with its horn.

"I've barely noticed it," Rir confessed. "An injury like yours can be terrifying, but I think you're making it into a bigger deal than it needs to be… and if this has to do with me teasing you earlier, then I want you to know it was just that. Just a tease. Nothing more."

"It wasn't anything you've said. I'd hate to lose us a mammoth."

Rir scoffed as he shook his head. "You're one of the best hunters our clan has seen. No limp will take that away. You just have to keep your mind," Rir pointed to Tor's head, "focused on what you can do."

Tor heaved a sigh. His friend was right. Years of hunting had honed his senses. He just had to remember that.

"Good to see both of you catching up." Daerk strode up beside them. Aiyre was attached to his arm, and every time she glanced up at her mate, her brown eyes would fill with light and love.

Longing entered Tor's heart. He wanted Ezi to look at him like that. With love in her eyes. Trust.

"Tor wasn't sure he should join in the hunt." Rir pointed at Tor with his hand and rolled his eyes like Tor had lost his mind.

Daerk's eyes narrowed on Tor. "You're our best hunter. Don't let your limp take that from you."

"Rir already convinced me that I was being foolish."

"Good." Daerk gave a solid nod of his head. "Now which of you wants to join some of the women while they go looking for plants."

"Not me!" Rir rushed to speak. up "I have to go out with some of the hunters to see where the mammoths are."

"Ezi will be among the women," Aiyre said.

Tor's eyes snapped over to Aiyre, who was smiling slyly at him. "I think I will join the women then." He wondered how much Aiyre knew about him and Ezi. Did she only suspect them of sharing furs, or had Ezi spoken about him to Aiyre? The idea that she was telling her clanmate about them caused him to smile.

"You'll find them gathering over there." Daerk turned and pointed over to a bunch of trees where several women stood, including Ezi.

"I will speak with the two of you later then." Tor walked away without so much as a glance behind him. His eyes could only focus on Ezi. The sight of her pulled him in, and a smile curved one side of his mouth. He would never be able to forget what they'd shared the night before. It had been more passionate than their first night together, and it still had his sabertooth purring in satisfaction.

"Tor!" One of the women smiled at him warmly. "Will you be guarding us against the scary predators?" She batted her lashes at him while giggling. Giggling because she was a sabertooth shifter and there were few predators who would dare to challenge her, so this was all a silly show for her.

Tor's eyes slid over to where Ezi was standing, feeding her child. She looked like she was giving her full attention to her child, but he could see the slight flush on her face. She was bothered with the other woman's attention being so focused on Tor.

"There will be a couple of other men." He replied easily as his eyes never left Ezi.

Right as he said that, a few hunters walked over to join them. The woman turned her attention to one of the men, batting her long eyelashes at him, and Tor chuckled as he rolled his eyes. The woman was either trying to find an unmated man to have some fun with or trying to see if any of the men could be her mate.

Tor was already taken though, and no woman would be able to distract him from Ezi. His eyes slid back over to her. "Will you be joining us?" He asked as he prowled closer.

Her head snapped up, and she nodded. "Eron asked me to find a few plants for him to replenish his supplies, so yes."

"Will you bring Flosa?" Tor waved a couple

of fingers at the baby in her arms, and he could have sworn amusement filled Flosa's little eyes. The baby was firmly pressed against her mother's teat, her cheeks working hard as she fed eagerly.

"No."

"We are leaving. Are you two coming or not?"

Tor glanced over at the group to see Ila facing them, her hands on her hips.

"Are you ready?" He glanced back at Ezi to see her shake her head. Turning back to the group not too far away, he said, "We will catch up to you. Go on without us."

The small group left as they chatted and laughed. There was a calm and ease to the clan now that the mammoths had shown up. The gods hadn't abandoned them, not yet at least.

"How much longer do you think we will be?"

Ezi pulled Flosa off the first breast and switched the child in her arms until Flosa was firmly suckling off her other nipple. "Until she is full, and then I'll give her to Ake while I search for the plants, Eron asked me to look for."

"She looks so like you," Tor commented as he watched the pair of them.

"Does she?" Ezi cocked her head to the side as she studied the infant in her arms. "I think she has a lot from her father." Her voice dropped lower, "Every time I look at her, I think of him."

There was sorrow coating her voice, and it twisted his heart. He wasn't sure he could replace what she'd lost, but he hoped to have the chance to repair any damage that'd been caused that night of the attack.

"I didn't know her father, so I can't say for certain, but she does look like you. There's a spark in her eyes that tells me she will be just as strong as her mother."

"Strong?" Ezi shook her head, denying his words.

Tor chuckled. "You have survived a lot more than most. You made it through a sabertooth attack. You lost everyone except Aiyre, and yet you stand here among us rather than sitting inside a hut ignoring the world around you. I call that strong."

"I don't know much about you." Ezi changed the subject of their conversation, raising a hand to her heating cheeks. "Are your mother and father still alive?"

"They are not." He wished his mother was still alive so he could turn to her for guidance. His mate was difficult to win over, and he was sure his mother would have had some sage advice for him.

"How long has it been?"

"Too many cycles to count." He waved a hand in the air.

Ezi nodded. "I'm sorry. It's never easy to lose someone so close."

Tor shrugged. "I miss my parents, but Daerk's mother has been there as a motherly figure. The loss would have been worse if she hadn't been so accepting of me."

They fell into silence, the only noise coming from Flosa as she continued to suckle and fill her belly with milk. Being near the both of them was comforting, and he found some of the stress in his shoulders sloughing off. He was still worried about joining the hunt with his limp, but this would be his chance to test out his leg and see if it really did affect his hunting.

Within a few minutes, Ake approached.

"Are you done with feeding Flosa?" Ake smiled down at the baby.

"Yes." Ezi groaned as she popped Flosa off her breast and handed the baby over to Ake. Rotating her shoulders, Ezi pulled her shirt back into place. "I'm not sure if she is drinking my milk or eating me." Ezi rubbed a breast through her shirt.

"A little of both." Ake teased. "I will be here with Flosa." She reassured the new mother before walking away until she was in the center of the makeshift camp.

"We should catch up to the other women before we lose them." Tor ushered her away.

Ezi raised an eyebrow. "Can a sabertooth shifter ever lose a fresh scent?"

Tor smirked. "Depends how interested we are in the scent."

She rolled her eyes, and without another word, she spun on a heel and followed after the group. Tor followed on her heels, eager to spend more time with her. He could feel her coming around to him. When she looked at him, there was less apprehensiveness and more light. A light skip entered his steps as they worked their way through the forest.

Chapter 18

Ezi bent over and picked a couple of small yellow flowers that waved in the slight wind. She wasn't entirely certain what Eron used them for, but he had described them to her perfectly. There were five little round petals around a darker yellow center.

Using two of her fingers, she clipped the small stem lightly with her fingernails. She gathered the flowers gently in one hand as she walked around, bent at the waist, as she clipped more of the flowers.

Standing up straight, Ezi glanced around to find herself slightly removed from the main group. Her eyes scanned through the trees until she spotted him. Tor. He stood off to one side of the main group, talking to another man, who she had yet to learn the name of, or she just couldn't remember. She'd have to remember to ask the man's name at some point.

Soft voices from behind Ezi caught her attention, and she walked a couple of steps back behind a large tree trunk so she could overhear the conversation without interrupting it. If she learned what the women in the clan talked about, then she could blend in easier when she started conversations with them.

"Have you seen his face when he looks at her?" One woman lamented.

Ezi cocked her head to the side, wondering who was speaking and who they were talking about.

"I know she's been through a lot, and our clan is responsible, but Tor is a good man."

Ah. They were speaking about herself and Tor. A frown turned down the sides of her mouth. She wanted to step out from behind the tree and stop the conversation, but she also wanted to hear what they thought of her.

"How long can Tor last?" A third voice asked, and without looking, Ezi knew the woman was looking around at the rest of the group.

"He's lasted this long without his mate."

"He's also been gone." Another pointed out.

"I feel sorry for him. He must look at her and see everything he is missing in his life. A mate is life. She is the source of happiness for the rest of his life. She will provide him with children."

Ezi glanced through the trees to where Tor still stood talking with the other man. Was he wishing for children of his own? And was she the one causing him to wait?

She licked her lips. Thinking back to the last time Tor held Flosa, Ezi searched her memory for any clues. He had stared down at Flosa with a glint of... something in his eyes. Even when the child wasn't his, he'd been able to cradle her gently and amuse her with his wiggling fingers. It wouldn't surprise her if he made a great father. He was tender, but she could also see him enforcing rules inside the hut.

Raising a hand, Ezi rubbed a couple of fingers over her left breast. It felt like there was something inside her breaking, like a thick ice sheet melting when the heat of the spring came to the land.

"Do you think she will ever accept him?"

"She hasn't yet."

Ezi smothered a snort that threatened to

come out her nose. If they'd seen her and Tor last night, this conversation might never have happened. She hadn't accepted Tor as anything other than a lover last night, but it may have stopped their tongues from wagging like the tail on a horse when flies were bothering it.

Rolling her eyes, Ezi opened her satchel, placed the small flowers inside, and cautiously walked away, making absolutely no sound. The women didn't bother her at all. Nothing they thought mattered to her, and nothing they said would influence her, and she found no need in interrupting their harmless conversation.

If Tor was the right man for her, then she had no doubt the gods would show her. They always had a way of showing what needed to be shown. At least, that was what she'd been told as a child.

"Finding everything you need?" Tor approached her, his arms relaxed by his sides, a small smile playing across his lips as his eyes lazily wandered over her.

"I still need some mushrooms."

The smile on his lips grew wider. "I think I spotted a couple of mushrooms over here." He raised a hand and pointed a finger away from both of the groups.

"Thank you." Ezi smiled shyly and brushed past him. His finger grazed along her shoulder, and even through the thick fabric of animal leather, she could feel the thrill pulse up into the base of her skull. All he had to do was touch her, and it would send her mind reeling.

Quickening her steps, she plowed ahead,

determined to find those mushrooms so she could get back to Flosa and away from Tor. Her feet crunched over fallen leaves and dry twigs that littered the forest floor.

The scent of freshly trampled foliage called to her. It begged her to shift into her pronghorn form and prance through the forest. She could hear that Tor was following her, but he was a good distance behind her.

Stopping, she dropped her satchel, shrugged out of her shirt, and shook her pants off her legs, and then toed her moccasins off her feet.

"Ezi?"

Turning her head so she could glance over her shoulder, she caught sight of Tor, who had stopped dead in his tracks. His eyes wandered all over her naked backside, his eyes gone wide out of shock, until his eyelids dropped, hooding his eyes.

"Ezi." He whispered, and when she glanced lower than his face, she noticed a sizeable bulge in his pants.

"Catch me, sabertooth." Whirling around, Ezi shifted into her pronghorn form, and leaped through the air, landing on four hooved feet, which swiftly carried her through the forest. Wind whipped through the brown and white fur that covered her large frame.

A growl pierced the air around her, and a skitter of excitement flew through her heart. Tor was after her.

Her hooves frantically beat against the ground as she tried to hold her lead. Trees flew past her in a blur of brown and green with a spot of color every time she sped past flowers.

Soon, she could hear his heavy breathing and his large paws landing against the ground with a soft thump. He'd shifted into his sabertooth form and was after her.

For a quick second, Ezi doubted she could do this. He was hunting her down like sabertooths the night of the attack, but this time her mind knew there would only be pleasure at the end of this hunt... no death... no blood. Only pleasure.

Tor landed on her, and they went down, but at the last moment, he shifted his large cat weight and took the brunt of the fall. They skidded across the ground for a second, and then they stopped.

Ezi shifted into her human self and found herself dwarfed by the large animal under her. Her heart skittered in fear before she took control of it. Bracing herself, she glanced down to find Tor looking up at her in silence. His large golden cat eyes were zeroed in on her face.

Her eyes skimmed down his short snout to the large canines that sprouted from his upper jaw, past his lower one, and still went even lower before coming to a sharp point. Reaching out a shaky hand, she gently poked a pad of her finger against the tip. It could tear into her flesh, and the rest of his mouth would easily make short work of her bones like they were the thinnest twigs.

Tor didn't move. All he did was breath, his chest carrying her up and down as she laid across his sabertooth body, and blink at her. He was giving her time. He was always giving her time.

Those women had been right. He was a

good man. He wasn't forcing her to do anything she wasn't comfortable with, and when they did do something, he took his time, allowing her the chance to refuse him.

Ezi wouldn't have ever expected a sabertooth shifter to be this kind.

It was unbelievable.

Yet, it was happening.

Next, Ezi turned her gaze to his massive front paws. There were sizeable claws on each toe and just as sharp as his teeth.

"The last time I was this close to a sabertooth, it was trying to kill me."

Tor shifted under her until he was a man, and his arms wrapped around her as his hands ran up and down her back. The gentle touch of his hands soothed her. She pressed her bare chest against his, her face close to his, and her legs entwined with his hairier ones.

Bending her head down, she planted a kiss against his soft lips. His beard tickled her skin as the prickly hairs pressed against her soft skin. She smiled against his lips as the hair tickled her.

One of his hands worked its way into her hair, pushing her lips more fully against his as his tongue darted out, slipping along the line her lips formed. Slowly, she opened her lips ever so slightly, allowing him entrance. His tongue slipped past her lips and into her mouth, and her tongue darted forward to meet his. Together their tongues danced as each fought to get past the other.

Pulling away with a loud smack, Ezi smiled down at him. Placing her hands against his chest, she heaved herself up. "Tor."

"Yes?" He rolled them over until they were both on their sides facing each other.

Ezi wanted to tell him how she felt. There was an ache inside her to join with him and to be his mate, but she still wasn't able to say it out loud. She wasn't ready.

Instead of answering him, Ezi reached between their hot bodies and grabbed a hold of his hard cock. Sunlight danced over his face as the leaves high above them shifted with the light wind.

A groan left his mouth as his eyelids sank closed.

Using her hand, she pumped up and down his cock, enjoying the feel of it in her hand. The weight of it. With just a few simple moves, she had him groaning like it was the best thing he'd ever enjoyed. She was the one in power right now, and she loved it. Loved the feel of him in her hand.

She ran a thumb over the tip of his cock, spreading the bead of cum around the head. Glancing down between them, she watched his cock pop in and out of her hand.

"I need you," Tor growled before flipping on top of her. He leaned back on his heels, his gaze raking over her naked form in the bright light of the day. "Spread your thighs and show me what I wish to see." A wicked smile curved his lips.

Biting the inside of her cheek, Ezi did as he bid. Spreading her thighs, she held her breath as she waited for his approval. This would be the first time he would see her spread out in front of him without the cover of night.

With a growl of appreciation, Tor ducked down between her thighs. His hot hands spread her thighs even wider, and the cooler air of the day brushed up against her lower region. It felt good. It felt exciting.

His hands skimmed down her thighs until they reach the apex of her thighs. Using only his thumbs, he spread her inner lips wide to his view. Ezi glanced down her belly to see him gazing at her with lust curling through his blue eyes like a wispy cloud.

Then his mouth landed on her. Hot and heavy.

The tip of his tongue slid up between her folds until it reached the nub at the top of her lips. His lips closed around her nub as he sucked the sensitive flesh into his mouth, lightly scraping his teeth against her.

Sensation flowed through her like a hot wanting that she was unable to name. Her mouth popped open, and her eyelids sank down.

"Gods." She panted under him.

A moan ripped up her throat, and her hands clawed desperately at the long grass beside her. A few of the weaker strands came up as she writhed in pleasure on the ground. The soft grass nuzzled her buttocks while Tor sent shivers of delight racing all the way to her toes.

Tor didn't give her any time to think about what they were doing or who could wander across them. He sucked and licked at her like he was desperate for all that he could get. A growl rumbled out of his chest and vibrated against her nub, sending a thrill of delicious sensations rolling through her. His thumbs kept her lips spread and out of the way.

The pressure built and then crashed down on her like the weight of a mammoth. Pleasure ripped through her body as she bucked and twisted below him. His tongue never slowed, sending her over the cliff. Moving his hands to her waist, he held her down as she threatened to buck his mouth off in her enthusiasm.

With a snarl against her flesh, he flipped her over onto her hands and knees.

"Tor!" She gasped in surprise. Glancing over her shoulder, she saw him sitting back on his heels, his eyes scanning over her buttocks.

A grin spread over her face right before she wiggled her butt in his face.

Tor groaned. "You are beautiful." He shook his head like he was at a loss for words. "I wish you could see yourself from my eyes."

Ezi wished she could too. Then maybe she'd understand what he was feeling and maybe it would help her feel safe with him, not that he made her feel fearful.

"I need to be in you." He groaned as he stood up on his knees and wrapped his hands around her waist. He drew her towards him.

Her heart sped up as she uttered, "I want to feel you inside me." The pleasure he brought her was like nothing she'd ever felt before.

Tor's cock rubbed up against her slick lips, the head sliding between them. It didn't enter her but just slid against her wetness, the tip rubbing against her nub. Thrills raced through her.

His hands tightened around her waist as his cock slowly entered her, spreading her wide. She loved the sensation of him filling her. There were no words to describe it. He pressed deeper and deeper, and a low moan escaped her mouth. He didn't stop until his entire shaft was penetrating her, his balls touching her flesh.

"Mate."

Instead of answering him, Ezi rocked back, enticing him.

Tor withdrew his cock to the head and then slammed back into her. His balls bounced against her wet flesh causing the pleasure to spike through her more intensely. With each thrust, Ezi cried out. Her entrance clamped down around him, the last time she'd climaxed still on her mind.

Her breasts jiggled back and forth as he pounded into her. The heavy weight of her breasts only helped to enhance the pleasure. Her fingers dug into the ground, finding purchase, so he didn't push her across the ground with the force of his thrusts. His groin pressed into her buttocks with every thrust and the head of his cock hit every delicious part of her.

It grew so intense that she began crying out in pleasure, her moans turning to groans. Then her body clamped down around his long length, tempting him to spill his seed deep inside her.

He came with a roar. "Take all of me!"

Tor jerked against her bottom, his cock blowing its load into her. Hot and searing.

Both of them slumped as the orgasm rocked through both of their bodies. She could feel his cock twitch inside her with a few last spasms. Bending her head down, she rested it against the cool grass. Tor was still slumped over her back, but he held most of his weight off of her.

Her eyes sank closed as she enjoyed the moment of peace. Then she felt Tor stir behind her. He lifted himself up off of her, his cock sliding free from within her, and then he placed a hot kiss on her shoulder. Slowly, his kisses made their way over to her spine and then down her back.

"You are beautiful." He repeated from earlier.

A small smile crept across Ezi's face at the compliment. It was nice to hear. Ever since having Flosa, there'd been some extra weight on her frame. It didn't bother her. Every woman who experience birth also experienced the added weight, and she knew in no time it would disappear like a lot of things in this world, but it was still clinging to her frame.

Tor rolled over onto his side and drew her down into his arms, turning her, so her head rested on his shoulder. His hand smoothed down her hair.

"I'm glad you can trust me."

Trust him. Did she trust him? She supposed she had to trust him if she felt this comfortable with him and was willing to let him hunt her in his sabertooth form.

"I do trust you." It was a shock to say the words out loud, but there they were. She wasn't sure she wanted to be his mate, but she knew he meant her and Flosa no harm. This man might be able to shift into a terrifying predator, but he was no monster.

Ezi ran her hands through her hair frantically as she tried to hide what she'd been up to with him. Tor watched on from a distance from within the camp. She still didn't want anyone to know they had shared a couple of intimate moments together, while he wanted to shout the news from the top of the highest mountain.

Tor glanced around wondering where exactly the highest point would be. Then he shrugged it off. He'd shout at the top of a mountain once he actually had his mate bonded to him in front of the gods. Until then, he still had a lot to do.

After their romp in the woods, they'd made their way back to the camp, and thankfully no one had seemed to realize they were missing.

"Ready?"

Glancing over his shoulder, he found Daerk nearby.

"For?"

"Meeting with the other hunters and getting our hunting area ready for the mammoths." Daerk raised an eyebrow. "Have you forgotten?"

Tor shook his head, driving thoughts of Ezi from them. If he wasn't careful, his mate was going to be the sole focus of his attention. He had other things to worry about as well, like providing for his clan, which would also provide for his mate.

"Wasn't Rir helping the hunters?"

"They need more men," Daerk explained.

With one last look over his shoulder at Ezi, Tor headed off, following Daerk as his leader led the way.

"How did the foraging in the forest go?" Daerk eyed him from the corner of one eye.

"I think Ezi found everything she needed."

"And more." When Tor raised his eyebrow in question, Daerk reached out and pulled a twig from Tor's hair. "There was more than picking flowers going on in the forest."

Tor reached out and smacked the twig from Daerk's hand. "It wasn't our first time together." Satisfaction flowed through him as he said it out loud. His sabertooth might give her pause, but she liked what he could give her, and he would give her more, like his heart.

Daerk's mouth hung open. "Ezi and you?"

His surprise wasn't unwarranted. Even Tor doubted those moments had happened. He wanted to share the news with every clan member but knew Ezi wouldn't want that.

"Don't tell anyone. Not even Aiyre." Tor shook his head. "I am so close to having my mate, and I don't wish to scare her away."

"I won't tell anyone. Not even the gods." Daerk promised. "But I am glad to hear you might yet win her over. You and her deserve to find happiness."

Tor chuckled. "I think the gods already know. This has to be a part of their plan."

They walked in silence. The makeshift camp long gone as their long strides carried them towards the mammoth hunting grounds. In some ways, Tor hated Brog, the past clan leader, for what he'd done to Ezi's clan, but at the same time, he wondered if they would have been brought together had that night not happened. There was no way for him to know. All he knew was that he now had a mate who he needed to help heal.

The further out they went the taller the grass became until it came all the way up to his thighs. This area was perfect for hunting mammoths. Their hunters would easily be able to hide away in the tall grass, letting them get closer to the ginormous beasts that could topple trees and cause the ground to tremble with each step.

"Eron prayed to the gods that our hunt would go well, and there would be no injuries, but I still worry." Daerk confided in him.

"As a new leader, you take everything onto yourself, but you shouldn't." Tor clapped a hand across his friend's back. "No matter what you do to protect our clanmates, the gods will find a way to affect our fates. Leave it in their hands."

Daerk sighed. "You're right." He brought a couple of fingers up to his forehead and rubbed his temple. "But he's still out there, and there's no telling if he will come back for revenge after what I did to him."

There was no need for Daerk to say his name. Tor knew exactly who his leader was talking about. Brog.

"We all fear his return."

"Brog was never a man to let others get away with insulting him, and what we did was much worse." Daerk glanced over at him. "If he comes back, it will be for me, you, or Rir, or any of our mates."

A growl threatened to spill from his throat as Tor thought about Brog trying to kill or harm Ezi... or Flosa. The banished leader had tried to kill Aiyre in the most cruel manner before the clan had forced him out... by trying to toss her into the village fire... Tor's skin crawled as he recalled that night. It would forever be seared into his mind.

"I will rip his throat out if he lays a single finger on Ezi or Flosa." The words were barely audible as his sabertooth threatened to rise to the surface.

"You won't be the only one. No one in the clan will let him do that without suffering."

They fell into a tense silence as they both thought about the man that still haunted their memories. With Brog as the clan leader, they'd had to tread carefully, and even with him banished he was still terrorizing them.

"We should try to find him after the mammoth hunt."

Daerk glanced over at him. "And kill him."

Tor nodded. "We should have done it instead of banishing him."

He knew Daerk hadn't wanted to start his leadership with a death but now they had a problem. A man who hated them all was roaming around out there, and maybe he would never strike, but Tor wasn't about to bet Flosa's or Ezi's life on it.

"We're here." Daerk drew their attention back to the area around them.

Tor glanced around to find themselves in a small valley and up around them were hills and further down the valley were cliffs. This would be the perfect spot for hunting mammoths.

"We can have hunters hiding in the tall grass on the hills driving the mammoths towards the cliffs where we can easily kill several mammoths with spears and rocks."

"Exactly what we were thinking," Daerk confirmed. "And hopefully there will be no deaths."

Deaths were common when mammoths were involved. Those beasts might look large and lumbering, but they could be fast and easy to anger. They had long ivory tusks that swept out in a magnificent arch, and with one swing of their heads, they could crush a man's ribcage.

"You've joined us!"

They both turned to find Rir headed straight for them with a bunch of warriors following right after him.

"We have." Daerk embraced Rir in a hug.

Then Tor and Rir embraced. With a pat to each of their backs, they separated.

"Do you have a task for us?"

Rir roared with laughter, his head falling back. "Do we have tasks?"

Tor rolled his eyes. "Is that a yes?"

"Follow me, and I will show you what needs to be done."

Chapter 19

"Oh, Flosa," Ezi begged as she jiggled the baby in her arms while walking around the makeshift camp.

Flosa let out a scream that had Ezi wincing as her ears rang with the sound. Couldn't Drakk have left her with a less fussy child? She was about to lose her mind, and it was her child causing the noise! Aiyre had tried a turn, but Flosa wouldn't let anyone soothe her. She was upset about something, and not even a nipple could convince the baby to quiet down.

"Have you tried feeding her?"

The male voice caused tremors of excitement to race through her, and bumps spread out over her skin. Turning on a heel, she found Tor standing behind her, a smile on his lips as he gazed down at the child in her arms.

"I have." Ezi snapped. She was in no mood for him to tell her how to handle her child. It wasn't like he had any of his own… not yet, but they had shared plenty of nights together… for all she knew, she could be carrying yet another child. Dismay roared through her. She could barely handle one child. There was no way she'd keep her sanity with two of these things crying.

"Let me hold her," Tor reached out his hands.

Ezi stood there, staring at him. The sun was setting behind him in a brilliant display of oranges and reds. He and the other men had come back from setting up the mammoth hunt area not too long ago.

"Let me hold her." Tor repeated as he kept his hands outstretched for the child.

"What could you do?" She doubted much, but it might give her ears some much needed rest.

In response, he wiggled his fingers at her.

With a small huff, Ezi gave up and handed him the child who couldn't keep her mouth quiet. It was like Flosa was trying to call out to the gods.

Tor wrapped Flosa up in his arms and bumped her bottom a bit as he made strange noises to her and she… quieted.

Ezi's mouth dropped to the ground as she stared in wide-eyed shock. "She's…"

"Quiet." Tor's blue eyes flashed in triumph.

The quiet was so peaceful, and when she glanced around the camp, she could tell a lot of the clan were thankful for the reprieve from the crying of the child. Then her eyes landed on Tor and Flosa. A baby looked good in his arms like he was meant to have a child in his strong arms.

"Do you want children?" The question escaped her mouth before she could stop herself.

Tor's head jerked up, and his eyes went wide in surprise. "I want to fill my hut with children."

Her heart sputtered around in her chest. And if she were his mate, then he would want to have them with her. An image of Drakk holding Flosa tried to surface, but she shoved it down. Drakk wasn't here for her and Flosa. Only Tor was here now, and he was offering her a hut and safety. She bit the inside of her cheek, and she would be foolish not to consider what he offered seriously.

Tor slowly walked away from her as he bounced the baby in his arms. Flosa's delighted thrills sang through the air as she giggled.

"If Tor has Flosa, then you can help us build some baskets near the fire."

Ezi glanced over to see a woman from the sabertooth clan standing near her. "I can't believe how much she likes him." Ezi shook her head in wonderment.

"We always knew he would make a good father." The woman smiled fondly as her eyes followed Tor, who moved around the camp.

"It's sad to hear that some never find their mates." Like Eron. He was nearing the end of his life, and he still hadn't found himself a mate. Ezi couldn't even imagine how he felt about that. If he'd dreamed of having children, then it would now be dashed, and it was sad.

The woman shook her head as she led Ezi over to the other women. "I know Eron wished for children and a mate, but the gods had other plans for him."

"Can he never take another?"

The woman shrugged. "He could take a woman as his partner, but what if she or he found their mate?"

That was true. It would make a bad situation even worse. If he took a woman, she could find her mate, or Eron could find his, and then that relationship and any children from it would be torn to shreds.

"Eron has come to accept what the gods have in store for him." The other woman said. "He is happy with the life he has, and you shouldn't pity him."

To have that much faith in his gods. Sometimes, like the days following her clan's massacre, she found it hard to trust in them. She still didn't understand why so many had to die and why the gods hadn't given them any warning, not that a warning would have done them much good against a clan of sabertooth shifters.

Ezi picked a seat near Aiyre, and the woman who'd grabbed her plopped a seat on her other side.

"Where's Flosa?" Aiyre glanced around.

"Tor has her."

Aiyre raised both her eyebrows, causing her brow to wrinkle.

"What?" Ezi snapped a bit more harshly than she meant to at the glance she was receiving.

"I figured you wouldn't want him to have her without you nearby."

"You told me to start trusting the people in the clan." Ezi frowned at her friend. "Should I not trust him?"

Aiyre frantically waved her hands in front of her. "No, no! I'm not saying not to trust him. I'm happy to see you trusting Tor and Ake. Just surprised."

Ezi glanced over to where Tor was still walking around the camp. His eyes only focused on the baby in his arms. "I don't understand why Flosa trusts him."

"Why wouldn't she?"

Ezi shrugged. "Shouldn't she sense that he is a predator?"

Aiyre chuckled. "If she can sense he is a predator, then she can sense he won't hurt her."

"I wish she would behave for me." The moment he touched Flosa, she would quiet down and smile up at him, while Ezi had the hardest time getting the child to calm.

"She does. You just forget when she starts screaming." Aiyre laughed.

"Flosa will cry for him." Another woman promised. "If he holds her more, you will hear her cry in his arms."

The rest of the women in the group nodded their heads in agreement.

"She's right." Aiyre laid a hand on Ezi's. "Let Tor hold her more often, and you will hear cries of displeasure ringing through the trees."

A smile cracked across Ezi's lips. "I wonder if he could handle a crying baby."

All the women peeled into laughter as they shook their heads.

"I can see his face now!" Ake bent over herself in laughter. "His eyes will go wide, and he'll look around in bewilderment, and he will either handle it or run around until he finds you."

The women around her kept laughing, and she had to admit the image of Tor running around in a panic was amusing. If Tor, a strong warrior, couldn't handle the cries of a baby and ran around with panic in his eyes, she would laugh a little before stepping in and saving him.

"The first time our child cried in my mate's arms, I could see the terror in his eyes." One woman confessed.

"I remember!" Another giggled.

"My mate was able to handle it." Another

pitched in.

      The rest of the conversation faded into the background as Ezi's eyes followed Tor. She didn't care if Flosa cried in his arms because the other women were right. If he held her more, she would eventually cry, and she wanted him to enjoy this moment with her child.

      Tor's head lifted, and his blue eyes connected with hers as the last few rays of day faded away. A spark of fire lit in those deep blue eyes, and she knew she would once again be sneaking into the forest with him later.

      The area between her legs heated as a blush of anticipation crept up her neck and cheeks.

      His nostrils flared in the waning light as if he could smell her arousal from across the camp. Swallowing harshly, Ezi bit the inside of her cheek as images of him above, below, and around her formed in her mind.

      Tonight would be a good night.

      Tor loved the weight of the spear in his hand. Hunting mammoths was going to be fun, and he felt like a young boy again, like he was going on his first hunt. His limp wouldn't get in his way, and he needed to remember that before he let his fears get the best of him.

      "I saw you and Ezi last night." Daerk walked up beside him, a spear in one of his hands.

      Tor grunted. He wasn't sure he wanted to

get into another Ezi discussion. "She found me. I'm not pushing her into accepting into her furs." It had been another passionate night for them with barely any sleep, but he still felt well-rested and relaxed.

"I'm not worried about her."

He cocked an eyebrow at Daerk. "Me?" He wanted to laugh in hysteria. Daerk was worried about him getting hurt?

Rir strolled up beside them. One spear was in his hands, and there were three strapped to his back.

"Do you have enough spears?" Tor shook his head as he glanced over at Daerk.

Daerk shrugged at Tor.

"You can't kill a mammoth with one spear," Rir stated defensively.

"Weren't we scaring them into a canyon where more hunters will be waiting to kill the mammoths as they panic?" Tor glanced between the two men as he wondered if he'd forgotten the plan.

"We are, but if I lose a spear in their thick hide, I want to make sure I have another."

"He must not be a good spear thrower." Tor chuckled.

Rir dropped the spear in his hand and tackled Tor to the ground. The spear in Tor's hand skidded across the ground.

"Get off!" Tor roared at his friend as he raised a hand to block a blow.

"Is this really the time?" Daerk said with exasperation.

"Take it back," Rir demanded as he rained blows against Tor's arms, but the punches were halfhearted and not meant to land a serious blow.

"It was a joke," Tor said before Rir landed a blow against his jaw and his teeth snapped together. "What's wrong with you?" Now he was pissed, and he threw a hand up knocking Rir against the chin.

They continued to roll around on the ground as each of them tried to get the upper hand, but they were evenly matched, and neither got anywhere.

"Enough!" Daerk hollered at them before grabbing Rir around the scuff of the neck and yanking him off Tor.

Brushing off his clothing, Tor sat up and stared up at Rir in confusion. "You aren't the hot-headed one."

Rir gripped the hem of his shirt and tugged it down, back into place. "Instead of talking, I will prove I'm the better hunter." A cocky smile spread across his lips before he bent over, snatched up his spear, and jogged off to join some other hunters.

Tor stood up and brushed off the bits of dirt and grass that were now adorning his tanned leather clothing. "Is there something wrong with him?"

Daerk watched Rir, who was now speaking with the other men in the hunting group. "I think he's worried about ending up like Eron. Mateless. And it's causing him to lash out."

"Why? He's young." Tor picked up his spear. "Eron might be passed his prime, but Rir has plenty of time to find his mate."

"We both have mates, and now he is left alone with no mate and no future children." Daerk supplied.

Tor and Daerk weaved their way through the tall brittle grass as they caught up to the other men.

"He needs to believe in the gods."

"I know how he feels."

Glancing over at Daerk, Tor caught a flash of despair in his friend's eyes. What did Daerk have to be sad about? He had a mate, and she loved him. Tor was still fighting to win over his mate. He and Ezi may be intimate, but that didn't mean he'd won her. He still hadn't won her heart, and she didn't want anyone to know they'd been together.

"How can you know how he feels?"

Daerk sighed and a couple of seconds passed before he said, "The gods have yet to bless us with any children. I'm wondering if they ever will."

"They will." Although it did disturb Tor a bit to hear of their troubles. He wanted offspring. Lots of offspring. He wanted them all to look like Ezi with cute little noses, and he could care less if they were pronghorns or sabertooths.

"Now isn't the time to think of this. We need to focus on the hunt." A smile spread over Daerk's face. "One problem at a time."

Tor nodded his head in agreement. "Yes." But now there was a trickle of fear coursing through his heart. Either the gods were being cruel to Daerk and Aiyre, or it meant sabertooths and pronghorns couldn't produce anything.

Shaking his head, he shoved his thoughts of Ezi and children away and replaced them with thoughts of mammoths. He would worry about children at a later time.

As they walked up to the rest of the group, Tor hugged each of the other warriors. Then Daerk pulled out a small bag made of an animal's stomach.

Pulling out a plug, he held it up. "May the gods bless our hunt. May no man get injured or die." Then he took a swig and passed it around to the other warriors.

When it came to Tor, he put the opening to his mouth, tilted his head back, and took a swig of the bitter liquid. His eyes and nose scrunched up as he swallowed the nasty tasting liquid. It was one of the herbal concoctions that Eron made for their hunts. It was supposed to bring them closer to the gods so their spears would throw straight and their stamina would be increased.

He wished he could wipe his tongue off with a leaf, but he didn't want to anger the gods. Their emotions could be fickle, and he wanted to remain on their good side.

He passed the stomach back to Daerk who capped it and tied it back to his waist.

"Eron needs to make those drinks better." Jirk's tongue shot out of his mouth as he used his teeth to scrape off the top of his tongue.

Tor raised a hand to his mouth, smothering the snort that threatened to come out as he watched Jirk's tongue shoot in and out of his mouth.

"You men ready to hunt mammoths?"

All the men spun around to find Aiyre leading a group of women who were participating in the hunt. Aiyre's hair was braided back behind her head, and her brown eyes sparkled with fire.

Then his eyes landed on Ezi. She didn't hold a spear like most of the other women, and he was relieved she didn't plan on participating. A mammoth hunt shouldn't be anyone's first hunt.

Stepping away from the men, he wrapped an arm around Ezi's waist and drew her away from the groups.

"Is Flosa with Ake?"

Ezi turned her head up, her big jade eyes swallowing him whole. His heart pitter-pattered around in his chest. His head dipped lower, but before he could plant a kiss on her luscious lips, she danced out of his arms.

"She's with Ake," Ezi confirmed.

Disappointment soared through him that she'd pulled away. Someday he would be able to kiss her in front of others, but it wouldn't be today. He reminded himself to be patient. All it would take was time, and he had all the time in the land.

"Have you been to a mammoth hunt?"

She shook her head, her brunette hair waving behind her. "I've seen them from a distance." She tapped a finger against her chin. "Or maybe it was a wholly rhinoceros."

Tor chuckled as he shook his head. "You would know the difference."

"Then, I have no idea what I saw." She shrugged. "But I will see one today."

"You should see more than one." Their hunt would be a disappointment if they couldn't kill a couple of mammoths.

"Ezi," Aiyre popped up beside them, and Tor jumped a little in his shoes. Aiyre made a great hunter because she was so quiet when she walked. It was like the woman never ran into any small branches or dry patches of grass on the ground. Her feet just dodged them. "If you come with me, I can find you a safe place to watch the hunt."

Ezi glanced up at him. "I will see you after the hunt."

"I will see you after the hunt then." He agreed.

Ezi nodded as she followed after Aiyre. He stood there and watched her walk away… and then she stopped, turned, and her jade eyes bored into him. "Be safe." And then she spun back around and left.

A slow smile crept across his lips as he realized she was worried about him. He would, of course, make sure to be safe, because he had a reason to live.

Sucking in a breath, he prepared himself for the hunt. He might have a limp, but he had to believe in himself. He was a skilled hunter, and no limp was going to ruin his ability to take down a mammoth.

With a small hop in his step, he rejoined the hunters, which were now a mix of men and women.

"Sorry about earlier." Rir bumped a shoulder against Tor's.

"Don't worry about it."

"I don't know what got into me." Rir ran a hand through his hair. "I've felt tense, and then you insulted me, and before I knew it I was on top of you."

Tor shrugged. "Don't worry about it."

"No one is to change into their animal form!" Daerk speared them with his eyes, and both of them snapped their mouths shut. No need to anger their leader. "We will hunt the mammoths from a distance with our spears from the cliff edge. If a mammoth charges, run and do not try to kill it." Then he pinned Tor with his gaze.

"What?"

"You tried to kill a wholly rhinoceros by yourself."

"I wasn't thinking straight." Tor grumped under his breath. Everyone was going to hang that above him for the rest of their lives, and he thought it was unfair. He'd been rejected by his mate and was going crazy.

"No hunting mammoths alone." Daerk pointed a finger at him.

Tor rolled his eyes as Daerk began telling the hunters where they should go. With his limp, he wasn't planning on doing anything risky.

Chapter 20

Ezi plopped down on the boulder. It overlooked the entire hunting area, and she would be able to watch everyone if she could drag her eyes away from Tor. He looked intimidating with the limp in his walk, and the spear clutched tightly in one hand.

Her mouth went dry.

She was worried about him. She feared his limp would endanger his life while hunting these giant beasts.

The ground below her vibrated, and as her eyes went wide, she glanced over her shoulder to see the mammoths coming. Her jaw dropped. Their enormous tusks jutted out from their upper lips sweeping out in giant arches. Their long trunks swept over the ground as they searched the area for something to eat, and she could have sworn their hair was long enough to hide in.

As they neared, the ground trembled under her, and she placed her hands flat against the boulder she sat on lest they bounce her right off the rock. There were so many, and among all the ginormous adults small babies ran about or trailed after their mothers.

Then sadness hit her square in the face, and she glared at the animals. They were the reason her clan had been slaughtered. If they had come earlier in the winter, then her people would still be alive, and she would be with...

Her eyes traveled over to where Tor stood. She wasn't sure she would want Drakk now that she'd gotten to known Tor. He was kind, and yes, he was a sabertooth, but he'd been gentle with both her and Flosa. Her heart hitched in her chest as she watched him.

Tor crouched low in the grass disappearing from view.

As her eyes scanned over the area, she found no hunters. Her head zipped back and forth on her shoulders as she tried to locate anyone, but she came up empty. They must have all crouched low in the tall grass.

The mammoths moved slowly over the land heading straight towards the canyon where half the hunting party would be waiting.

Small rocks around her bounced with the heavy steps of the mammoths, and she watched them tremble around her.

When Ezi glanced back up, she spotted the lead mammoth heading straight into the canyon. The hunters in the tall grass bounced up and ran towards the rear of the herd. The mammoths raised their trunks and trumpeted in alarm. The air filled with the sound, ringing off her eardrums, and she raised her hands, covering her ears.

Then the mammoths stampeded straight towards the canyon.

Despite trying to pick him out, Ezi couldn't spot Tor among the hunters. They all loped after the mammoths, jabbing their spears in the air to keep the mammoths going on track.

One mammoth broke loose from the rest of the group and charged the hunter closest to it. The hunter rolled out of the way, but then the mammoth set its eyes on yet another hunter, and this time she could make out exactly who it was.

"Tor!" She bellowed even though she knew from this distance, he wouldn't be able to hear her.

The mammoth moved faster than she would have ever been able to guess. With such a large frame, she would assume it'd be slow and lumbering. It shook its head, waiving its large white tucks through the air.

Ezi sucked in a breath as she stood up in horror. The tip of its tusk brushed past Tor, dangerously close to clipping him. Tor darted out of the way, and another hunter poked his spear tip into the mammoth's flesh.

The mammoth trumpeted again, but this time there was a high-pitched tone at the end as the tip of the spear met its flesh. The mammoth rounded and went after the hunter who'd poked it. It let out a bellow of challenge and barreled down on the man.

Ezi's breath caught in her chest as both of her hands came up to her mouth.

Tor bolted forward, braced a foot, drew back his arm, and threw his spear. The long wooden shaft soared through the air before landing in the thick mass of hair covering the mammoth's body. It let out a bellow of pain, its trunk rising high into the air, but it stopped charging the other man, allowing him time to get away from the mammoth.

More mammoths bellowed from down in the canyon, and from her position she could see hunters throwing spears down at the mammoths from high up in the cliffs. From the pained sounds coming from the mammoths, she knew some of the spears were hitting their mark.

Ezi's eyes flickered back over to Tor, who was drawing the angered mammoth away. His limp slowed him down, but he managed to keep ahead of the enraged beast. She wanted to leave her boulder and help, but Ezi knew she would only get in the way.

Tor ducked behind some trees, and without a visual threat, the mammoth spun around searching for another target for its anger. When it didn't see anyone else, it lumbered away, back to the rest of the herd, which was now fleeing the canyon in a frantic rush to get away from the hunters.

When everything quieted down, she once more searched for Tor but came up empty.

"Ezi." A deep voice came from behind her.

Spinning around, Ezi clasped her hands together in front of her. "You're safe!" She cried out before flinging herself into his arms.

Tor chuckled, and the vibrations flowed through her as she pressed her chest up close to him. "I was never in danger."

"The mammoth wanted blood." She buried her face in his shoulder and enjoyed the scent of man, leather, and trampled grass.

"You were worried about me?"

Ezi pulled away and straightened her shirt as she glanced up at him from under hooded eyes. "A little." She had no idea why, but she had been worried. "I was afraid your limp would allow the mammoth to catch up to you."

"But it didn't."

"It was brave of you to charge after it to save your clanmate." She blinked. The man in front of her was selfless and courageous. Sucking in a deep breath, she studied him. He was strong and kind, and though he had stormed away for many moons, he was being patient with her now.

Feeling awkward about where her thoughts were headed, Ezi asked, "Should we join the others and see if they got a mammoth?"

"Yes, let's go." Tor reached out and placed a hand against the small of her back as he directed her down from her boulder. He leaped down to the ground and then held his arms up.

"I can climb down."

"Jump, Ezi. You can trust me to catch you." And then he whispered under his breath, "I will always catch you." But it was just loud enough for her to hear.

Ezi's heart hitched in her chest as her pulse raced under her skin. He would always catch her. And she wasn't sure how to take that. Either he was saying he would always be there to catch her before she fell, or he was saying he would always catch her if she ran.

Either way, it excited her and reminded her of the times when she'd changed into her pronghorn form and demanded that he catch her.

"Trust me." He repeated.

"I do." And she leaped from the boulder.

Tor's hands wrapped around her ribcage and brought her down against his chest before letting her feet touch the ground. His head descended, and his lips came down across hers. The kiss was demanding and sent heat coursing through her body. Her toes curled in pleasure as his kiss deepened, and then his tongue slid across the seam of her lips. Popping her mouth open, she welcomed him in. The tip of his tongue danced with hers before scraping across her top teeth and then pulling back into his mouth.

Tor broke away with a chuckle. "We need to meet up with the others before they worry about us, or come looking for us."

"I don't care if they see," Ezi was delirious with desire and could care less if someone in the clan caught them. Leaning up on her toes, she pressed her mouth to his and he purred against her.

Tor's hands clamped down around her waist, and gently he lowered them to the ground, the tall grass protecting them from any wandering eyes. He pulled her into his arms, and one of his hands worked its way into her thick mane of hair. Then he pulled away and began kissing a trail across her cheek down to her neck and then she heard him take a deep intake of breath.

"You smell delicious, mate."

Ezi's blood froze in her veins at his words.

"Now you smell like fear, mate." He pulled back until his blue eyes met hers. "I would never harm you."

"Sorry." She shook her fear away. "I know you wouldn't hurt me."

His eyes searched her face. "You do?"

Ezi nodded her head.

A smile cracked across his lips. "Good. I never want you to fear me." One of his hands came up to caress the side of her face, and she leaned into his palm enjoying the contact.

Her heart swelled in her chest, and when he leaned in to kiss her again, she met him halfway. She murmured against his lips, "Take me, Tor. Take me."

A growl left his lips vibrating through his chest and into her body. It only warmed her blood and sent tingles of excitement straight to her toes. Her hands wandered over him until they reached the leather ties of his pants. With quick fingers, she undid the strings and reached her hand into his pants where she found his cock hard.

A smile spread across her lips as they continued to kiss. Her fingers wrapped around his cock, and she stroked it with long pumps. He groaned against her lips.

"I need you." He moved his hips, withdrawing his cock from her grasp. Placing his hands on her shoulders, he pressed her back against the ground before undoing the leather straps holding her shirt together halfway and then popped her breasts up above the collar. "You're beautiful, Ezi. So beautiful."

A blush crept up her face. She knew she shouldn't compare Drakk and Tor because they were different men, but Drakk had never said anything like this, and he had never made her heart flutter in her chest like Tor did. There was something different about this sabertooth shifter.

Reaching out, he cupped one of her breasts and caressed her creamy orb. One of his fingers circled her nipple, causing her breath to catch in her throat as she waited in anticipation. He captured her nipple between two fingers and pinched it lightly. A twinge of lust pierced her.

Ezi's back arched under him, and he sucked in an audibly harsh breath. His blue eyes flashed with hunger, and she could've sworn she saw his sabertooth in there. Instead of scaring her, it now comforted her. She'd seen it up close and had even touched it without getting her throat ripped out or her hand bitten off.

Tor couldn't believe this was happening, and he hadn't even started it. She'd asked him to take her! She was gorgeous as she arched under him. To him, Ezi was stunning with her jade eyes and long brunette hair, and he loved the width of her hips. She had birthing hips. She was a woman who would fill his hut full of cute chubby-faced children.

"More." She begged, and he was happy to oblige.

Reaching between their aching bodies, he wrapped a hand around his cock and released it from the loose folds of his pants. Then he undid the leather straps of her pants and pulled them down her legs and kicked them away. Settling between her legs, Tor placed one of his hands on either side of her head. Bracing himself, he stared down at her.

"I love everything about you." And with that said he slammed his hips forward, entering her fully in one stroke.

His cock throbbed inside her. His sabertooth wanted nothing more than to fill her with his seed and his children.

"Yes," Ezi panted under him as her hands came up to his shoulders before one of them dug into his thick head of hair.

"You're mine," Tor growled, and the words that came out were guttural.

Her hips bucked against him, and he pumped in and out of her in smooth strokes. "You're so wet." His cock slid easily in her core, and her warmth welcomed him.

The scent of her lust wafted through the air, and he sucked it in greedily. The scent went straight to his mind, and he clutched at her waist as he pounded into her. Her breasts jiggled wildly in front of his face. They danced and teased him.

Bending over her, he sucked one of her full breasts into his mouth and licked her teat. Her back arched as she met each of his thrusts. Her tight inner walls began to pulse around him, drawing him in with eager and equal pressure. He could feel himself nearing the edge.

"Ezi." Tor groaned as his fingers dug into the flesh of her hips. His sabertooth tried to show itself wanting to be a part of this, but he shoved it back. This moment was for him and not his animalistic side.

Then she crashed. Her inner walls clamped down around his cock, milking it for everything he had. His seed flowed out of him and filled her with every strong thrust. His groans mixed with her moans as she arched below him and he continued to thrust against her wet center.

And then they both crashed as pleasure rolled over them both.

Ezi cracked her eyes open as Tor nibbled the outer rim of her ear. Ducking her head to the side, she tried to bush him off, but he wouldn't be deterred that easily and continued his quest at eating her ear.

"We should get back to the group." He purred in her ear.

"I need to rest."

Tor chuckled in her ear. "We can rest later. We have to help with the mammoths."

She sighed. She was comfortable, and she wanted to stay for the rest of the day in his arms. It felt nice and right now, she could even see herself waking up in his arms for the rest of her mornings, but the moment they got back to the others, she knew it would change.

"You're right. We should go back before they look for us."

Ezi sat up and began tying the front of her shirt. When Tor stood next to her to tie the leather straps at the front of his pants, she stared openly at his flaccid member. He was impressive, and her tongue darted out to lick her suddenly dry lips.

"Don't tempt me again."

Startled by the sound of his voice, she turned her gaze upwards to see a smile dancing in his sky-blue eyes. Then her gaze fell back to his waist where his cock was twitching back to life.

Quickly, Ezi glanced away, not wanting to entice him. They really did need to get back to the others before people began to wonder about them. She finished with the ties on her shirt and then stood and tugged her pants back over her legs.

Tor motioned her forward, and she took the lead heading straight towards the canyon.

Ezi wiped the sweat off her brow as she stood and looked at the giant carcass in front of her. The hunters had taken down two mammoths, and now they had to break the animals down so they could be transported back to the village.

"Look at these tusks!" One woman exclaimed as she motioned to the ginormous ivory tusks. "We can create so many statues for the gods with these."

"Eron will be a happy shaman." Another agreed.

Aiyre stood and wiped some sweat off her

brow and ended up smearing a large line of blood across her forehead. "We might need to come back to get all this back to the village."

"Then we should leave some hunters to guard the carcasses." Daerk strode up to them with a bone knife clutched in one of his hands and blood covering his arms all the way up to his elbows.

The women nodded. Then one of them raised their hand. "I will stay to guard the mammoths."

"Now we just need a couple more. These mammoths will attract a lot of predators tonight." Daerk smiled at Aiyre, pulled her into his arms, and planted a deep kiss on her lips before breaking away with a loud smack. Then he walked away, and Aiyre gazed after him with lust-filled eyes.

"I never thought I would love a sabertooth, but I do." Aiyre smiled at all the women around them, and they smiled back.

"You both are perfect for each other." Ezi smiled at her friend glad to see she and Daerk were doing so well. She knew they were both worried about creating offspring and she really hoped the gods would bless them soon. Aiyre and Daerk would make wonderful parents. She had no doubt about that.

Aiyre bent back over the mammoth and carved away at the red meat. Ezi scooted closer to her friend so she could speak without anyone overhearing her.

"Tor and I have been together… in each other's furs."

Aiyre paused mid-swipe. Glancing up, Aiyre's mouth popped open. "When?"

"A few times now, and once today." A blush

crept up her neck and cheeks as she cast her friend a shy smile. It felt good to admit it out loud.

"Ezi!" Aiyre whispered. "Will you accept him?"

"I'm not sure what I am doing," Ezi confessed. It felt good to have this off her chest. She'd been wanting to tell someone how she felt for so long.

"And Tor?"

Ezi shrugged not sure what the question meant.

"Does he know what this," Aiyre waved at her, "means?"

Blinking dumbly, Ezi's mind raced back to all their moments together to figure out how to answer her friend. "I think he knows I'm not sure."

"You think?" Aiyre shook her head. "You can't tease him, Ezi. If you don't want him as a mate, you shouldn't be with him. You'll..." Her friend faded off as she looked over Ezi's shoulder.

"What?"

"Ezi." A deep voice caressed her. It stroked her from the inside out.

Spinning around, Ezi wondered if Tor had heard any of their conversation, but there was no evidence that he had, and a sigh of relief left her. "Tor?"

"I brought you some water." He held out an animal stomach that slowly leaked a couple of drops of water. "I thought you might need some with this heat."

She accepted the gift, unplugged it, and took a few swallows before handing the stomach back to him. "Thank you."

"Let me know if you need anything else."

And then he strode away, a little hop to his step that even she could spot. Providing for her pleased him, and it pulled at her heart with little tugs of delight.

"Don't hurt him," Aiyre whispered. "We aren't sure he could take it without losing his mind."

Ezi's jaw dropped as she turned to stare at Aiyre. She blinked and then blinked again. "Me? Hurt him? He's a sabertooth."

"A kind man." Aiyre corrected her.

"I don't want to hurt him." And she really didn't. He was a kind man who was being patient, but maybe Aiyre was right. Was she even going to consider the mate hood he was offering?

"Please be careful, Ezi." Aiyre's brown eyes begged her.

"I will." Ezi bent over the mammoth and hacked and sliced at the beast under her. She wasn't sure she wanted to talk about this anymore. The conversation hadn't gone in the direction she would have thought.

Once she had a slab of red juicy meat cut, she hefted it into her hands and then dropped it onto a sled they'd created out of leather straps and wood. Then she walked back to her position and began cutting another slab. This was a lot of hard work, but it would fill their meat hut and relieve the massive amounts of stress everyone felt. The mammoths had come, and the gods hadn't abandoned them.

After she'd cut a few more slabs of meat, she pulled back from the mammoth and glanced around. The massive white bones of the mammoth were finally showing, and soon they could work on breaking down the skeleton so they could use the bones for tools and building more huts within the village.

A knocking sound had her head swinging around to the head of the mammoth she was working on to see another clan mate swinging a club against the mammoth's jaw.

"What are you doing?" Ezi approached the woman, curious what she might be up to by swinging a club against the mammoth's face.

"Knocking the teeth loose so we can use them for jewelry and decorations."

Ezi watched as the woman slammed the club down. After a few more swings, the woman put the club down and opened the mammoth's mouth to collect the teeth that'd come loose. The woman stood back up and held out her hand so Ezi could see the teeth. Then the woman threw the teeth into a pack, picked up her club and hammered away at the mouth of the mammoth again. The large teeth would make some impressive jewelry.

Ezi arched her back as she pressed her hands against her spine, and she heard a few satisfying cracks. Then her eyes caught on something moving through the tall grass in the distance.

"What's that?" She raised a hand and pointed at the thing loping through the tall grass.

Everyone stood and looked off into the distance.

Aiyre raised a hand to her forehead, blocking the sun. "It looks like a person."

"Who could it be?" Another woman asked.

"I think I know who it is." A woman off to Ezi's left said. "It looks like Hirt. I would recognize him anywhere." The woman's voice turned silky smooth as her knees buckled visibly at the sight of Hirt. It looked like they might have another mate hood ceremony coming.

"Daerk!" Aiyre called out. "We have a warrior from the clan coming!"

Daerk darted past the women, leaping over the mammoth carcass in a smooth stride, landed on the other side and then weaved his way through the tall grass. A couple of other men came forward, ready to assist their leader at a moment's notice.

"What could it be?"

Ezi had no idea, but it couldn't be good. Maybe Eron had joined the gods in the Eternal Hunting Grounds. It seemed like a mean thought, but he was older, and it wasn't completely out of the question.

"Wasn't Hirt staying with the other women at the camp?"

Ezi's ears perked up at that tid bit of information. "Could it be about Flosa?" Panic sent her heart rate spiking, and she could hear the roar of blood in her ears.

"Ake is with Flosa." Aiyre walked over to her and wrapped an arm around her waist. "Nothing has happened to your child."

Ezi forced herself to suck in deep and even breaths. Aiyre was right. Ake was with her child, and she was just panicking because she was a first-time mother, and there was nothing else for her to worry about.

From this distance, the conversation couldn't be heard, but in no time Daerk loped back through the grass. When he reached the waiting group, his eyes briefly flickered over her before he turned to

Aiyre, put a hand to her lower back, and guided her away from the group.

As their heads bent together, Ezi strained to hear what was being spoken.

"Do we know what's happening?" Tor strode up beside her.

"Daerk only told Aiyre, but he hasn't said a word to us yet." Ezi supplied as she watched Aiyre's eyes widen, and then they flickered over to Ezi. Her heart rate sped up again. What were they talking about? The anticipation was killing her!

"Ezi?" Aiyre spun around and met her gaze.

"Yes?" Her answer was barely audible.

"I…there…we…" Aiyre shook her head and looked up to Daerk for help. "I can't." She muttered.

Daerk placed a comforting hand to Aiyre's shoulder. "Brog and his men attacked our camp."

"What?!" Tor stepped forward, and a growl vibrated through the air.

Ezi stared at all the people around her dumbly. She wanted to ask about Flosa, but she couldn't form the words. She didn't want to hear the answer to her question. Her stomach plummeted to her feet as her throat closed up.

"Flosa?" Tor growled, and when she glanced up at him, she saw his canines extending. This man was going to kill something… he was going to kill someone.

Then she looked back at Daerk, trying not to get her hopes up that he had good news for them all.

"After Brog and his men attacked, they stole Flosa." Daerk said.

Her legs buckled.

"Ezi!" Tor jumped forward, and his arms scooped her up before she could collapse on the ground. "Ezi?" He slapped her face lightly.

"Flosa." Her voice was barely audible as her heart shattered in her chest. She hadn't been pleased with the child Drakk had left her, but this clan had made motherhood easier, and then there was Tor. A man who was willing to accept a child that wasn't even his.

"We will get her back."

"Do you think she's alive?" Ezi remembered Brog. That sabertooth had soulless eyes and a crazy temper. The man had tried to burn her and Aiyre alive in the village fire. She didn't even want to begin to think about what he might do to Flosa, a baby who couldn't fight back.

Then a thought smacked her in the face. "Can he even feed her?"

"We will get her back," Tor promised as he looked over at Daerk.

"We will." Daerk promised, then he turned to Aiyre, "Can you take over with the mammoths and directing our clan?"

Aiyre nodded. "Yes. I will worry about this." She waved a hand at the mammoths. "You take whatever hunters you need."

"I'm coming." Ezi straightened in Tor's arms.

Everyone stared at her without saying a word. They were stunned… or thought she wouldn't be able to go after her own daughter.

"I'm going." Ezi glared at each of them in turn.

"Brog can be violent. You should stay here where he can't hurt you." Tor placed a hand on her arm.

Shaking his hand off, she backed away as she continued to glare at him. "He's already hurt me, Tor."

"You two figure it out while I gather the hunters we will need." Daerk had enough of the conversation and stalked off. She could see the steam rising off his shoulders. She wasn't sure who was more upset, her or Daerk at Brog's audacity.

"Are you sure you should go with them, Ezi?" Aiyre asked as she stepped a bit closer. "I have to stay here to oversee the clan, and I won't be there for you."

"If it were your child, what would you do?" Ezi folded her arms in front of her chest. Why was everyone against her on this?

"I'm a hunter. If you go, Brog might try to kill you as well."

"I'm going." She glared at Aiyre and Tor. "You won't convince me otherwise." She didn't wait for an answer. She marched after Daerk, and she heard the clan members behind her erupt into conversation as they crowded Aiyre.

"Ezi!" Tor yelled as he jogged to catch up to her.

She increased her pace as she tried to put distance between them.

"Ezi!" His hand wrapped around her upper arm and yanked her around and into his chest. Then his other hand captured the back of her head and tilted her head.

"I need to go." Her eyes bored into his as she did her best to communicate her need.

He closed his eyes, and she felt his chest expand and then contract as he steadied himself. Then his eyes opened, "If you go, please do what I say. I don't want Brog to harm you more than he already has." She opened her mouth, but one of his hands came up to place a finger over her lips, stopping her. "If you're in harm's way, I won't be able to save Flosa and kill Brog. I'll be too worried about you."

She wanted to protest, but when she actually looked into his blue eyes, she could see the worry for her safety swirling through his eyes. "I will be safe." She would say whatever he needed to hear, as long as it got her there.

He smiled down at her. "Then let's save Flosa."

Chapter 21

Tor's paws ate up the ground as he and the rest of the hunters raced back to the camp. Ezi was beside them in her pronghorn form. Their animal forms were faster than their human forms, and it wasn't like they would fight Brog in their human forms. This fight would be done sabertooth to sabertooth.

When the camp came into view, some of them skidded to a stop and shifted back into their human forms while others shifted mid-run. Tor raced into the camp, his human feet pounding over the ground.

"Ake?" He asked as he knelt down by the woman who'd been taking care of Flosa. "Are you sure it was Brog?" There was no time to waste.

She nodded her head, and then he noticed the bruise developing around one of her eyes.

"Did they?" He pointed to her face.

Ake nodded her head again. "Brog stormed into the camp." She glanced over his shoulder, and he knew she was staring at Ezi who was now directly behind him. "It was like he knew about Flosa, and he wanted her. I refused to give her to him, so one of his men attacked me and ripped her out of my arms." Ake choked on a sob. "I'm sorry."

"It isn't your fault," Ezi said with compassion coating every word.

He sniffed the air and although there was fear coating Ezi, he could tell she truly didn't blame Ake. She shouldn't, but with all her trust issues with sabertooths, he wouldn't have been surprised.

"Can you tell us anything more?" Daerk asked as he came up beside them, his bare chest pumping in and out as he did his best to maintain his calm.

"Brog told me to tell you that he will ruin you all for what you did." Ake winced as she raised a hand to her eye and felt around the bruised area. "I think he wants you to come after him. It's a trap." She glanced between them all.

"She's right, Daerk. This has to be a trap." Tor glanced up at Daerk from where he crouched on the ground in the buff.

"We have to go." Daerk looked down at him. "We have no choice. We can't let a member of our clan go without a fight." He glanced over at Ezi. "And Flosa is a part of this clan, like you Ezi."

Tor stood and glanced over at his mate. Her eyes were wide, and then a shy smile spread over her face as a light blush crept up her cheeks.

"Thank you." She murmured as she realized everyone here considered her and her child a member of the clan, even if she had a hard time trusting them.

"Where did they go after taking Flosa?" Daerk asked Ake, not wanting to waste any more time.

Ake raised a shaking hand and pointed off in a direction. They all turned to follow her finger.

"Will you be fine if we leave?"

Ake nodded her head. "I didn't get the worst of it so that I can help the others with their wounds. Go and save Flosa, and finish off Brog." She growled their past clan leaders name in disgust.

The rest of the hunters waited around the

camp or assisted their clanmates.

"Two hunters stay here and help the injured back to the village. The rest will come with us." Daerk directed the men before shifting back into his sabertooth form and racing off.

Tor shifted and took off, and within a second Ezi was beside him in her pronghorn form. She was sleek and beautiful. Every step was graceful and perfect, and even in this time of urgency, he wished he could chase her down and plant his mark on her.

Another scent had his head swiveling around. Rir was running beside him in his sabertooth form, and a smile spread across his sabertooth face. Rir turned, and he returned the smile. Earlier Rir had said how tense he was, and a fight was one of the best ways to get it out. Then hopefully Rir wouldn't punch him into the ground again the next time he joked with his friend.

Lifting his nose into the air, Tor sniffed as he raced after Daerk. The scent was faint, and he could tell they were about a day behind Brog. If Flosa were injured or hungry, Tor would rip out Brog's throat and enjoy the feel of blood on his tongue. His sabertooth purred in agreement. Both of them loved Ezi and Flosa, and neither of them were pleased with the situation.

They should have killed Brog instead of banning him from the clan. It was a mistake they were all regretting now. He understood why Daerk hadn't killed Brog, but there were some people in this land who weren't worthy of breathing.

Tor had never met a demon before, but he'd heard about them at clan gatherings, and he wondered if Brog was one of them. He couldn't be a sabertooth. He was selfish and cruel. There was no doubt in Tor's mind that when they killed him, Brog wouldn't be joining anyone in the Eternal Hunting Grounds.

When the men called a stop, Ezi wanted to shout at them all in frustration, but she held herself back. She didn't need to anger them when they were helping her save her daughter.

"We should continue." She grabbed a hold of Tor's arm and used her eyes to beg him to help her.

He placed a comforting hand on one of hers and squeezed her fingers. "Night is falling, and the scent is growing stronger. We want to fight Brog in the daylight, so we know we aren't running into a trap."

Tor's words made sense, but her motherly side wanted her to tear the entire forest up as she searched for her child.

"I can't lose Flosa." She'd never been close to her daughter, and now she regretted it. If Flosa died, Ezi would blame herself. She'd wasted so much time with Flosa, and she wanted a chance to make it up to her child.

"We won't lose her, Ezi. I won't let it happen."

She could see the conviction in his eyes. He meant every single word. It floored her.

"Why do you care so much about Flosa?"

Tor leaned his head closer. "She's a part of you, and you love her. If anything happens to her, it will hurt you, and I will never let anything hurt you now that you're in my life." His blue eyes never glanced away as he said every word with such an intensity it made her blush.

It was then that she realized Aiyre was right. Tor wasn't going to hurt her... she was going to hurt him, and that thought had her heart-shattering in her chest. She didn't want to hurt Tor.

Ezi pulled away from his arms and put some much needed distance between them. "I'll never be able to thank you enough."

A smile cracked across his lips. "There's no need to thank me, Ezi." One of his hands reached out to bring her back into his embrace, but she moved her feet quickly and danced away from him.

Without looking back, Ezi found a spot by the small fire Daerk was busy building.

"How will we get Flosa back from Brog?"

Daerk's hands paused as he was about to strike a couple of stones together. "It depends on what Brog wants."

Tor walked up and took a seat not too far from her. His eyes never left her as his long legs folded underneath him. He was no doubt wondering why she was pulling away from him, but she had to end this before it went too far.

Then why was her heart protesting so much? She rubbed the area above one breast as she looked back at Daerk. "How can we be sure he won't harm her?"

"He either wants Tor or me." Daerk glanced

over at Tor, and a look passed between them.

Rir stepped out of the dark. "He could want me."

"Or all three of us." Tor offered and then glanced at Daerk's hands. "Need help starting the fire?"

Daerk frowned in the dark. "I'm good." He struck the stones together, a spark flew through the air, and it caught the tinder. The small orange flame flickered as it licked the thin branches with delight. Slowly, Daerk added more to the fire until he had a small fire going.

Ezi glanced off into the darkness that surrounded them on all sides. She felt closed in and knowing Flosa was out there somewhere drove her insane. Ezi could only hope her child wasn't scared or hungry or both.

A hand landed on her back, and she knew it was Tor without having to look. His hand moved in slow circles that she knew were meant to be comforting but ended up having a sexual note to each small caress.

The area between her thighs heated and her inner pronghorn nickered with delight. She shoved the daft animal away. They needed to put space between them and Tor. She couldn't let him get close if she didn't know her own feelings.

Ezi did her best to scoot away from him, breaking the contact. When she glanced at him from the side of her eyes, she caught a wounded look flash through his eyes. Maybe it was too late for her to pull away before hurting him.

Her pronghorn urged her to cuddle up to him, but again she pushed the animal back into its place. They had more important things to worry about, like Flosa.

All the men settled around the small fire, and she felt comforted by their presence. She might be a pronghorn shifter among so many male sabertooths, but they were here for her. It warmed her heart. How had it taken her this long to realize how close this clan was?

Because she was a horrible clan mate and hadn't tried to get to know any of them. Shame crawled through her.

"Would you like some?"

Startled by Rir's voice, Ezi glanced down at his outstretched hand to see a bag of dried meat. She wanted to tease them about not bringing any fresh meat from their mammoth hunt, but it felt strange making a joke when her daughter's life was hanging in the balance instead, she said, "Thank you, I would enjoy a couple of pieces."

After selecting a few, she passed it to Tor, who was still sitting on her other side. As he took the leather bag from her, his fingers skimmed over the back of her hand, and a sizzle of awareness flowed through her. Her eyes shot up and collided with his fiery blue eyes.

Yanking back her hand, Ezi cleared her throat and turned away from him. He was so intense, and she was addicted to him.

She shoved a piece of dried meat into her mouth and chewed vigorously on it. Saliva filled her mouth as her mind finally thought about something else other than Tor.

When she finished her meal, she excused herself and picked a spot to settle down for the night. She wasn't sure how much sleep she would be able to get when her child's life was in danger, but she had to try.

Tor watched Ezi stand in one graceful fluid motion and then stride away into the darkness. Listening, he made sure she didn't walk too far away, but within a couple of seconds, he heard her settling down in the grass.

Good.

Brog had already taken Flosa. Tor didn't need their banished leader coming back and taking Ezi. He was still angered that he'd let Brog take Flosa in the first place. He should have stayed back at the camp and guarded Flosa. It wasn't like they hadn't known this moment would come.

"We should have killed Brog," Tor grumbled.

Daerk buried his face in his hands. "I know." His words were muffled, but Tor was able to make them out.

"It wasn't like we had much time to think about our decision." Rir jumped into the conversation. "That night was a blur of decisions."

"He tried to kill Aiyre and Ezi. It was foolish of us to think he would leave and never come back."

"I won't deny that." Rir agreed.

"If he kills Flosa, I fear that I will lose Ezi." Tor glanced over his shoulder to where Ezi had disappeared into the dark. "I can already feel her pulling away from me."

When he looked back at the other men, they were just shaking their heads, uncertain what they could say to reassure him. Probably because they knew no words would ease his panic that his mate was once more pulling away from him.

"I wish we could promise to get Flosa back safely, but Brog is unpredictable." Rir frowned.

"Don't let Ezi hear you say that," Tor growled as he pointed a finger at his friend. He didn't need anyone causing Ezi to worry more than she had to right now.

Rir raised his hands. "I would never."

"We will get her back."

The conviction in Daerk's voice had hope blooming in Tor's chest. Maybe he could get Ezi back once they rescued Flosa. Hopefulness flowed through him… but he wasn't just doing this for Ezi. Flosa was a part of their clan now, and no one here would turn away in her time of need.

"How did you win Aiyre over?" Tor was desperate for some advice.

Daerk shrugged in the flickering firelight as he leaned back on his hands. "I'm not sure our situation is the same. Aiyre is a hunter, and although that night haunts her, she was able to move forward."

And Ezi was still plagued by nightmares as Tor knew all too well. She would wake up in a cold sweat gasping for air or lightly screaming. He wished he could have been there for her that night of the attack. He could only imagine what she'd seen. If he'd watched his clan being torn apart by sabertooth shifters and was unable to assist, he knew it would drive him insane.

"At least you have your mate," Rir said before taking a bite of some of the dried meat.

Tor glanced over at his friend. The words hadn't been harsh or hateful, just matter of fact. "You will find her. I doubt the gods would let you down."

"I don't think so. Maybe the gods want me to be the next shaman." Rir grumped. Tor chuckled, and Rir glared at him. "What's so funny?"

"Eron already has an apprentice that the gods chose for him. And it isn't you."

Daerk chuckled beside him. "Be patient, Rir. She's out there."

Rir shook his head. "Maybe I should go to the next clan gathering. No one in our clan is my mate, but I might meet her at the gathering."

Tor nodded his head. "It's a good thought."

"What will you do if she doesn't want to leave her clan for ours?" Daerk asked, still leaning back on his hands with his legs outstretched towards the leaping flames of the fire.

Rir's face turned thoughtful while he pondered that question. "I suppose I could join hers."

"We will miss you," Tor said solemnly.

Rir's lips turned down in a frown. "This is no time for joking, Tor."

Tor raised his hands in the air. "You haven't even met your mate yet. I'm not about to worry about you leaving the clan for a woman you haven't found. Find her and then I will worry about losing a friend and a brother."

"He's right. Don't worry about anything until you find her, and you will find her Rir." Daerk said with a pointed gaze.

"I know. It's hard to see you two with your mates, though."

"Don't be too envious of me. I might have my mate, but she hasn't joined with me." Tor looked at each of them. "And with mention of my mate, I'm going to search for her." And make sure she was holding up alright.

Daerk and Rir winked at him in unison, and he rolled his eyes. He wouldn't be asking his mate for anything tonight. Her mind would be on other things, like her daughter being in Brog's clutches.

"Ezi?" Tor whispered as he approached her resting spot. He could barely make out her form in the dark. She was curled up with her legs up against her chest and her arms wrapped around them.

At first, she didn't answer, and he was contemplating going back to Daerk and Rir when she said, "Yes?"

"May I join you?"

Again, she took her time with her answer before saying, "You may."

Tor stepped forward cautiously until he stood beside her, and then he crouched before laying down beside her and drawing her tense form into his arms. "We will find her."

"Alive or dead?"

Her words caused him to pause. "If we find her alive, I will rip Brog's throat out with my teeth." He felt her shiver in his arms at the venom in his tone. "And if we find her dead? I will make sure his death lasts for an eternity."

"Strangely, your words are a comfort, although I do want to find her alive."

"As do I."

Ezi shifted in his arms and then turned until their chests were pressed together firmly. "I still don't understand why you care so much. I know you say that I'm your mate and you want me happy, but is there no part of you that wants Flosa dead so we can have your young and only your young?"

Tor shook his head as he stroked a hand through her soft hair. "Flosa won't prevent us from having our own young. And there is no part of me that would wish her dead. She is a child who was created before I met you. I know our world is cruel, and there are many men who would prefer their own young, but I am not one of them."

She bit her bottom lip in the dark, and he knew she was processing the words he'd spoken. "Hold me?"

"As long as you need." Tor used a hand at the back of her neck to push her head into his chest. Then he placed his chin on the top of her soft head of hair and closed his eyes. Tomorrow was going to bring blood and heartache, but this moment of peace couldn't be passed up.

Chapter 22

"We're getting closer." Tor shifted out of his sabertooth form and walked up beside Ezi's pronghorn self. He felt the urge to reach out and stroke her fur, but without an invite, he was uncertain how she might react to such contact.

Within the blink of an eye, Ezi shifted and where her pronghorn once stood was her human self. She was stunning. The bright sunlight streaked through the leaves above them to highlight her in glowing yellow light. She was brilliant, and although she didn't have a hunter's body, she was toned with a little extra flesh around her hips and thighs.

She glanced over her shoulder at him, and the breath left his lungs. She probably didn't know it, but she had the ability to knock him to the ground with just a single glance.

Raising her nose in the air, she sniffed. "I smell sabertooths, but," she waved towards him, "you're a sabertooth, so it means nothing to me."

"Our sense of smell is better, and we can smell Flosa and Brog." Tor sniffed the air. "He has several other sabertooth shifters with him, which means he must have found even more sabertooths to join him since leaving the clan."

"He has more men than us." Daerk approached as he sniffed the air, and his eyes turned thoughtful.

"Are you… are you going to let him have Flosa?" Ezi's voice trembled as her eyes darted between the both of them.

"Never!" Daerk looked like she'd reached out and slapped him. "We wouldn't leave anyone in Brog's clutches. We just need to think about how we should approach."

Tor nodded, and the rest of the men crowded around while they waited for their leader to guide them.

"If I'm picking up the scents correctly, they have about five more men," Rir commented.

"Sounds correct." Tor agreed.

"We should have a few men split off and come around." Rir continued as he looked to all the other men for ideas and support.

"Good idea." Daerk nodded his head. "It will surprise Brog and make us look like a smaller group."

The men murmured in agreement.

"You, you, and you go around and take out any men you come across, and the rest of us will meet Brog head on." Daerk ordered them. "He'll be expecting us to do that, so we should so he doesn't suspect we have men surrounding him."

Three of the men shifted back into their sabertooth forms, and when Tor glanced over at Ezi he didn't see her give a single flinch. Another spark of hope fluttered through his chest. This was a good sign.

The sabertooths melted away into the forest as they rushed to do their leader's bidding.

"May the gods bless us and provide us the strength to do what needs to be done," Daerk said before shifting into his enormous sabertooth form. Then he launched himself forward and disappeared from sight.

Everyone else shifted and followed close on their leader's tail. Tor felt excitement flow through them. They were finally going to end this reign of terror. Tor's paws eagerly tore up the ground underneath him. His claws dug into the soil, allowing him to gain traction as he raced forward.

Ezi was beside him. He did his best not to allow her to distract him, but her long neck was outstretched as she sprinted beside him, and she was glorious. Shaking his head, he focused on the battle that was ahead of them. He would do anything and everything necessary to save Flosa. All that mattered was his mate's happiness.

Brog's scent grew stronger until the air was filled with the sour scent of sweat and blood. He sniffed the air, making sure the blood wasn't Flosa's, and it wasn't.

Relief swept through him.

When they broke out of the forest, all of them came to a grinding halt as their eyes landed on a group of men before them. Tor waited for Daerk to make the first move, not even his short tail twitched.

After a tense second, Daerk shifted into his human form so he could communicate to Brog who stood a mere few feet in front of them. Tor and the rest stayed in their sabertooth forms until Daerk gave them a signal. In his human form, their leader would be nearly defenseless. He was naked and without a single weapon. They were his weapon.

"Taken my spot as leader I see." Brog tossed them all a smile that would kill if it could spit venom. Then Brog's brown eyes flickered over to Tor's side, where Ezi stood in her pronghorn form. "A pronghorn?" Brog spit as his mouth curled in disgust at the sight of her.

Tor's muscles tensed, and he suppressed a growl of displeasure. Brog might not like pronghorns, but this was Tor's mate he was sneering at, and it caused Tor's hackles to rise in irritation.

"We've accepted two pronghorns into our clan after you destroyed their clan," Daerk informed their past leader, sounding proud.

Brog sneered. "You're weak."

All the men around Brog nodded their heads. No wonder they were following Brog and fine with taking a baby. They held exactly the same views.

"Where's Flosa?" Daerk demanded.

Brog stood there in silence, and Tor knew he was trying to get the upper hand. He was drawing out the tension, to see who would break first.

Tor could feel the tension vibrating off of Ezi's pronghorn form as she waited impatiently. She wanted to know her child was safe, and so did he. The moment Flosa's dead body was produced, he would pounce, and no one would stand in his way. Tor would rip out Brog's throat.

After several tense moments passed, Brog raised a hand, and Tor's hind legs bunched, ready for an unpleasant surprise. Brog snapped a couple of his fingers together. A man in the back stepped forward, a small bundle in his arms. Tor's ears pricked forward as his eyes locked onto that small bundle. Then the man flipped off one of the sides of the fur and revealed Flosa. Her small eyes looked around at the world around her with wonder and innocence. She had no idea how dire the situation was around her.

"Why did you take her?" Daerk asked.

Brog snorted as he glanced around at his men who chuckled with their leader. The sounds were false and brought a frown to Tor's face. He must be ruling over his men with force, yet again. The man would never change.

"You stole my clan from me, and I've been forced to live out here." Brog swept his arm around the forest. "Now, I want to see you endure the same pain I had to when I was forced out."

If Brog asked for Daerk to back down... they would be in a tough position. Tor wasn't sure what they would do. They couldn't let Brog back into the clan. The man would take out anyone who hadn't been loyal to him.

"What do you want?" Daerk growled, his patience growing thin.

Brog's mouth dropped before he snapped it shut. Clearly, he hadn't expected Daerk to cut straight to the matter at hand. "I want Tor." His hand rose, and Tor found their ex-leader pointing straight at him.

Now it was his turn for his mouth to drop. Him? What had he done, other than support Daerk? Glancing over to Daerk, he realized what Brog was up to by asking for him. Daerk's eyes were filled with turmoil as he thought about Brog's demand.

Tor shifted into his human form and went to stand beside his leader. "There is no reason to think on it, Daerk. If Brog wants me, then he can have me." Tor faced Brog without a single sign of fear.

"He will kill you," Daerk whispered out the side of his mouth, "after days of torture."

Tor knew this, but they couldn't sacrifice a baby to Brog. "We have no choice," Tor whispered back.

"I know." Daerk met his eyes and a message passed between them. Once they had Flosa, they could attack, but first, they needed the child.

A small hand pressed up against his back, and Tor turned to find Ezi looking up at him. "I don't want you to be harmed…" She trailed off as she turned to look over at her child being held by a strange sabertooth shifter.

But she wanted him to save her child. His mate didn't need to finish her words for him to know what she was going to say.

Stepping forward, he announced, "You may have me, but you must hand over the child at the same time."

A slow smile crept across Brog's face. "Agreed." He nodded his head as he waved the man holding Flosa forward.

Each time the other man stepped forward, so would Tor, until he was face to face with Brog. The man's stale breath washed over his face, and he barely suppressed a cringe. He couldn't wait to dig his teeth into Brog's flesh.

"We have Flosa!" Daerk called out, and that was the signal Tor had been waiting for.

Tor shifted in the blink of an eye and lunged, but Brog dodged and slipped away like the serpent he was. Instead, another sabertooth filled his vision, and he could smell that the man wasn't a clanmate. He charged the male.

They met with a clash of teeth and claws as

each of them tried to get the upper hand. A paw slashed dangerously close to his throat, but it left the other man open to attack. Pushing forward, Tor went for the throat, his mouth wide, and then he closed his long canines down on the man's throat. Thrashing his head, he ripped the man's throat out, and he went down in a gurgling mess.

Tor's sabertooth purred in happiness at the taste of blood. These men had harmed his mate and stolen her child. Their lives were forfeit.

A clan mate rushed up beside him and together they targeted another of the sabertooths on Brog's side. While his clan mate distracted the male, Tor snuck up from behind and then leaped on top of the man's back, his claws digging into the man's back. The sabertooth under him roared in pain and attempted to buck him off, but Tor wasn't letting go. His clan mate came in for the kill, crushing the man's throat with a single bite.

Letting go of the now motionless sabertooth, Tor pulled away, and his eyes searched the writhing mass of sabertooth bodies. He caught sight of Ezi in her human form with Flosa clutched to her chest as she watched the bloody fight in front of her. She was being guarded by a couple of clan mates, which meant he had time to search for Brog.

Tor's eyes scanned over the area again, but he didn't spot the sabertooth he was searching for. Huffing, his large cat's body turned as he continued to scan over the area, and then he caught sight of a sabertooth fleeing the area.

The coward!

Brog was fleeing while his men stayed and

died.

Tor flung himself forward. His claws dug into the ground as he tore towards the retreating back of Brog.

A roar behind him had his ears flickering back, and as he turned to see what the commotion was about, he spotted a sabertooth aiming straight for him. His eyes widened as he realized he couldn't do anything about the incoming attack. Then Rir shot out of nowhere and tackled the sabertooth.

The air whooshed past Tor's face as he watched the two sabertooths battle it out with their teeth and claws.

Shaking off the surprise, Tor whipped around and sprinted after Brog who had disappeared. Thankfully the man's sickly smell filled the air, leading a trail straight to him.

Trees and bushes flew past in a blur of green as his nose led him in the direction of Brog. There was no way he would let Brog slip through their fingers. Once this man was laying on the ground dead, their clan wouldn't have any more reasons to fear his return.

Grinding to a halt, Tor paused as Brog's scent ended. Confusion flooded Tor as he looked around, his cat eyes scanning over the forest as he searched for his prey. How had he just disappeared in the middle of a forest?

The ground rose up and slammed into his face as something heavy landed on his back. Twisting around under the immense weight, Tor found Brog's sabertooth snarling into his face. Brog's large canines were dangerously close to his throat, and for a brief second fear froze him, until his sabertooth instinct kicked in.

Thrashing under the weight of Brog, Tor got a paw up blocking Brog's strike, which was aimed straight for Tor's neck. Brog's mouth locked onto Tor's arm and got a mouthful of hair.

Using his own weight, Tor flipped them, breaking free from Brog's mouth. A trickle of blood tickled its way down his front leg, but he ignored it. Letting out ferocious growls, the two men circled each other.

If they'd been in human form, they would have been throwing insults at each other, but in their sabertooth forms, they could only growl, slash their claws through the air, and flick their small tails in annoyance.

After several circles, Brog made the first move. He leaped forward, a claw swiped through the air, and Tor dodged, but not soon enough. Some of his fur was shaved off as he flung his body out of the way, but the skin wasn't broken.

Tor twisted back around and swiped his own claw at Brog. Satisfaction flowed through him as his claw hit its mark, and red-hot blood covered his sharp claws. His sabertooth purred with excitement. When he pulled his paw back, Tor launched himself at Brog in another onslaught of sharp claws.

One of Brog's paws came up to deflect the attack, and their claws hooked together as they tumbled over each other. Kicking out his hind legs, he attempted to scrape his claws across Brog's exposed belly, but the man was stubborn and refused to die. Brog twisted onto his side, and Tor only ended up clawing his side.

Brog roared in pain, before shoving Tor through the air.

Twisting his body in mid-air, Tor landed on his feet, and they began circling each other again.

A growl from behind him, had Tor tensing, but he didn't turn. It would either be a friend or a foe, but he definitely knew he had a foe in front of him, and he didn't want to give Brog an opening.

Rir came around the other side, a snarl curling his upper lip as his large sabertooth form circled Brog. Brog's ears went flat as he moved backward trying his best to keep them both in his sights.

Then another growl pierced the air and Daerk melted out of the shadows of the forest.

A smile curved Tor's sabertooth lips. Together, they were going to bring down Brog once and for all.

Ezi watched the fighting in front of her with horror. Fur and blood flew through the air, but she had two sabertooths guarding her and Flosa, so she felt decently safe as the fighting continued around her. She managed to keep her eyes on Tor for a few seconds before all the sabertooths blended into one massive pile of predators.

Her pronghorn form begged her to flee, but her feet felt like large boulders. Her heart skipped a beat when she watched a sabertooth go down. Was it Tor? Her eyes skimmed over the motionless form until it transitioned into its human form.

Relief washed through her. It wasn't Tor, and it wasn't one of her new clanmates.

A sabertooth broke off from the rest and fled the area. Then another sabertooth followed after, and she immediately knew it was Tor. He was chasing Brog down. Her heart shot into her throat as she feared for his life. She wasn't sure how skilled a warrior Brog was, and she worried about Tor's safety.

Stepping forward, she intended to follow, until one of the sabertooths guarding her stepped into the way. It lightly growled up at her, and she paused, and when she looked back up the two fleeing sabertooths they were gone.

One of the sabertooths guarding her shifted into his human form. "Get on Lers back." He ordered her.

Turning, she eyed the sabertooth beside her. "I don't–"

"Get on!" The man beside her growled.

Her pronghorn forced her feet into motion. There was no need to anger a sabertooth shifter. She clambered onto Lers back, positioned Flosa in her arms as she laid down slightly, and then they were off.

Ezi felt horrible fleeing with her child when the fighting was still going on behind her. All those men in the clan were putting their lives in danger for her, and Tor was one of them. Her heart pattered uncomfortably in her chest.

The next time she saw Tor, she was going to give him a chance at being her mate. She wasn't ready to say she was in love, but she definitely hated the idea of seeing his lifeless body. And he was wonderful with Flosa. He was gentle with her, and even without her accepting his matehood he looked out for her by allowing her to use his hut.

She was going to give him a chance if he came back alive. The thought of him dying had her throat closing up as she choked on her emotions. He'd better live. She wasn't ready to lose another who was so close to her.

Epilogue

Tor braced himself outside his hut. He, Rir, and Daerk had successfully killed Brog, and scattered his men to the four winds. It was nice to have the pressure off their backs. The clan would be able to sleep easier, and they would be able to reduce the number of hunters in the forest around their village.

A couple of clan mates passed by, and Tor smiled at them until they left and then he faced the entrance to his hut again. Sucking in a breath to calm his nerves, he pushed the fur entrance aside and popped his head inside.

"Ezi?"

"Tor?" Ezi glanced up from where she was feeding Flosa.

"May I come in?" It felt strange asking her permission to enter his own hut, but he'd given her free use of the hut, which meant it was no longer just his.

"Yes." She pulled Flosa off her nipple and placed the child in her fur-lined basket.

Slowly, Tor entered the hut, which looked no different since the last time he'd been in here. He took a seat by the fire and sent her a smile.

"I'm glad to see you alive." Ezi's eyes skimmed over him before landing on the scrapes on his arm. "Do those hurt?"

Tor shrugged. "They are healing. They itch more than anything," he reached over and scratched around his wounds, "but Eron has been kind enough to make me a couple of salves. We are lucky we made it out of our fight with Brog with just a few scrapes."

"Brog?" Ezi asked as her jade eyes searched his.

"Dead."

Relief washed over her face. "Flosa will be safe from him."

"We all will be safe from him." Tor reached out and grasped one of her hands, and satisfaction pumped through him when she didn't flinch or pull away from his touch. "I should never have left Flosa unguarded. We knew he would be back for one or all of us."

Ezi shook her head, her loose brown hair swirling around her shoulders in hypnotic waves. "You didn't know when or if he would come back. It's not your fault, and Flosa," she glanced over at the child who was sleeping soundly, "wasn't harmed. She doesn't even know something happened."

"But it could have gone wrong." It broke Tor's heart in half to think that Brog could have killed Flosa so easily, and destroyed his mate in the same strike.

Ezi leaned in, and before he could react, she placed a gentle kiss to his cheek before pulling away. A light blush stained her cheeks. "Thank you for saving her. And thank you for," she glanced away, "giving yourself over to Brog."

"He wanted me more than he wanted your child."

"His plan to get his hands on you seemed poorly planned."

Tor nodded his head. "Brog was never good

at being a leader. It was one of the reasons our meat hut was so empty last winter." Tor squeezed her hand, which was still clutched in his.

"Tor?"

"Hmm?" He glanced over at her.

Ezi's hand tightened around his as she stood and brought him up to his feet as she guided him over to his bed of furs. A place where he used to sleep until he'd given her his hut, so she and Flosa could get out of the women's communal hut.

"What are we doing?" He asked cautiously as his heart pattered in his chest. He didn't want to get too hopeful, but as she laid down on the pile of furs and drew him down on top of her, his heart soared straight into his throat.

"Ezi?" Tor tried again as she spread her legs, and he settled between them.

"I want…" she took a moment before raising her eyes and meeting his, "I want your mark."

His heart thundered in his ears, and he feared he hadn't heard her words correctly. "Wh– what did you say?" He stuttered a bit.

A smile curved one corner of her lips as she weaved her hands into his long hair and pulled him down for a passionate kiss. Then she broke away and said, "I want your mark, Tor."

"Why?" He had no idea why he asked, and his sabertooth growled at him in frustration. Why was he questioning something so perfect?

Ezi laughed. "Because I was blinded by you being a sabertooth shifter, but you're more than that. You're gentle, and you accept Flosa. I want to this."

Tor didn't need to hear anything more. He

sank down until his chest was pressed firmly against her breasts, flattening them between their hot bodies. His lips skimmed over hers in a fleeting kiss, before he worked his way down her neck until he reached the neckline of her animal skin shirt.

Tor leaned back on his legs, and his fingers quickly undid the leather straps that held her shirt together. He folded back the parts, exposing her breasts to his view.

"Perfect." He growled before his head dipped down, and he sucked a nipple into his mouth. His tongue swirled around the tight bud, drawing mews from her mouth as her back arched. His other hand took hold of her other breast, and he rubbed his palm over her nipple. He loved the sensation of the tight tip tickling his palm.

Her hands pushed his head closer to her breasts until he felt like he was one with her body. His sabertooth growled at him to give her his mark before she pulled away. Tor calmed his sabertooth. Ezi wasn't going to pull away. He could feel the intensity of her emotions as they vibrated through him.

But he still broke away from her nipple and drew back until he could untie the leather strings at her pants. Then he gripped the pants and yanked them off with a solid pull. He flung them through the air, grabbed her waist, and flipped her onto her hands and knees. When he gave her his mark, he was going to do it from behind, like it should be done.

Knocking her legs apart with a knee, he pulled her into him and entered her in one smooth thrust. His cock filled her, and his eyes slid shut. "Gods, Ezi, you are perfect."

"Mmm." She murmured underneath him as her hips moved against him, pulling away and then pushing back into him. "Mark me, Tor."

She was begging him for his mark?

Joy spread through him, and he leaned over her back as he moved in and out of her in slow, passionate thrusts. Pressing his face into the crook of her neck and shoulder, he breathed in her wild flower scent before opening his mouth, his canines extending, and then bit her shoulder.

Immediately, her entrance clamped down around him with enthusiasm, and a groan of pleasure left her mouth as her head pitched forward, and her body pitched against him.

He had his mate, and a sense of completeness filled him to the brim.

Made in the USA
Lexington, KY
07 December 2019